THE DISSENSION PROCESS
PROCESS
INSURGENCE

C000147303

THE DISSENSION PROCESS

INSURGENCE

Markus James

First paperback edition February 2022

ISBN: 978-1-7397284-1-0

www.thedissensionprocess.com

Hatred is the real *weakness.*

Chapter 1

"Impressive, eh?"

"Man, you haven't seen anything until you see what I can do!"

"Can you show us again, babe?"

"Yup, stand back."

Bill stood with his arm outstretched towards the low brick wall in front of him. Behind him was Johnny, a teenage boy and two girls, one of whom he could refer to as his girlfriend. A second later, another beam shot out from his pointed fingers and tore out a chunk of brickwork.

"That's so cool!" one of the girls exclaimed.

"You know it!" Bill responded before briefly looking up to the sky as a large shadow, presumably a low flying bird, brushed over the group.

"Wait 'til you check me out!" the other male member of the gang said aloud.

"Go on, Nate, show us what you've got," Johnny said, oblivious to the annoyed and envious look Bill was giving him in response.

"Alright, hope you're checking this out," Nate replied.

"Same old self-indulgent rubbish, huh?"

Nate turned around towards the source of the voice, as did the rest of the party, seeing a black-clad, hooded individual standing looking at them.

"Bitch is back," Bill grinned.

"Such an unimaginative comment, Bill," Jamie replied. "But then, you're not much of an imaginative person anyway."

"Who's she?" one of the girls asked aloud.

"A pain in our butts," Johnny replied unreservedly.

"Not for long," Bill said, looking towards Nate. "How about that demonstration, Nate?"

Jamie looked on as the unknown male behind Bill vanished into thin air, feeling a sense of unease for a moment. She then felt a hand being placed on her shoulder as her viewpoint then changed out of nowhere like a blink of an eye to that of being thirty feet in mid-air before feeling herself plummeting to the ground as a very audible scream cried out from below.

"Shut up, she had it coming!" Bill snapped at the horrified girl beside him as he looked upon his loathed enemy falling through the air with Nate teleporting back down to the ground.

However, glee then quickly turned into shock as he witnessed the girl slowing her rapid descent to a complete halt as she approached the concrete floor.

Responding quickly, Jamie launched dual kinetic energy waves at Bill and Johnny, striking them both and knocking them to the floor before either had a chance to react.

8

Jamie suddenly felt someone grabbing her from behind once more and pinning her arms to her side, countering by taking to the air using her flight ability once more and flying at a considerable velocity.

Unable to hold on, Nate teleported back to the surface as he lost his grip, only to tumble heavily against the ground from the speed and momentum he had carried over from his prior position.

"For the record, I never tire of seeing you laid out on your backsides," Jamie taunted Bill as she floated down beside him.

"Never know when to keep your gob shut, do you?" Bill growled as he fired a quick laser beam, only to see it blocked by an invisible shield.

"What else you got?" Jamie mockingly said in response. Bill glared in response but noticing Johnny already fleeing the scene with the two girls and Nate in tow, he begrudgingly opted to follow suit.

"You're going to get it one of these days, you grunge freak!" he yelled as he departed the desolated industrial area.

Not from you at least.

As she watched the hapless miscreants disappear from view, Jamie felt her phone vibrating in her pocket, seeing that Jesse was calling her.

"Yo!" she said.

"Hey, Jame. Do you think you could swing by mine?"

"Can do, what's the occasion? Thought we weren't meeting up until tomorrow."

"Well it's to do with Kayleigh; she's acting a bit strange and I'm a bit clueless on how to deal with it."

"What do you mean 'strange'?" Jamie replied, taking on a more serious and worried tone.

"She's being extremely over-emotional for one, just lying on her bed upset. It's not like her at all and has nothing to do with anything she's ever gone through."

"Alright, I'll head over. See you in roughly ten minutes," Jamie said before hanging up and taking to the air as she activated her borrowed hazing ability. Though she found what Jesse had explained to her weird, she also had a gut feeling about what might be going on with Kayleigh considering it allegedly had nothing to do with her disruptive upbringing. Her lingering absorption of Dawn's ability analysis power would likely be of help if it turned out to be enhanced human-related but she had no other reason to suspect any foul play at hand.

She had been conservative with her use of the ability seeing as Dawn was no longer around to attain more of it. Not that she really had a specific need for it anyway since the encounter with and subsequent defeat of Ryan Sharp in his empowered form a fortnight ago – she had kept good to her word in promising Gabrielle and Jesse not to go looking for trouble anymore (humiliating Bill and his friends in revenge for their previous attack on her at the fun fair being the exception), especially now that she was more content with her life as a whole and had no desire to vent her negativity using her powers as she once had.

Jamie couldn't help but think about Sharp and his current predicament, or at least how the police had chosen to deal with him given the extreme nature of his powers. And that was if they were even aware of super-human powers being the actual reality that they were. It still amazed her that her kind wasn't widely known in public by now but she had no complaints, even less towards the fact she hadn't received any blowback from breaking Miles out of prison in order to stop Sharp either.

Jamie touched down in the small, forested area near Jesse's house and deactivated the haze before making her way onto the street. Using her own innate ability to sense nearby abilities rather than Dawn's, she could already feel a large swelling of power nearby as she gradually approached the Webster siblings' abode. Whatever was going on with Kayleigh definitely appeared to be power-related but just in what manner Jamie imagined she was about to find out.

"Jamie," Jesse said as he opened the front door.

"How is she?" Jamie asked.

"Still pretty bad, I have no idea what's going on with her."

"Let's try and find out," Jamie said as she followed Jesse up the stairs to Kayleigh's room. The whole time she could feel her passive power sensing peaking.

"Kay," Jesse said as he opened the door to his sister's room. "Got your best bud here to see you!"

Jamie walked in to see Kayleigh lying on the bed with her back turned. The sensation being caused by her power sensing was almost overwhelming.

"Everything alright, Kayleigh?" Jamie asked softly as she approached the other side of the bed to face the stricken girl.

"No..." Kayleigh whimpered back, clearly having been crying.

"What's the matter?"

"Everything hurts..."

"You're in pain all over?" Jamie asked, feeling confused.

"She doesn't mean physically," Jesse cut in. "Like emotionally."

"Like she's depressed?" Jamie inquired. "What's making you feel that way, babe?"

"Everyone suffering..." Kayleigh replied meekly. "I can't stop it."

"That's what she's been saying the whole morning since she woke up," Jesse said. "I had to take the day off work and call her school to say she was ill but I've been at a loss at what I could do to stop her feeling like this. What do you think brought it on?"

Jamie thought to herself for a moment, then placed her hand over Kayleigh's face.

"I'm going to try something," she said to the young girl. "It might feel weird but it won't hurt. Ready?"

Kayleigh gave a feeble nod as Jamie began initialising the deactivation part of her base power, seeing the youth slowly coming out of her miserable stupor. Jesse looked on curiously.

"Is that better?" Jamie asked.

"Yeah!" Kayleigh responded in a much more cheery tone. "What did you do?"

"Yeah, what *did* you just do?" Jesse chipped in.

"I deactivated her ability."

"What?" Jesse replied in disbelief.

"Kayleigh's ability was exaggerating her emotional responses. It's probably just gotten too naturally strong for her to manage passively but I've turned it off for now."

"What ability *has* she got though?" Jesse continued, with Jamie quickly remembering that he had not been made aware of it yet.

"She has the power of empathy – she can feel how other people feel by skin contact, but it seems to be making her feel too much of her own emotions now."

"Well, that's something," Jesse remarked, still trying to process the revelation that his sister was an empowered being just like him and Jamie. "This mean you'll have to keep deactivating it from now on then?"

"Maybe not," Jamie answered, taking Kayleigh's hand and reactivating some of her ability before taking it for herself. "I've just absorbed an amount of it, not enough to turn me into an emotional wreck but it should last me to try and figure out how to control it so I can teach Kay how to deal with it herself."

"Do you know anything about it at all other than it making Kayleigh feel too much?"

"I did give it a quick scan with that Dawn girl's analysis power just before I turned it off and all it had to tell me was that the user can feel what other people feel."

"In which case, I just hope you can figure out how to prevent it happening again," Jesse said. "Though it worries me a bit that the same thing could happen to you, especially with everything you've gone through."

"It probably would've happened already and I feel the same as always," Jamie replied. "Trust me, I've got little interest in going back into full-blown depression mode."

"Want to try and see what I'm feeling?" Jesse asked, offering out his hand.

"Couldn't hurt," Jamie responded, curious herself to see what exactly Jesse was feeling.

Or dare I?

She decided to throw caution to the wind and find out. Closing her eyes, she took hold of his bare hand and, having no idea how the ability worked precisely, tried concentrating on Jesse's emotions. Almost to her dismay, she found herself simply feeling a neutral sensation, if not slight contentment.

"Well this is a bust," Jamie griped out loud.

"It's not working?" Jesse asked.

"No, you're not feeling anything in particular!" Jamie retorted, still holding onto Jesse's hand.

"How about now?" Kayleigh said with a mischievous grin as she dug her fingers into Jesse's ribs.

"Kay, no!" Jesse exclaimed, trying to stifle a laugh from the unexpected tickle attack. Suddenly, Jamie gave out a squeal in response before covering her mouth in embarrassment.

"Looks like it works," Kayleigh smirked.

"You're such a terror!" Jesse remarked with a playful ruffling of his sister's hair.

"I know," the girl smiled. "Ready for a round of board games, Jamie?"

"Like I have a choice?" Jamie gave a happy sigh.

Nearly four hours of board games followed by another four hours of watching films together later, Jamie departed the household to get home for dinner with Gabrielle. In the midst of the first film, she had cheekily grabbed Jesse's arm in another attempt to deduce his emotional state of mind, again being disappointed by a lack of proper sensation. Yet she considered it lucky that the empathy ability didn't work both ways, not wanting Jesse to know of her own uncertain feelings towards him when he apparently did not feel the same towards her.

Being her turn to prepare the evening meal, Jamie had found herself enjoying being creative in the kitchen. It was heartening also that Gabrielle complimented every meal she prepared, almost feeling guilty that she hadn't been doing the same the whole time.

"Dinner, Gabby!" she yelled up the stairs.

"So what have you got for us tonight then?" Gabrielle asked, wearing a dressing gown with a towel wrapped around her head.

"Meatballs and spaghetti. Could you have not at least thrown on your pyjamas before coming down?!"

"You were in your towel to eat breakfast only yesterday, you cheeky sod!"

"Yeah but that's just breakfast."

"And there I thought it was the most important meal of the day," Gabrielle quipped as she sat down at the table. "Must say, looking mighty fine as always."

"You mean me or the dinner?" Jamie joked.

"Well the dinner's looking fabulous too," Gabrielle laughed. "Bit ironic you favour Italian meals over French ones all the time though."

"Didn't think you'd care too much for snails and frog legs(!)"

"Ha! Well guess I'll find something more France-based sometime to try out," Gabrielle remarked as the two made a start on their meals. "What did you get up to all day anyway?"

"Well Jesse called to tell me Kayleigh was off school ill," Jamie said after swallowing a mouthful of spaghetti. "So I went round there and annoyed them both all day long."

"Aw, how's the poor girl doing?"

"Oh she cleared up soon enough. She even managed to beat me at Monopoly for the first time ever too."

"That mean she and Jesse are still coming to the shopping centre with us tomorrow?"

"Yesssss," Jamie replied in a mock huff.

"Oh it'll be fun, sourpuss," Gabrielle smirked.

"Yeah, for you and Kayleigh. Me and Jesse have little interest in trying on clothes."

"It's not *all* we'll do there y'know, besides you can drag Jesse over to the games shop or something while we do that."

"Sounds like a good idea."

"(Or a romantic meal)," Gabrielle muttered under her breath.

"I heard that!" Jamie fired back with an unimpressed look.

"You're so easy to wind up," Gabrielle chuckled.

After dinner, Jamie retreated to her room while leaving Gabrielle the living room television to herself, curious to engage her absorbed empathy in order to discover how it exactly worked.

Despite what she had told Jesse earlier, however, the analysis ability had also informed her that it was possible to feel someone else's emotions without physical contact, a trait that Kayleigh apparently wasn't aware of herself. Jamie hoped to be able to feel Gabrielle's emotions from the fifteen feet that separated them between floors, helped by the fact that the film she was watching would probably bring out a myriad of different emotions within her to sense.

As she focused, her concentration was broken momentarily by her absorbed analysis ability flaring up out of nowhere, detecting a teleportation ability being used. Oddly, the use of it did not feel localised but quite distant which was unusual to be able to detect something so far away while being used passively and not directly focused on anything in particular.

Maybe the empathy ability enhances the analysis power?

As she continued her concentration, Jamie suddenly felt a jarring pain go off in her head minutes later as though she was suffering from the worst migraine she had ever had before subsiding just as fast as it had struck.

Confused and slightly disorientated, Jamie tried to gather her thoughts. Almost on instinct, she could feel the empathy ability within her trying to detect the source of the painful sensation as though it had a mind of its own. It then began informing her brain that the culprit was situated not too far away, though also not within walking distance without giving her an exact location.

Could it be the same teleporting prat of that Bill idiot's group from earlier on?

Concerned that she had just been subject to some form of enhanced human attack, albeit a telepathic one from the individual being picked up by her borrowed empathy ability, Jamie decided to head them off where they were currently being located in her mind, seeing as she was still fully dressed.

"Just going out for a walk quickly, Gabbs!" Jamie yelled as she clambered down the stairs to put her shoes on.

"Don't be too long, it's getting dark out!" Gabrielle called back.

"I'll be fine, I've got your ability and Jesse's flight if need be," she called back before exiting the house through the front door.

Chapter 2

Nate sat on the floor of the warehouse, furiously waiting for his ability to recharge enough for him to at least teleport out of the building and on to the street. He knew he had completely made a mess of stealing the game consoles he had been tipped off about and it had been easily avoidable. Using the future sight aspect of his powers to see where he was teleporting to took up a lot of energy alone but choosing to then teleport from his home as opposed to having walked to outside the warehouse first out of laziness and impatience had just been idiotic.

But the damage had been done. On the plus side though, his presence had not set off an alarm and there appeared to be no obvious security cameras monitoring his activity. Even if there were any, however, it would be hard to believe a human being had teleported inside the building in the first place despite video evidence to back it up.

To try again so soon though would inevitably cause the usual pain in the head to occur; he figured it best to wait another few minutes before attempting to escape to the outside street with his swag.

Jamie tried her best to maintain focus on her multiple abilities simultaneously working together. The combination of flight and hazing was more accustomed to her by now but trying to utilise the empathy power as well was proving tricky, in addition to keeping an eye out where she was flying.

The analysis ability would have been the easier choice to make use of but the teleporter had failed to activate his power again since the initial occurrence. Empathy, on the other hand, appeared to be keeping track of the individual rather than the power which was proving more valuable despite Jamie's inexperience in handling it. It didn't surprise her now that it had begun to overwhelm Kayleigh considering it had since expanded into also acting as a form of clairvoyance.

Jamie began to descend over a warehouse in an industrial complex to where the empathy ability had directed her, of which had been seriously drained from maintaining its usage the entire flight. If it was the 'Nate' individual from earlier, he was likely still inside the building and would possibly be making an appearance soon if he planned to teleport straight outside.

Jamie decided to give it a few minutes before giving in and heading back home. After all, it was the side of her she didn't really want to be engaging in anymore; the incentive of once again thwarting Bill and his moronic crew was the only reason she had even bothered to do so to begin with, her ego and bruised pride still proving a hindrance in that regard.

After nearly three minutes of hovering above the warehouse, Jamie's absorbed analysis power suddenly activated. She then spotted a figure on the far side attempting to creep around the building with two boxes under each arm.

Nate slowly inched towards the other side of the warehouse where the exit to the industrial site was located. It was unlikely there were any security guards around but being hasty was still a chance not worth taking, especially with his teleportation ability still currently incapable of getting him anywhere near his home but while he was now outside he could make up the distance on foot until it had fully replenished.

Seeing the coast being clear, he then decided to make a break for it.

Nate then found himself being struck from behind by something with significant force which knocked him down to the ground, dropping the two console boxes in the process.

"I'm sure the shops would've restocked them in the morning if you're *that* desperate to have one," Jamie taunted Nate as she floated down to the surface.

"You following me or something?" Nate angrily replied, distracted by the pain emanating from between his shoulder blades.

"Maybe I just haven't forgotten the attempted death by teleportation from earlier," Jamie responded with a menacing glare. Nate felt his heart beginning to race; his powers still hadn't recuperated enough to escape the scene and as much as he hated to admit it to himself, the interfering girl and her seemingly multiple powers scared him.

With no other option, he attempted to run towards the entrance gate, deciding he would be better off trying to reclaim the stolen consoles later when his powers had fully restored. However, he found his route being blocked off by the girl swooping quickly in front of him from out of nowhere, being forced to retreat back towards the discarded console boxes.

Jamie essentially had little left to deal with – she had effectively intimidated Nate into submission, the only thing left to do now was let him escape for real without his ill-gotten gear and head home.

Though being able to teleport would probably come in handy…

Jamie stared down Nate, biding her time until her analysis power detected the teleportation ability being activated, in which case she would quickly fly towards him and absorb it whole.

Nate by now was left in a desperate state, frantically waiting to be able to teleport again to get away from the lunatic girl. Deciding to take the chance anyway, he threw caution to the wind in anticipation of either pain or disappearing from the scene.

Here we go!

Jamie took to the air and sped straight towards Nate, immediately grabbing the side of his face with her bare hand as she felt his ability reactivate.

Except this time, Nate's eyes were completely glazed over and his pupils faded.

What?

Suddenly, with her hand still on Nate's face, the empathy ability reactivated by its own accord. Jamie saw her vision then fade to darkness, taking the rest of her senses away with it.

*　　*　　*

Jamie found herself standing in what appeared to be a Central London street, or what it seemed like judging by the surrounding tall buildings and familiar landmarks she could just about make out. Unlike London though, there was a complete lack of activity accompanied by an eerie silence.

Jamie looked around, seeing absolutely no sign of any other human being around at all, not even Nate who she assumed was responsible for transporting her there.

But how? she thought. Her power analysing ability detected teleportation and nothing else which meant if Nate had teleported her to there, he should at least be standing in front of her now. Did he have another hidden aspect of his powers that were responsible?

Whatever the reason, Jamie began to feel a cold sensation of fear and anxiety running through her as she finally heard a noise in the background that echoed around the empty street. She turned around to face it.

Jesse?

Jamie looked bewildered but felt relief as she saw what appeared to be Jesse as the source of the noise, apparently having just flown down to the surface.

"Jesse, what's going on?" she called out.

Jesse simply stared back at her, expressionless. Jamie then noticed the dark shading under his eyes, like he was wearing make-up on his lower eyelids. His pupils appeared heavily dilated too, almost black in appearance instead of his normal brownish colour.

"Jess?" Jamie tried again in a more worried tone.

Jesse then spread his arms wide either side of his waist with his fists clenched. Jamie then saw the sky become blanketed in dark clouds as gale force winds accompanied them from out of nowhere, feeling sheer terror at the unexpected turn of events.

"Jesse!" she cried out as she looked up to see the huge streak of lightning coming down towards her from above.

Jamie then found herself staring Nate right in the face with her hand still clutching his cheek as he appeared to come out of his trance.

"Wha...?" Nate stuttered as his vision returned to see the hooded girl right before him. Her hand quickly pulled away from his face before gripping the neckline of his t-shirt.

"What the bloody hell did you do?!" Jamie snapped at him.

"Did you just see that too?" he responded. Jamie could tell via the empathy ability still within her that he wasn't faking his surprised reaction.

"How did you just do that?" she growled, intimidating Nate further.

"I-I can see the future to an extent," he panicked. "I use it to picture where I can teleport to and if I'm going to be seen doing it when I do. I have no clue why it self-activated just then."

Jamie realised her empathy ability must have caused her to see the same future vision that Nate had via her hand being in contact with his face at the time.

"What did *you* see?" she asked.

"An empty street. Nobody was around at all."

The same thing as me, minus Jesse.

Jamie let go of Nate's t-shirt and immediately took off into the night sky without bothering to cloak herself with her borrowed hazing ability, feeling that coming out in the first place had been a gigantic mistake.

"Quick walk, eh?"

"How long was I gone?" Jamie asked as she closed the front door.

"About half an hour," Gabrielle replied from the living room.

"Isn't that quick for me?" Jamie sarcastically responded.

"I guess! Was it alright?"

"Absolutely dandy," Jamie answered before heading up the stairs, considering herself lucky Gabrielle wasn't able to read *her* emotions and finding out what she had really been up to. But her curiosity had nearly gotten the better of her again; if the buck hadn't stopped with Ryan Sharp, it sure did now. It just wasn't worth chancing it anymore.

Nonetheless, the supposed future vision of Jesse had been unnerving. It had appeared to be him, just not the benevolent, friendly version she had come to know. It was something she unfortunately was going to have to keep on her mind whether she wanted to or not depending when, or if, the future state would come to fruition.

Jamie awoke in the morning to smell breakfast cooking. The time on her phone read 8:20am, a rare occasion where Gabrielle hadn't tried to wake her up. She realised she was slowly becoming accustomed to rising at a relatively early time on her own now, thankful also that she hadn't woken to a bizarre, nightmare version of London again.

"Morning!" Gabrielle said cheerily as she entered the room and climbed into Jamie's bed.

"Gabbs!" Jamie yelled as she shook from the cold feel of Gabrielle's hands being placed on her bare back under the duvet.

So much for not being disturbed.

"Just seeing if you were awake," Gabrielle sniggered before wrapping her arms around Jamie's torso and pulling the front of her body into the back of her friend's. "Here, I'll warm you up."

"A shame you couldn't have done that to begin with," Jamie replied, settling back down into the warmth.

"I've got breakfast waiting for us downstairs if you want to get up."

"Do I have to?" Jamie bemoaned, albeit in a joking manner.

"I can help if you need."

"Don't you dare touch me with your cold hands again!"

"Alright, promise," Gabrielle replied. Jamie then felt the duvet lift up as Gabrielle seemingly got out of the bed, only to then let out a shriek and fall out herself as she felt the icy sensation of her friend pressing her freezing-cold toes square into her back.

"Gabby!" Jamie growled from the floor with the duvet still partially wrapped around her.

"No hands, you said," Gabrielle jested. "See you downstairs."

Jamie settled down to her breakfast two minutes later, enjoying the scrambled egg, beans and sausage ensemble enough to forget about the latest rude awakening she had received. Due to pick up

Jesse and Kayleigh from their house at ten o'clock, Jamie opted for the shower while Gabrielle occupied the bath (with Gabrielle mockingly pointing out from the bathtub the water bill being run up by Jamie's excessively long shower). By the time Gabrielle had finished doing her make-up at half nine, the duo set off in her car hoping to miss the worst of the Saturday morning traffic.

"Race you there!" Kayleigh yelled as she stepped out of Gabrielle's car and began making a beeline to the entrance of the shopping centre.

"Kayleigh! Back here now!" Jesse called back to her.

"Aw, killjoy," the girl stropped as she ambered back towards the group.

"Don't want you getting hit by any careless drivers, sweetness," Jesse said as Kayleigh grabbed Jamie's hand and began forcibly dragging her forward. Jamie gave a quick glance back towards Jesse.

How can he be the same person I saw in that future vision?

The previous evening's events were still playing on her mind, though she was determined to cast it aside and not bring it up lest she ruin a perfectly good day out for everyone, especially after what happened on their last outing to the fun fair. Plus she didn't want Gabrielle finding out that she had lied about the whole incident occurring to begin with for obvious reasons.

"So where are we going first?" Gabrielle asked.

"Toy place?" Jamie quickly replied, eyeing Kayleigh suggestively.

"I thought we could go to a clothes shop first," Kayleigh surprisingly replied.

"Huh?" Jamie said in astonishment, until she noticed Gabrielle trying to cover her mouth while stifling a laugh.

"Good job playing along, Gabby!" Kayleigh said jokingly.

"You ganged up on me? Traitor!" Jamie smiled at Kayleigh. "So what do you *really* want to do first?"

"Well actually, I want to go clothes shopping first," Kayleigh answered, to the surprise of everyone.

"You do?" Gabrielle chimed in.

"Yeah, I want to do something *you* want to do for a change."

"Aww," Gabrielle replied with Jesse giving a prideful look at his sister.

"Sure you don't want to check out all the toys first?" Jamie jokingly argued.

"Well it's two against one at the moment, babes," Gabrielle rebutted humorously.

"Ah, but Jesse can cancel that out with his vote," Jamie continued the mock farce. "Which way do you swing, Jess?"

"Well…" Jesse pondered briefly.

"Jessss-seeee," Kayleigh stared intently at her brother.

"I abstain," he quickly uttered.

"Coward!" Jamie exclaimed with the two girls laughing in victory.

"In we go then," Gabrielle said, hand in hand with Kayleigh.

Jamie sat with Jesse on a set of stools next to the changing rooms where Gabrielle and Kayleigh were trying on matching dresses.

Despite her distain for clothes shopping, she was actually happy for the outing to be Gabrielle-centric to begin with seeing as she was always doing things for everyone else.

She then looked at Jesse while jabbing her finger into his back.

"Er, you rang?" he said.

"Ah, so you *do* have a spine after all," Jamie joked.

"Like *you* could ever say no to her," Jesse joked back.

"Excuses, excuses(!)"

"Whadya think?" Gabrielle stepped out of the booth in her black dress.

"Still sure you're not interested in modelling?" Jesse replied affirmatively.

"Jamie?" Gabrielle asked.

"I feel like I want to take you out to dinner," Jamie replied, to the laughter of Jesse and Gabrielle.

"Thanks," Gabrielle beamed. "You kitted out yet, Kay?"

"You tell me," Kayleigh said as she stepped out from behind the curtain in her matching dress, to the audible adoration of all three teenagers around her.

"So cute," Jamie remarked.

"Cute? I was going for 'hot'," Kayleigh cheekily replied.

"Stick with 'cute' for now," Jesse jumped in, being ever protective. "You can be 'hot' when you're older."

"Yes, *dad*," Kayleigh sassed. "Oh, we found something for Jamie to try on!"

"What is it?" Jamie asked wearily.

"It's in my changing booth, Gabrielle's got one to put on too."

"Am I going to like this?"

"You can always find out," Gabrielle encouraged.

"Yeah, come on, Jamie!" Kayleigh excitedly said.

"Yeah, Jamie(!)" Jesse gave her a gentle nudge. "Don't want to say no to Kay now, do you?"

"Cheeky git," Jamie quipped as she got up and headed into the booth, closing the curtain behind her. Kayleigh sniggered as she sat down beside Jesse.

"Oh Gabby, no!" the siblings heard Jamie erupt from the booth.

"Now, now, no backing out!" Gabrielle replied as she changed out of the dress while putting her own clothes on. "Alright, I'm sorted. You ready?"

"I guess," replied a sullen voice.

"Okay, out!"

Jesse and Kayleigh looked on at amazement as the two girls stepped out of the changing booths, both wearing cropped t-shirts with a rock music-influenced logo emblazoned across them.

"You look so awesome!" Kayleigh said.

"You really do," Jesse agreed, almost in awe.

"See, you look fabulous," Gabrielle said to Jamie who was trying to quell a smile she felt attempting to emerge.

"How come Gabby has a bellybutton piercing and you don't, Jamie?" Kayleigh asked, something made apparent by the fact the girls' midriffs were both exposed in their tops.

"Because Jamie here backed out at the last minute after agreeing to get hers done with me 'cause she got scared," Gabrielle mockingly responded while looking at Jamie.

"I wasn't scared, I just didn't really want a needle jammed into my navel," Jamie retorted.

"(Scared)," Gabrielle jokingly whispered to Kayleigh.

"At least you got it done!" Jamie replied in an annoyed tone. "You were the one who really wanted it anyway!"

"I know, just winding you up as always, you doughnut," Gabrielle said while kissing the side of Jamie's head. "C'mon, we'll change out of these and head to the toy place."

"Are we keeping the dresses?" Kayleigh asked.

"My credit card says yes," Gabrielle replied as she and Jamie returned to the changing booths. After closing the curtain, Jamie took another look at herself in the mirror and put on her jacket while keeping the crop top on. She gave a smile as she stared at herself for another few seconds before changing back into her regular t-shirt.

"Y'know, I'm actually amazed you managed to come home without buying everything in sight as always," Jamie said as she pulled out Gabrielle's bought clothes from the boot of the car.

"Oh, I do not spend that much," Gabrielle replied as she locked the car with Jamie following her towards the front door. "Besides, pay day's not until next week and I can't leave myself short."

"You're never short," Jamie refuted.

"Your money is your own, sweetie," Gabrielle responded. "But always appreciated."

Jamie smiled as she followed Gabrielle into the house.

"The bathroom's mine while I take my make-up off, just to pre-warn you."

"There *is* a downstairs toilet, Gabbs!" Jamie called back up the stairs as she heard the bathroom door close. Almost simultaneously, she heard the front door knock.

"Jamie Avon-*noit*?"

Jamie froze as she stared at two men standing before her on her doorstep.

"Avon-*wah*," she corrected. "And yes."

"We would like for you to accompany us for questioning in regards to a prison break that we believe you were involved in," one of them spoke while brandishing what appeared to be a police badge. Jamie felt a chill run through her spine.

"Just to be clear, we would like to do this the easy way, Miss," the other individual said, cutting off an attempt by Jamie to respond. "We really don't want to have to bring out the special ops, if you catch our drift."

Jamie stood helpless. She couldn't believe she had been found out and unlike Ryan Sharp's shadow operation grunts, she was unable to fight back against the law. The fact that they appeared to know of her true nature based on the threat of being in a special unit to handle her only terrified her more. She quietly closed the front door behind her as the two plain-clothed police officers led her to an unmarked armoured van in the near distance.

Chapter 3

"Hard to imagine just how much power is actually within her."

"Which surprises me she decided to come quietly. I'll give you credit, Brody, you know how they think."

"I just did my research, Layne. Plus after taking down a fugitive like Ryan Sharp, she can't be all that bad."

"What I see is someone who broke a criminal out of prison."

"Well if you're finished holding things up for the sake of worrying her more than she already is, I sure would like to get down to finding out why she did that."

"Like it even matters in the scheme of things."

Jamie sat motionless in her chair, too afraid to do anything in front of the two armed guards monitoring her from the opposite side of the room. She had felt her phone going off at least twice followed by another quick vibration indicating a text message which was probably Gabrielle trying to find out where she was. It surprised her that she had even been allowed to keep it on her.

Most of all she just wanted to know why she was being kept under guard for as long as she had been without anyone coming to speak to her.

After a few more minutes, she finally saw the door open as the two officers who had arrested her earlier entered and sat opposite the table to her.

"Okay, let's get the introductions out the way with: my name is David Layne and I'm with the Criminal Investigation Department and this here is Detective Lawrence Brody. We've been assigned to deal with you on the basis of your unique attributes, which is the technical term for saying you have super-human powers."

Jamie simply maintained her gaze upon Layne, trying her hardest not to show fear as she processed what was being spoken to her.

"However, it's what you chose to do with those powers that actually interests us, namely breaking someone out of prison. Detective Brody here is actually intrigued to find out why you did so."

Layne then leaned forward with his arms on the table.

"But to tell you the truth Miss Avon-*wah*, I'm not really bothered knowing why you did it," he said in a sterner tone of voice. "Far as I'm concerned, you broke the law and caused property damage in the process with those abilities of yours and from what evidence we have amassed on you, you have the potential to be a great threat to the city of London and beyond. Quite frankly, it would be the easiest solution to simply have you locked up under sedation for the rest of your days."

Jamie suddenly felt another wave of terror flowing through her body mixed with a feeling of injustice – she had actually *saved* the city from potential destruction at the hands of Ryan Sharp as opposed to trying to purposely cause any herself, not to mention also stopping a criminal gang of youths from plunging it into anarchy, yet she was the one facing punishment for it. She also didn't want to lose the life she had just managed to gain for herself after all the years of loneliness and misery she had suffered.

"But lucky for you, higher powers have taken an interest in your capabilities and potential," Layne continued, eliciting a small amount of relief in Jamie. "As you may have gathered from what I've said, we are aware of the existence of people with powers like you and aside from causing the government a monumental headache trying to cover up your acts and prevent the general population being aware of them on a constant basis, we do occasionally offer opportunities to the ones considered to be useful."

Opportunities?

"My own personal thoughts on you aside, my superiors were impressed with you being able to take down Ryan Sharp and deliver him to the police completely neutralised, given what he was later discovered to be capable of."

"What did he do?" Jamie decided to finally speak.

"If you must know, he was taken into custody but not only did he try to break out several hours later, he also tried to kill several responding police officers who attempted to prevent his escape. They were able to taser him into submission in the end but two of them are currently in critical condition owing to the extensive injuries his powers dealt them."

Jamie couldn't help but feel some guilt regarding the officers' injuries, having known Sharp's powers were always going to eventually restore after she had deactivated them.

"So despite you being entirely at fault for those servicemen and women being thrown into harm's way, as well as another empowered criminal being let loose upon the streets, the top brass want to offer you the chance to work with our operation in combating special ability-based crime, which to sum up involves doing what you did to Ryan Sharp on a more regular and controlled basis."

Jamie took a moment to think to herself, realising she probably didn't have a choice in the matter but would effectively be doing the same thing as she had been doing the months leading up to befriending Jesse; the very thing she had vowed to stop doing. Except now she would be doing it with an actual proper agenda.

Not that Jesse and Gabrielle would be any less annoyed by it though...

"On that note, I have other things to be doing so I shall leave you in the capable hands of Detective Brody here who I'm sure has plenty of further things to discuss with you. Good day," Layne dismissively stated as he got up and left the room. Jamie turned her attention to Brody who looked at the guards behind him.

"I think we will be alright alone from this point," he said.

"Are you sure?" one of them asked.

"Yes," he assured them, watching as they both left the room. He then turned his attention back to the timid-looking teenager with colourful hair in front of him.

"Why did you send them away?" Jamie asked.

"I trust you not to attack me," Brody answered.

"Why?"

"Because I don't consider you to be the malevolent n'er-do-well that Detective Layne does. Far as I'm concerned, you stopped a potential rampaging maniac who I'm convinced was responsible for that double-decker bus being twisted into oblivion. But I am still curious as to why you broke that other person out of prison though, if you wouldn't mind enlightening me?"

"He had a specific power I needed to stop Sharp with, which is how I ended up defeating him," Jamie said. "The only way I could get him to agree to give it to me was to set him free in return. I didn't want to do it but I figured the positives of doing so outweighed the negatives."

"From a neutral stance, I'm inclined to agree with you," Brody sympathised. "We were able to re-arrest that Miles Donwick fella yesterday with some help from our other resources so at least he's back in jail, albeit in the right environment this time that prevents his powers from creating havoc now that we are aware of what he actually is. For a gang leader though, he didn't seem too hesitant to co-operate with us in revealing who busted him out."

"So *he's* the reason you found out who I was," Jamie said.

"Not directly – he couldn't give us your name on account of not knowing it but he did mention the previous encounter you had with him in Cerulean Park which just happened to have been caught on videotape by Ryan Sharp's little clandestine project."

"You know about that?"

"He didn't exactly employ an effective 'scorched earth' policy regarding that facility of his to be honest. We were able to recover the digital logs and video files of his operation, including everything on you, which ultimately led to us identifying you. I'm going to assume you're the one who blew that hole through his building?"

"Yeah, I was. He had held me against my will for experimentation purposes regarding my powers."

"In which case, I give you my thanks for helping to expose his activities. Prosecuting him for serial kidnapping and human rights abuses would be otherwise straightforward if not for the nature of his abilities."

"Where is he now?"

"In an induced coma in a special holding facility of our own design to confine the more dangerous and unmanageable empowered criminals we deal with, ironically not unlike what he did to many of his captured test subjects. Until we can figure out how to disable or even remove his powers permanently, putting him in a regular prison is unfeasible."

"Poetic justice I suppose."

"Well, as part of your co-operation with us, telling us what powers he actually possesses would be a good start," Brody said while taking out a notepad and a pen.

"His main power is to be able to absorb the powers of others," Jamie answered. "According to the person who helped him locate the original ability, it is activated when the holder feels a strong desire to attain someone else's nearby powers. He's used that to gain the abilities of solar manipulation, magnetism and power analysis and detection. He also has access to flight as you may already be aware."

"Any more?"

"Not that I'm aware of," Jamie replied, choosing to keep the rest of Sharp's inherited powers from Jesse to herself for her friend's sake.

"And if you don't mind me asking, what can *you* do precisely?"

"I can manipulate abilities; deactivate them, make them stronger or even absorb them for myself if I choose to."

"That definitely explains what I saw in that park footage of you," Brody remarked. "And why were you engaging that gang in the first place out of curiosity?"

"I caught them discussing starting a riot in the city so I did what I had to do to stop them."

"So, you consider yourself a vigilante then?"

"No, I just had a lot of angst to release."

"That wouldn't be down to your parents both having died, I'm guessing?"

"...Partially," Jamie hesitantly responded. "I was also the victim of an attempted sexual assault at the hands of another empowered piece of scum and I was just feeling run down so I thought it would relieve the misery I was going through to experiment with my powers when I discovered them."

"If I'm being up front with you, you really don't come across as a trouble-making miscreant to me," Brody said.

"Too bad your partner doesn't feel the same way about that."

"Not that I will lie and say he isn't a handful to deal with and I have to admit he doesn't exactly view each case with an unbiased mind but he has his uses."

"Such as?"

"Dealing with the more hostile empowered beings we arrest mainly. We're practically two different sides of the same coin: his straightforward, no-nonsense approach and my more clued-up and restrained manner. We balance each other out in that sense."

"He doesn't exactly make anyone want to co-operate with his attitude," Jamie said.

"That attitude is mainly to let people know not to mess him around, at least with the ones we offer amnesty to in exchange for their service."

"And how long would I be expected to work for you guys?"

"That's to Layne's discretion I'm afraid," Brody replied. "I can't honestly tell you when he would consider letting you go but with his preference to having you imprisoned instead and that this offer of co-operation is for all intent and purposes an alternative to jail, it could be a while."

"Great," Jamie lamented. "And I actually told my friends I wouldn't be doing this anymore too."

"If it's any consolation, your involvement will be on a per-case basis. Which means that unfortunately you could be called upon at any given time but at the very least, you will be paid a basic wage for every case you participate in."

Jamie suddenly felt far less optimistic towards the endeavour upon learning of the erratic schedule that had the potential to really disrupt her blossoming personal life.

Her thoughts were then disrupted by the vibration of her phone going off again in her pocket. She decided to pull it out, seeing that it was Gabrielle trying once more to get through to her.

"Can I take this quick?" she asked Brody. "I left the house without saying where I was going."

"By all means," he replied.

"Hello?" Jamie answered.

"Jamie, where the hell have you been?!" Gabrielle responded in a furious tone. *"You can't just go off without at least telling me where you are!"*

"I know, I'm sorry," Jamie replied sheepishly. "I'll be home soon, I just had something important to deal with. I'll explain everything when I get back."

"This better be good, Jamie."

"I'll see you in a bit."

"Okay, bye."

Gabrielle then abruptly ended the call, Jamie feeling the venomous sting of her anger as she turned her attention back to Brody.

"So where do we go from here?" she asked.

"Well you're free to go of course," Brody replied. "You won't be monitored or tagged or anything of the kind, you can go about your daily life and you'll only be contacted if a situation arises that really needs your specific aid. So you don't have to worry about your life being disrupted too heavily but be aware you could receive a call or text at any given time."

"Okay."

"And probably to your relief, you'll be dealing directly with me for the most part. Layne will only pop up every now and then but as he has a key role in the operation and can insert himself into anything he wants at a moment's notice, you can expect him to be involved in virtually every case you undertake."

"I've dealt with more toxic personalities than him I suppose."

"Before you go though, I would like to introduce you to two other individuals with special abilities that are working with us using their specific skills."

"If you want," Jamie meekly replied, her social anxiety suddenly flaring up as Brody led her out of the room and up a flight of stairs.

"This is our general office area where our main officers conduct their work," Brody said while walking Jamie into a large room with multiple cubicles being occupied by uniformed individuals. "Over in the corner is where one of the people I want you to meet is situated."

Jamie followed Brody to the end of the room where he approached what appeared to be a young woman with raven-black hair and brown eyes sitting at a desk with three computer monitors.

"Rachel, you got a minute?" he asked the person.

"For you, Brody, I have two," Rachel quipped back in response. "Who do you have there?"

"This is a young lady by the name of Jamie Avonoit who will be joining us on the field from time to time. I thought you might like to make her acquaintance."

"My, she's a pretty one," Rachel exclaimed. "And such awesome hair, I think I'm going to like her."

Jamie couldn't help but smile a little to herself.

"So what did you pick her up on then?"

"Well not to embarrass her too much but you have the distinction of meeting the person who singlehandedly took down Ryan Sharp."

"Hmm, impressive. Especially with what a nightmare he turned out to be. I'm guessing you're packing quite a powerful ability then?"

Brody gave an encouraging look towards Jamie.

"I can manipulate abilities and absorb them," she replied, feeling intimidated but also in awe of the friendly young woman before her.

"Very intriguing indeed," Rachel replied.

"And Rachel here has the also intriguing ability to manipulate computers and other various technological devices, and came up on our radar when she very carelessly decided to try and hack into our mainframe a year back."

"Guilty!" Rachel shamelessly remarked to Jamie's amusement.

"But rather than lock her up for ten thousand years as suggested by Layne–"

"Urgh, what a tosser," Rachel interrupted.

"...we decided to give her a full-time role working for the department instead," Brody finished. "As it turned out, while Rachel is obviously adept at commanding certain technology at will, she lacked the expertise and knowledge behind her powers so we've been slowly building her up on said knowledge to aid us in cracking down on techno-terrorists and general internet criminals and scam artists."

"Was pretty fun bringing down that online paedophile ring three months back, I must admit," Rachel replied before putting the back of her hand to her mouth in a secretive manner towards Jamie. "(Was also fun signing Layne's phone up to receive special offer text messages from every pizza place in the local area)."

"Which of course I'm sure she will have undone by the time I see her again later on(!)" Brody replied with Jamie smirking in the background.

"Of course," Rachel said with a sarcastic wink.

"Anyhow, it's time I introduced you to the other recruit," Brody addressed Jamie before beginning to walk back towards the door.

"Catch you around, Jame," Rachel said flirtatiously as Jamie followed Brody out.

"She seems fun," Jamie remarked as they walked through a corridor.

"Definitely brightens up the place when she's not playing pranks," Brody replied.

"Is the other person as interesting?"

"Turns out you already know this one, and I don't think it'll be as pleasant as meeting Rachel but I feel it's necessary for the sake of moving forward," Brody said as he opened the door to another room, one similar to the interrogation room the pair of them had spoken in earlier with Layne.

"Alright," Jamie said as she followed him in, wondering which of her previous opponents it could be. She suddenly felt a flash of anger upon seeing who was seated at the table in the centre of the room.

"Don't let her near me!" Dawn yelled as she jumped out the chair.

"Nobody's hurting anybody in here," Brody responded, holding an arm out in front of Jamie.

"Why is she working for you?!" Jamie furiously demanded. "She helped Sharp abduct dozens of people with abilities and experimented on them, she deserves to be left to rot!"

"You're sounding like Layne there, Jamie," Brody responded in a more unpleasant tone. "Like you, she has a specific skill that we can utilise to aid our operation, and like you she has been offered amnesty in exchange for her co-operation."

"What I did is hardly comparable to what she and Sharp were responsible for doing."

"I don't disagree but now you are both working for a common cause and I think it best to sort out your differences so we can all co-operate better in the future."

"How on earth do you expect me to work with someone who twice had me imprisoned against my will?" Jamie protested.

"Hey, I'm not keen on being anywhere near you either," Dawn fired back. "But it's either I do this or I end up in prison for the next ten years. I think I know where I stand."

"Well you can stand on your own, love!"

"Jamie, you're going to have to find some mutual ground here," Brody attempted to mediate. "This is not an ideal situation I admit and I can understand your anger but sometimes we have to do things we don't like with people we're not fond of. It's life. Now I recommend calming down a bit."

Jamie seethed but then thought of a way to work the situation to her advantage.

"Give me your hand," she said to Dawn.

"Why?" Dawn responded.

"If I'm going to be working on this project, I need more of your power to determine what I'm dealing with in the future."

"How can I use it myself if you have it? That's the whole point of me being here!"

"You know it replenishes itself after a while," Jamie rebutted. "But as a gesture of good will, I will restore it to normal levels upon absorbing it for myself. How does that sound?"

Brody looked towards Dawn, finding the proposal to be unconventional but meeting him halfway at the least. Dawn hesitated.

"Okay, fine," she finally responded, not feeling as though she had much of a choice anyway as she held out her arm and activated her ability. Jamie took hold of her bare hand and quickly absorbed the maximum amount she could before replenishing what she had taken in Dawn's body.

"Are we done here?" Jamie brazenly said to Brody.

"Yes," he simply replied while leading her to the closed door, leaving Dawn behind.

"Was that really necessary?" Jamie asked Brody upon the door closing.

"In my opinion, yes," he answered.

"What did it even prove? I still don't want anything to do with her."

"I would imagine not but I just wanted to see if you could compromise, and I'm glad to see that you did to an extent. If anything I learned from seeing that footage of you in the park, you can be brash and even a little arrogant in your approach which leads to recklessness. I'm not going to claim to know you inside out, which I don't, but I want to make sure you approach every situation you engage in with a rational mind."

"You don't have to worry about me," Jamie replied, not disagreeing with what Brody was saying based on her other previous skirmishes.

"I'm afraid I do; I'm in charge of you and that makes you my responsibility also, so anything that you do reflects on me, good or bad. But on a more personal level, you're a bright young woman with your whole life still ahead of you – I would rather see you still have that life to live despite the situations you may be thrown into while working for us."

"Alright," Jamie replied after a brief pause, having not expected Brody to empathise with her. The truth was that she did not like the fact she was on a leash to effect and under the control of law enforcement but it did at least help that she had some allies within the organisation. Working with someone like Brody probably might make the whole thing bearable at the least.

How the hell am I going to explain this to Gabrielle?

Jamie stood outside her front door, fearful of Gabrielle's reaction upon entering. It was definitely a déjà vu moment from the previous month. Having been present for the Ryan Sharp bout, Jesse would've been the one to be more understanding of everything that had transpired but Gabrielle would only see it as another betrayal of her trust, regardless of the circumstances in which the incident had come to be and everything leading up to it.

She hesitated a few more seconds before finally choosing to enter the house, for better or worse. The moment she closed the door behind her, she heard the television immediately turn off and an irritated-looking Gabrielle storming towards her from the front room. The situation was almost borderline terrifying.

"Feel free to speak," Gabrielle said in an unimpressed and demanding tone.

"Okay," Jamie spoke softly. "I was at a police station."

"Why?" Gabrielle's demeanour quickly changed to concern. "Did something happen to you?"

Jamie stalled. She couldn't go through with it. Somehow she had to come up with something that wasn't completely the truth but enough to keep her out of the doghouse, something that would also play off Gabrielle's concerned tone. She knew she would hate herself later for it but it was better than the alternative.

"No...the police, when conducting their investigation into Ryan Sharp, discovered that he was running a secret project that involved abducting and experimenting on humans with powers like us."

"Is that the actual reason why he was abducting people as reported?" Gabrielle asked.

"Yeah, he was trying to discover how to replicate abilities and be able to implant them into normal human beings," Jamie continued, surprising herself just how coherent she was making everything sound so far. "They also discovered an archive of videos that he had amassed which involved spying on people using their powers. I was in one of those videos."

"What, did they arrest you for having super powers?" Gabrielle asked, confused and worried.

"Not exactly," Jamie replied, knowing she had to make sure the rest of the story was nailed on. "They told me that they know of our existence and had built a special operation entirely around preventing ability-based crime and activity, aiming to keep us out of public knowledge. But rather than put me away, they offered me the opportunity to help in their cases instead."

"I don't understand," Gabrielle said. "Are you saying they're forcing you to do their dirty work to avoid being locked away just for having powers?"

"Kind of," Jamie sombrely replied, feeling guilt-ridden but mildly relieved at Gabrielle not being mad at her.

"How is that fair?!" Gabrielle exasperated. "You've done nothing wrong!"

"They said it may not be forever if I prove that I'm not a threat in any way," Jamie lied. "And it's only whenever they actually need me for anything involving my specific powers, they're not just going to order me into every given situation that arises."

"Am I supposed to take comfort in that?"

"Well...no," Jamie despondently replied.

"I don't know what to say, Jamie," Gabrielle said, almost on the verge of getting upset. "How am I supposed to deal with the fact some arsehole police operation is going to be practically throwing you into all kinds of danger on a general basis?"

"I promised you that I wasn't going to do anything stupid anymore and I intend to keep that," Jamie tried to calm the situation. "I will be working with their forces, not being sent in as a sacrificial lamb. I'll make sure I have regular amounts of Jesse's shielding ability and flight to protect myself no matter what issue I'm to deal with."

Unable to say anything, Gabrielle simply grabbed Jamie in a tight hug.

"Nobody's taking you away from me," she quietly sobbed.

"I'm never going away," Jamie replied while holding Gabrielle back. Despite the embellished tale, if ever she needed a reminder of how much her friend truly loved and valued her, the current moment was probably it. She just hoped that she could literally live up to that pledge in the face of her new engagement.

Chapter 4

Marcella stared through the window of the small flat, not in the least bit concerned that anyone down on the street might glance up at her completely naked. Not that it mattered to her what anyone thought in general, seeing as it wasn't hard for her to twist people's minds to however she wanted them to anyway. She knew in the grand scheme of things that she served greater forces than anyone could humanly imagine and her life in addition to everyone else's was nothing compared to that cause.

"Babe, come back to bed," a male voice stirred.

"Busy," Marcella replied without turning around.

"You know there's no lace curtain over that window?"

"All the more for everyone looking through to enjoy the view of."

"Well I'm sure I'd enjoy it more than them, if you were to join me back over here."

"Was last night not enough for you?"

"A guy could easily get used to that," the male flat occupier seductively replied.

"I'll bet," Marcella responded bluntly.

"Not short on confidence, are you?"

"Call it a gift."

"The gift you got handed in that body alone was one hell of a doozie, love."

"That's not my greatest gift though," Marcella said as she climbed onto the bed and straddled the young man on top of the duvet cover. "You ever think about where we go when we die?"

"Doesn't really interest me," he replied.

"That's too bad. Some believe they'll join the angels in the sky. But I know my place – right by the throne of Hell itself."

"Huh?"

"I suppose to an atheist like you it won't make a lot of sense but the dark prince has his plan for me," Marcella spoke as her eyes began to glow an eerie shade of crimson. "Why else would I have been given such power to manipulate people's mental states?"

The male simply stared back in a hypnotic trance.

"How does the old saying go? 'Better to reign in Hell than be the servant of Heaven'?" Marcella continued while climbing down from the bed and getting dressed. "My time on this earth will be well spent serving my master below, but your pointless existence has come to an end I'm afraid."

Marcella put on her boots and opened the flat door before turning back around towards the entranced flat owner.

"When you take your plunge off the top of the building after I leave, please make sure you tell them who sent you when you arrive in the abode of the damned."

*   *   *

"So when I play this G chord, all you need to do is play the root note on the third fret of the E string."

"The *what* note?" Cecelia replied.

"It's the same G note that my guitar chord is based on," Jamie answered, indicating on her guitar fretboard the note in question.

"Easy in theory, not so much in practice," Cecelia said as she haplessly tried playing the note on her bass guitar, eliciting a lot of buzzing noise from the barely correct finger positioning she was applying to the fretboard.

"Chuck it here, I'll show you," Jamie said as she put her own guitar down. Flipping the bass to accommodate her left-handedness, she began playing the G note flawlessly.

"Guess I've got a while to go."

"Just pick the string while watching TV or something with your finger holding down the same note, you'll get a feel for it eventually."

"Well I really want to see where we can go with being a band so I'll work on it until my fingers bleed," Sissy joked. "Are you alright, Jamie?"

"Why, do I look sad?" Jamie responded.

"Well I was going to ask when you arrived earlier but you seemed a bit off, like something was bothering you."

"Just some minor bullshit from yesterday."

"Boy troubles?"

"I wish. Just a run-in with some arsehole coppers."

"What'd they do?"

"Stop and search," Jamie lied. "Probably down to the appearance."

"The boys had that once, luckily they were alert enough to discreetly shove their weed down their pants when they saw the pigs walking over."

"They get off scot-free?"

"Yeah, Rob knows how to make friendly chat with anyone anyway. They *did* bring it on themselves though for choosing to congregate in a cemetery, probably got grassed up by a visitor."

"Eeep."

"So you got any guys on your radar at the moment then?"

"Oh y'know, just trying to win over that mate of mine," Jamie mockingly responded, though noticed Sissy giving her an intriguing look in return. "I was *joking*."

"Or maybe you're not," Sissy joked back. Jamie could only think to herself just how accurate to a degree that probably was.

"And have *you* got someone on your mind?"

"Nah, still trying to put the last relationship behind me really. But I'm still down for some fun in the meantime."

"Reckon your powers are better under control now regarding that?"

"I'd hope so, don't want them wrecking my love life in the future," said Sissy. "Speaking of which, do you have any cool new ones?"

"I don't know about 'cool' but the one I recently absorbed was interesting to say the least." Jamie replied. "Being able to feel what other people are feeling is a bit trippy."

"Where'd you get that from?"

"Someone who didn't know how to control it themselves," Jamie replied vaguely, wishing to protect Kayleigh. "I've been trying to avoid dealing with folk with powers lately to be honest."

"The thrill of it gone?"

"A little, though it's mainly wanting to make the most of my social life more. And I had an insane encounter only a fortnight ago that was a bit much."

"What happened there?"

"You know that guy that was in the news for kidnapping – *Ryan Sharp*?"

"Yeah," Sissy answered, curious.

"He managed to gain several powers himself and I took him down."

"Say *what*, girl?" Sissy reacted with astonishment.

"Not that you'll read about it online or anywhere but he had been abducting and experimenting on people like us to get the abilities in the first place. Managed to get the best of him though and drop him off at the cop shop."

"Wow, never a dull moment with you," Sissy remarked.

"Not a moment I want to relive either," Jamie replied. "I nearly bit off more than I could chew, if not for the abilities I absorbed beforehand to fend him off and defea–"

Jamie abruptly paused towards the end of her sentence as something passed through her head.

John…

"You alright?" Sissy asked.

"Yeah, I just remembered something I nearly forgot about," Jamie replied.

"Well if you need to go deal with that, I can work on getting the hang of the bass in the meantime."

"You sure?"

"Well Rob needs it back for his rehearsal in two days' time so the more I work on it now, the better."

"I'd hate to just bail on you though, I've only been round an hour."

"Jamie, I'll be dragging you round here to jam every other day once I'm able to play properly!" Sissy laughed. "If you've got something to take care of, sort it out while you can."

"Thanks," Jamie smiled while packing her guitar away in her case. "Do let me know later how you get on."

"I'm hoping to be able to play without getting that buzz noise by the end of the day," Sissy replied. "Text me when you get home though."

"Will do."

Jamie stood before John's building on Denington Street, having dropped her guitar and portable amp off at her house beforehand. The scene felt extremely similar to their last encounter, only this time it was a courtesy call as opposed to asking a favour. John unlikely was even aware of the fact she had blatantly lied to him about absorbing his powers to begin with, yet she still felt bad for having done so regardless. Several months ago she would have hardly even cared but she felt a goodness in John that she rarely came across that didn't deserve to be taken advantage of.

Walking inside, Jamie quickly caught glimpse of a figure sweeping the corridor.

"Miss Jamie," John said as he noticed the person standing at the other side of the hall. "I'm surprised to see you here."

"Thought I'd drop by," Jamie replied. "How have you been doing?"

"I am fine, thank you for asking. Just having a quiet day so I thought I'd get ahead of keeping the place clean. Did that situation you had going on end up being resolved?"

"Thanks to you, yeah," Jamie sheepishly replied.

"I'm not sure I understand?"

"How long did it take for your ability to restore to normal in the end?"

"I don't know exactly but by the time I attempted to see if it had returned three days later, it was back to normal."

"That was not unexpected if I'm honest with you," Jamie said, slowly building herself up. "I wasn't completely truthful though when I said I was deactivating it at the time."

"You took it for yourself?" John replied, in an unsurprised tone.

"Yes. I know I shouldn't have lied to you about it but had I not, my friend would've probably been killed."

"Deep down, I probably already knew," John said. "Or at least subconsciously I was glad to have been able to help you without having advertently given you my powers. Not that I condone being mislead of course but I'm happy that someone who obviously means a great deal to you is still alive."

"Are you mad though?" Jamie asked.

"Life is too short and too precious to get angry over unnecessary matters, Jamie. And I know that trying to strip myself of my ability was wishful thinking anyway. It will always be a part of me, testing me to avoid the temptation of trying to use it until the day I die, something that I plan to do with a lot more devotion in the future."

"Well I won't be tempting you to break that pact again," Jamie said. "Anyhow, you want me to take care of that sweeping?"

"I've got the whole building to do still," John responded.

"I owe you that much."

"If you really want to," John said, holding the broom out for Jamie to take.

Jamie walked up to her front door two hours later, feeling glad to have made amends with her unwitting ability donor while considering herself lucky it had been an amicable affair, though mainly due to John's forgiving nature.

She didn't see herself meeting up with him again though, finding very little shared interests or anything really in common to fully enjoy his company. Though she was far less bothered about indulging in her powers than in previous weeks compared to John's open reluctance, she still found the religious angle the most off-putting. Not that she had a problem with his faith at all but she just couldn't relate to it.

The only thing that she remotely held in relation to any of that was the hope that her parents were enjoying a heavenly afterlife, which only off-set her anger at having lost them so young to begin with. Maybe she would revisit the possibilities of a belief system when she was older but for now she just wanted to continue trying to carve out a life for herself after having lacked one for so long, in spite of her new 'career' potentially getting in the way of that.

After quickly texting Sissy that she had made it home, Jamie scrolled through a few online videos demonstrating how to prepare several different meals. She hoped to surprise Gabrielle with a Spanish-esque paella meal upon her return to work, something that they had never eaten while living under the same roof but something Jamie assumed her friend would enjoy.

At around 6:30pm, Jamie finally heard the front door open.

"Heeeey!" she called out lovingly as she got up off the couch to greet Gabrielle. "Hope you're in the mood for something different for dinn–"

"I'm sorry, I'm not feeling hungry right now, Jame," Gabrielle replied sullenly, her eye make-up appearing to have been smudged from tears.

"What's wrong, babe?" Jamie asked, concerned.

"It's nothing, just had a massive row with my mum."

"That where you just come from?"

"She wanted to have a chat so I swung by hers. Wish I hadn't now," Gabrielle sighed.

"Anything I can do to help?"

"Nah, I'm just going to go to bed and forget this day ever happened."

Jamie watched on as Gabrielle walked dejectedly up the staircase, hearing her bedroom slam shut moments later. Disappointed, she took the bowl of paella into the kitchen and wrapped it in cling film before putting it in the fridge.

She then crept up the staircase and carefully pressed her ear against Gabrielle's door, hearing muffled sobs on the other side. She reluctantly decided to give her space and check up on her in the morning but couldn't help but wonder what her mother had discussed with her to bring on such a reaction to begin with.

Chapter 5

Jamie awakened in the morning to find that Gabrielle had already left for work, notably earlier than usual. Either it was a coincidence or she had deliberately planned to evade any questioning regarding what had happened with her mother.

Whatever her stance, Jamie sent a text message to her reminding her that she was available to talk it out. A belated reply came through an hour later, simply stating 'Xx'.

Before she could ponder on the matter any further, her phone began ringing with 'Detective Brody' coming up as the caller.

Oh, perfect...

"Hello?" Jamie spoke into the receiver.

"Hello, Jamie," Brody replied. *"I've got a matter to discuss with you that would be a decent introduction to your co-operation to the department. If you would like to head down here for noon, I'll be able to go through it with you in person."*

"Yeah, that's not a problem," Jamie responded.

"Okay, see you in a bit then."

Jamie ended the call, still feeling uncomfortable with the involuntary arrangement. With the time currently being half past nine, she decided to shower and put on her usual clothes as opposed to anything formal, opting to appear unapologetically defiant while begrudgingly complying with the assignment bestowed upon her. She almost hoped Layne was there to witness her showing up as such.

"Afternoon, Jamie."

"It's still technically morning," Jamie replied to Brody as she entered his office at five minutes to midday.

"Touché," he responded. "Well let's get right down to business: we've had an incident brought to our attention that may have involved super-powered activity."

"So what went down?"

"A young man was found dead on the street yesterday, having apparently jumped off the top of the flat he was inhabiting."

"Yikes," Jamie tamely replied, though feeling slightly uneasy at the same time. "Am I going to have to see the body?"

"No, nothing involving that," Brody answered. "But we have reason to suspect that foul play may have been involved in the individual's death."

"Somebody with powers, I'm guessing?"

"That's the intriguing part," Brody replied. "We interviewed a woman in her early twenties yesterday in regards to the incident; she was seen on security footage leaving the same property approximately ten minutes before the victim plunged to his death and she isn't a resident of the place so it got us wondering if she was the last person to interact with him. We had actually brought her in to ask her if she had known the deceased or visited him prior to his fall, which she denied, but she unexpectedly became a person of interest upon her arrival to the precinct anyway."

"And what was the reason for that?"

"As we led her through the building, Dawn noted the use of a telepathic, mind-manipulation ability within close proximity. And soon after this discovery, the ability completed disappeared from detection."

"So you think this person has that telepathy power and used it to make the victim commit suicide?" Jamie asked.

"It's not completely unlikely," Brody responded. "The power flare-up could've just been a coincidence or it could have been the young woman using the same power to read the minds of the people in the precinct including Dawn and deciding to deactivate her ability upon realising it was being detected."

"Not a bad theory," said Jamie. "But as you say, it could just be a coincidence."

"Well so far we've not attained much evidence that the victim was looking to end his own life in the first place," Brody replied. "His colleagues all noted that he wasn't depressed leading up to his alleged suicide and his quite active social media activity in his final days appears to back that up. Additionally, he had just booked a ticket to attend a music festival in July only two days before he took that leap off the top of his building. So at the moment it's the leading theory but nonetheless, we have a potentially dangerous empowered human walking the streets right now with the ability to control the minds of anyone around her."

"And you want me to subdue her?" Jamie asked.

"No, not given the nature of this ability but Layne has pushed for it so you're officially on the case now," Brody answered, with a tinge of reluctance in his voice. "However, I don't want you directly engaging with her. Instead, I want you to monitor her and try and detect any power use with Dawn's ability so we can confirm she is what we suspect of her."

"Why not just haul her in anyway just to be safe?"

"Because then we really *would* be as bad as Ryan Sharp," Brody asserted. "And for the sake of the secrecy of the operation, it's best not to risk bringing in potentially innocent persons with no knowledge of super-human abilities to begin with."

"Smart," Jamie replied, thinking to herself that Layne probably disagreed with that notion.

"Ah, Miss Avonoit," a familiar voice emerged from behind.

Oh, great...

"I'm guessing Detective Brody has just clued you in to our latest caper," Layne brashly spoke to Jamie.

"Indeed," Jamie replied, pretending to sound interested.

"Goodo, and do try *not* to break this one out if and when we apprehend her(!)"

"I'll keep it in mind," Jamie replied with a roll of her eyes. Layne then brought his face a few inches forward.

"Next time you feel like giving me sass, young lady," he growled. "Just remember where you could end up if you get on the wrong side of me. Understand?"

"Yes…" Jamie responded, silently seething.

"Now get to work," Layne remarked as he turned to Brody. "Got any further updates, Larry?"

"Nothing at the moment, Layne," Brody answered.

"Then let's hope Miss Avonoit here can prove she's not as hopeless as she looks," Layne bullishly said before walking away.

"Before you go," Brody said to a clearly agitated Jamie. "Go speak to Rachel."

"Any particular reason?" a fuming Jamie asked.

"Because I reckon she's the best person for you to vent your annoyance and clear your head," Brody smiled before walking away.

Jamie entered the first floor of the precinct, still feeling thoroughly wound up by Layne's indignant attitude towards her. Not that it was anything she hadn't previously experienced but it was frustrating not having the option of garnering some small means of petty revenge without risking being indefinitely locked up for her trouble. Clearly, Layne was going to be a constant thorn in her side during her tenure as part of his operation; it was just a matter of being able to learn to tolerate him in the long run for the sake of the overall arrangement.

"Jamie! How are ya?" Rachel said enthusiastically as the sullen-looking teenager entered her workspace.

"Been better," Jamie replied while attempting a smile.

"Layne?"

"Yeah. How did you know?"

"Brody told me to expect you following your briefing. I guessed that the blowhard was involved."

"Pretty good guess," said Jamie.

"Don't worry, he's an arse to pretty much anyone with powers."

"There a reason for that specifically?"

"Pfft, I assumed he just has a personality defect," Rachel nonchalantly replied. "He's easy to deal with anyhow."

"Not so easy when he's holding your freedom in his hands," Jamie dismissively responded.

"True, but you just haven't proved what a valuable commodity you are yet. Once you nail that, he's just blowing hot air. How else do you reckon I'm still sitting here in spite of all the pranks I pull on him?"

"How long did it take you to get to that point?" Jamie asked, intrigued.

"*Well*, it did require a successful effort on my part in setting up a trap on the dark web to snare a drug trafficking ring but once I had achieved that, I knew Layne would have a hard time touching me afterwards."

"Why's that?"

"Well often people like that take the precaution of making their internet footprint practically untraceable with advanced encryption methods that even the boys in blue have problems cracking, but my powers allow me to uniquely bypass those encryptions without much effort. So thanks to me, Brody and co managed to make a huge bust in a short matter of time that otherwise might've taken months to do. I went from being an unwilling tool to a valued asset practically overnight."

"And Layne doesn't give you any grief?" Jamie inquired.

"He did try to continue his antipathy approach but I then let him know who's boss by subtlely flooding his work e-mail with spam. He threatened me over it but he then discovered his personal e-mail inbox had received the same treatment. Funnily enough he hasn't really bothered me too much since then apart from giving the odd glare when he walks nearby."

"Nice," Jamie replied, feeling her sour mood suddenly lifting. *Kudos, Detective Brody.*

"I guess the drawback is that he's taking that out on you now though," Rachel grimaced. "But whether Layne wants to admit it or not, we're the ones making the difference between catching criminals and letting them slip away, powers or otherwise. The fact you were even offered a deal in the first place means you have some use to them that they wish to make the most of. Many other captured guys and girls just end up in the cells as they're simply considered a hindrance."

"Are they really just left to rot?"

"I don't know, never been too interested in finding out. It's not like they're my brethren or anything; Ryan Sharp certainly isn't someone who deserves to be walking about free right now with his capabilities so I guess the means are somewhat justified to an extent in this case. More than what he himself was doing with his little science project anyway."

"Well I know what that felt like," Jamie replied. "Suppose that's the only way to look at it."

"Like I'd let that douchebag Layne throw you down there too," Rachel said. "I can tell you're one of the good ones. Plus I love your style!"

"Thanks," Jamie responded, feeling overwhelmed by appreciation.

"But alas, I need to crack on with bolstering the place's firewall. You'd be amazed just how many viruses are on these computers in the office. Hit me up when we're both free sometime though."

"Will do," Jamie said, aware that she had her own task at hand as she proceeded to leave the area to head outside.

"Do you feel anything?"

"Not really," Kayleigh responded. "Are you sure you were able to feel a person's emotions without physical contact?"

"Well I did also use my power analysis ability at the same time," Jamie replied. "But you might be able to do the same if I'm standing right next to you."

Kayleigh attempted once more to tap into Jamie's emotions, eventually giving up.

"Nothing?"

"Nowt," Kayleigh replied.

"Strange," Jamie replied, surprised that Kayleigh wasn't even able to feel what she was feeling from a foot away when she had sensed Nate with the same ability from halfway across town, power analysis ability combined or otherwise. "At least you're handling your empathy powers better as a whole anyway."

"How did it feel when you experienced what that guy was feeling? Y'know, just so I can get a rough guide."

"Surreal would be putting it mildly," Jamie answered. "And I wasn't even trying to do anything initially, it just spontaneously happened. Then I felt a sharp pain but I think that had something to do with the clown misusing his powers or something."

"Well I definitely don't want to feel that!" Kayleigh butted in.

"Just don't focus on anyone getting hurt," Jamie joked. "Might as well pack it in for now. Mind if I bug your brother for a few minutes?"

"Sure, you can *hug* him for a few minutes!" Kayleigh teased.

"Sooooo clever, aren't cha?" Jamie replied, feeling relieved that Kayleigh was unable to feel her emotions at that current moment as she got up to leave the room. But then her lingering mixed feelings towards Jesse wasn't the worst thing his sister could have picked up on compared to the nightmarish vision of him she had seen through Nate's future sight ability, whatever the reason behind that was.

"Yo, Jess," she said as she opened the elder sibling's bedroom door.

"Have fun with the munchkin?" Jesse replied, lying on the bed with a magazine in hand.

"As always, though seemed to hit a wall with her empathy training today."

"How so?"

"Well I was able to use it to empathically track a rogue teleporter the other day from across town, albeit in combination with my analysis powers but Kay couldn't even feel me from close range."

"Might just be that you have more experience with it?"

"It was like my first proper go with it and I didn't exactly plan it either, it activated on its own."

"Weird," Jesse replied. "Maybe it varies with each user. But still, the aim for Kayleigh was at least to get a handle of it so it won't leave her catatonic again and at least that's been successful thus far."

"True," Jamie relented. "Puzzling nonetheless."

"Knowing you, I can imagine it's winding you up. Can take your mind off it with a round of dominoes with Kay if you want?"

"I did actually come in to let you know something," Jamie replied, awkwardly. Jesse's eyes narrowed, sensing something was up from the tone of voice.

"Doesn't sound like I really want to find out," he remarked.

"Well it's best you do anyway," Jamie responded. "After we got back to my house following the shopping trip the other day, I was arrested by two detectives for having broke that guy with the power dampening abilities out of jail."

"Say what?" Jesse said in shock.

"I've not been charged with anything," Jamie quickly followed up. "But they've effectively drafted me into working for them as part of a clandestine operation to round up hostile empowered humans."

"You're kidding, right?"

"I wish," Jamie glumly replied. "I'm actually technically on duty right now."

"Doing what?"

"Trying to detect a potential telepath/mind controlling individual who may have caused someone to commit suicide recently."

"Is that all they're making you do?"

"At the moment. One of the two is a complete arse but the one I deal with on a more regular basis seems to be looking out for me. He's told me to not approach the suspect for the most part, just try and catch her in the act."

"Does Gabby know about this?"

"Regrettably, yeah."

"Didn't take it well?"

"Not in the slightest but at least she understood that I wasn't deliberately going back into my old ways. Did hide the fact I engaged with that teleporting muppet the other day though."

"Well I would be lying if I said I wouldn't feel slightly aggrieved by that myself," Jesse said, a look of discontent on his face.

"Curiosity got the better of me, I admit," Jamie sheepishly responded. "But I really am trying to avoid being back in that environment as much as I can. I've got much more going on in my life now than concerning myself with gaining new powers for the fun of it."

"How long are they making you do this for?" Jesse shifted the conversation onwards.

"I don't know but at least I'm on their books officially so I technically have a job at long last if that's anything positive to go by."

"I suppose that *is* something positive regarding the situation."

"You're annoyed, aren't you?" Jamie said, not needing empathy powers to pick up on her friend's dissatisfied mood.

"I don't really know how I feel. Worried would be one part of it, and I guess some annoyance at the least that you're being forced to work against your will for something that's like the very thing you pledged to avoid in the future."

"It's unfortunate, I know." Jamie replied. "Ironically I'm effectively being punished for saving the whole city whereas I would be free to do what I want if I had just let Ryan Sharp have his way with everything. And you, I suppose."

"It's there I suppose I can't complain about the situation too much," Jesse admitted. "Had you not gotten involved in the first place, I probably would be dead right now. And Kayleigh would be without her brother."

Jamie gave a wordless smile, still absolutely confounded by the supposed future vision she had seen of Jesse attempting to kill her with a lightning strike compared to the real-life version before her who only cared that his sister still had him around to watch over her as opposed to losing his own life. *Would there be any point in revealing this to him at all?*

"Is Gabby talking to you at least compared to the last time after finding out what's happening with you now?" Jesse asked, abruptly changing the subject.

"Well yes and no," Jamie cryptically responded.

"Care to elaborate?" a confused Jesse replied.

"It's not actually my current situation that's the cause of anything. She's been real quiet since she came back from her mother's last night and hasn't mentioned what the reason behind the falling out was."

"That unusual for her not to spill the beans?"

"Quite. I know I'm one to talk considering how much of my super-powered malarkey I kept from her throughout the last few months but we normally don't keep much from each other in regards to personal stuff. Then again, I've never known her to ever have a row with her mum, let alone one that would cause her to be in such a despondent mood."

"I suppose if she's being that private about it, it's going to have to be worked out between her and her mum ultimately."

"Well I do currently have access to a certain ability that could help me find out..." Jamie responded, alluding to her borrowed empathy power.

"Think you'd be crossing a line there, Jame," Jesse interjected. "One: I don't think you can read minds with that power to my knowledge as opposed to just people's emotions and two – she clearly doesn't want to talk about it yet and you'd be invading her privacy doing so which I doubt will be appreciated."

"I guess," Jamie relented, knowing Jesse was right. "And there's why I have you around, to keep me on the straight and narrow!"

"Ha! And there I thought it was my sparkling personality," Jesse joked back.

"Guess I'm just going to have to see if she'll bring herself to tell me."

"I figure she will at some point if you're her best friend."

"Bit of a bummer having her avoid me all the time though," Jamie bemoaned. "Guess that was what I put her through last year with my constant moping around after my mum died. I was all but pretty absent to her the whole time with my catatonic-like depression."

"She stuck by you through that of course," Jesse replied. "You'll just have to show similar patience, I'm afraid."

"Joy(!)" Jamie gruffly responded. "Still going to ask her later anyway though."

"Maybe she'll want to answer you by then if you're lucky."

"I hope so, never thought I'd miss her winding me up as much as I do right now!"

"Speaking of being wound up, wanna entertain the Kay-ster for a bit?" Jesse reiterated from a moment ago.

"As long as she doesn't mind me beating her at Monopoly again," Jamie answered as she opened the bedroom door.

"I resent those remarks!" Kayleigh said in front of the doorway, scaring the life out of Jamie.

"And how long have you been standing there?" Jesse asked in an accusing tone.

"Only the last minute," the young girl replied. "Just trying to feel what you're feeling."

"Any luck?" Jamie asked, regaining her composure.

"Nope. Seems you just have a knack for it."

"Well I've been using my abilities for a lot longer than you, you'll get the hang of it eventually."

"As long as I can trust you to not use it on people without their knowledge," Jesse cut in with a light rebuke towards his sister.

"Of course…" Kayleigh replied in a light-heartedly devious manner. "At least I'm in control of it and not the other way around now."

"True, don't want to see you in that state again."

"Confident about it or do you want me to drain some excess?" Jamie asked.

"Nah, I think I have a better chance of controlling it if there's more to work with," Kayleigh replied. "Now are we playing Monopoly then?"

"Must be psychic(!)" Jamie jested.

Jamie arrived at her front door at six in the evening, having spent nearly three hours entertaining Kayleigh before watching a film on the downstairs television ahead of the siblings' aunt arriving home (with Jesse abruptly ending it prematurely upon the sound of the door opening to hide the fact he had let his young sister watch a horror film).

Though Jamie loved Kayleigh immensely, she did also want to spend time hanging out with Jesse too which was nearly impossible while they were in the house. She would have to invite him out to go someplace sometime or even just have a joint flight over the city.

More to her own surprise, she hadn't bothered to attempt using her empathy powers to read Jesse's emotive state again while in her

75

presence, though probably out of fear of finding out exactly how he felt towards her. Her own mixed feelings withstanding, it felt safer that she didn't know his thoughts on the matter anyway. She could deal with society rejecting her, not so much one of the closest people in her life.

But she had other issues at hand – namely the situation with Gabrielle who, judging by the parked car outside, was already home from work. Whether she was in a talkative mood about what had occurred between her and her mother, Jamie was about to find out.

"Gabbs!" Jamie called out to no response. Finding the kitchen and living room both empty, her friend's bedroom seemed the most likely place to look next.

"Gabby!" she called out once more only a few feet away from Gabrielle's bedroom door. With no response, Jamie opted to walk in.

"Hi," Gabrielle replied while lying on her bed, hurriedly pulling out her phone and pretending to read it.

"Why didn't you answer me?" Jamie asked.

"I was just really into this work group chat, I didn't hear you," Gabrielle quickly replied.

"Gabby, you don't have to bottle up what's eating at you," Jamie responded, immediately seeing a tired look manifest in Gabrielle's facial expression. "You know you can share whatever it is with me, I'm here for you."

"Jamie, honestly, I had a bad blowout with my mum. That's it," Gabrielle asserted. "It doesn't happen very often and I admit it was the worst I've ever had with her but I just needed some time to myself and I'm nearly past it now. You know what I'm like with taking a day or two to get over something that really annoys me."

Jamie gave a conflicted smile back. Against Jesse's advice, she allowed her enduring empathy ability to remotely pick up on Gabrielle's emotional state and the sensation felt overwhelmingly heavy, tinged with a great deal of hurt that could only be coming from someone with a deep and unresolved internal issue.

"You want dinner?" Jamie then asked.

"I've already eaten, I'll be fine," Gabrielle replied. Jamie knew that to also be untrue as there had been no evidence of a meal having been prepared in the kitchen or any plates washed up when she had looked a minute prior.

"Alright, I'm going to make something then. Let me know if you want anything."

"Okay," Gabrielle replied as she went straight back to looking at the phone screen.

Jamie descended the staircase, irritated by Gabrielle's lack of transparency. But despite using Kayleigh's empathy on her, she knew she ultimately had to respect the fact her friend did not want to divulge what was bothering her precisely regarding the argument with her mother, even if it was starting to become disruptive. With any luck, Gabrielle could come to terms with it sooner rather than later.

"Come on, Issy! You can do it!"

"Liv, this is never going to work!"

"Well I wouldn't be saying it would if I didn't think so, now would I?"

"Are you sure your powers are working properly and I'm not just wasting my time?"

"They've never failed me personally, though I'll add it is the first time I've used them to try and figure out another power's adaptability."

"And it really believes that I can push through solid matter using my super speed? Really does sound too good to be true, you know."

"Well that's what it's telling me and it's always been spot on so keep trying to make it work."

"I don't even know what I'm really doing here."

"Apparently you have to vibrate your molecules at a rate fast enough to physically pass through solid matter."

"I wasn't aware I was a science boff, Liv(!)"

"Focus your power internally instead of externally, that's the best way I can really explain it."

"I'm only giving this a try a few more times, then we pack it in and think of something else."

"If you don't think it's possible, just remember that you're the girl who can run as fast as a speeding car."

".......Okay, fine. Just a while longer."

Chapter 6

Jamie stirred in her bed as she found herself waking up at just after 8am. She had gone to sleep at around 11pm with Gabrielle never having come down for dinner, or doing virtually anything else either. While she tried to respect her friend's privacy, it was starting to really drive her insane not knowing what the issue really was.

As she tried to doze further, Jamie heard the faint, muffled sound of sobbing through the wall.

Oh, Gabby...

Forcing herself to get up, Jamie slinked through the corridor and opened the door to Gabrielle's bedroom, only for a loud creak to emerge as she did so. Upon the door opening, Gabrielle could be seen sitting at her dresser table wiping her eyes with a cleansing tissue.

"You alright?" Jamie asked.

"Yeah, just removing my make-up," Gabrielle replied. "Messed it all up."

"Sure?"

"Absolutely. Y'know what, I'll just go without it for a change just as you suggested I should."

As Gabrielle got up to leave, she was met by a forceful hug from Jamie.

"I'm always here," Jamie said lovingly.

"I know," Gabrielle replied softly before embracing Jamie back. "I'll see you later."

Jamie watched her friend walk down the stairs before grabbing her coat and car keys and heading out the front door. All she could think to herself was that respecting Gabrielle's privacy didn't really seem worth the effort of continuing to see her in such an unhappy state while denying it all the while.

Maybe it was time to talk to the source of the problem.

Jamie felt nervous about approaching the door of Gabrielle's family home but she knew if she wanted to be a step closer to helping deal with the situation at hand, she would have to bite the bullet. She seldom visited the house without Gabrielle but she was treated as a family member by her parents nonetheless, having provided additional comfort to her following her own parents' deaths. She wasn't even sure if Gabrielle's mother was in having not phoned ahead of time but it was now or never.

Without further hesitation, she knocked on the door.

"Jamie!"

"Hello, Imogen," Jamie responded to the blonde, wavy-haired woman standing in the doorway. "How are you?"

"I'm okay, it's quite the surprise to see you."

"Yeah, I know it's been a while, sorry about that."

"Is Gabby with you?"

"No, she's at work."

Jamie immediately saw Imogen's face drop slightly.

"So what brings you round?" she asked with a noticeable worried tone. Jamie could easily feel the unease emanating from her with the empathy ability despite it having very noticeably weakened greatly from the constant passive use of it.

"I think you probably may already know," Jamie replied.

"Is this about Gabrielle?" Imogen sighed.

"Yeah. She said you had an argument and she hasn't been the same since that day. It's been worrying me."

"You and me both," Imogen glumly said.

"Are you willing to talk about it?"

"Think you'd best come inside," Imogen replied, leading Jamie into the living room. Jamie honestly did not know what to expect the sorry tale to be but felt high anticipation to finally be finding out what had led to her friend being so uncharacteristically despondent.

"Would you like some tea?"

"I'll be fine," Jamie replied.

"Aye, I forgot you don't drink the stuff."

Jamie gave a puzzled look. *Did she just pronounce that in an Irish accent?*

"Surprised?" Imogen continued. "I guess it would be after hearin' me speak in an English accent all your life."

"What's going on?" Jamie asked.

"This is the reason why Gabby has been acting up – I had decided to tell her the true nature of who she is after a lifetime of keeping it a secret."

Jamie assumed Imogen wasn't referring to Gabrielle's powers. "And what is that exactly?"

"That she was born in Belfast, Northern Ireland to myself and her actual, Irish-born father."

Jamie felt her jaw drop slightly.

"You mean, Gabby's not actually from England?" she responded.

"She's lived here since she was one year old," Imogen answered. "For all intent and purpose, she was raised English but her heritage is completely based in Northern Ireland."

"But why? And why cover it up to begin with?"

"Well that was down to the nature of what caused us to move away from Northern Ireland to begin with all those years ago," said Imogen. "I suppose you're aware of the decades long conflict that occurred over there on the island of Ireland?"

"A bit. Wasn't sectarian tension behind a lot of that?"

"It was more along the lines of politics and nationalism for a good part of it. Either way, it was a period I grew up through and the acts of violence that occurred during all those years were horrific, some worse than others with it even spilling over to mainland Britain at times.

"It was towards the end of the seemingly endless conflict that I met Gabrielle's father. Her *biological* father. He was a recent addition to the insurance company that I worked for at the time and we just clicked immediately. Meanwhile, in the midst of our early romance, each of the combatants in the conflict were trying to negotiate a permanent ceasefire. There had been attempts before to end the violence but they had always ended up being temporary.

"It was soon after that I became pregnant with Gabby. Me and her father did discuss moving away to raise her in a more stable environment but we both loved where we lived and we just hoped that the talks to end the perpetual mayhem were actually looking prosperous this time round."

"This is so surreal," Jamie remarked aloud. "Hard to believe you and Gabrielle were close to never being in England. I do feel selfish for being glad that you did though."

"Well, that was one of the most difficult decisions of my life," Imogen replied. "It was close to a year following Gabrielle's birth that her father went out into town one day. Next thing I know I'm hearing a huge bang in what felt like the not-so far distance, a sound that I was all too aware of by this point."

"Gabby's dad?" Jamie asked solemnly.

"I had no idea what had happened but I grabbed Gabrielle from upstairs and turned on the television set. Eventually a breaking news bulletin came on and announced that a car bomb had gone off in the centre of our small town. There were early reports of fatalities; I just prayed that her dad wasn't one of them.

"It was a day later that his body was identified as among those who had been killed in the blast. I had never felt so distraught in my whole life."

"I know how you felt," Jamie sympathised, still in awe at the story. "There's really no other pain like losing a loved one."

"I took Gabby and stayed with my parents for a bit following that. The house just felt so empty without his presence. It was during this time that I began looking back on our decision to stay put and lamenting that we didn't get out while we had had the chance. We would've been away from everything and everyone we loved but we would've been a family.

"It was then that I decided to move over to England with my daughter. I spent a few weeks preparing myself for it, including learning to speak with a moderately English accent and my parents helped me travel to the mainland."

"How did you get on once you settled in?" Jamie asked.

"My parents kept me and Gabby afloat for a while; they also managed to sell the house I had shared with Gabby's father so we were quite comfortable during that time. I even managed to get a job once I felt comfortable hiring a babysitter for Gabrielle."

"Another insurance company?"

"Waitressing," Imogen replied, somewhat indifferently. "It was different but I didn't feel comfortable going back to selling insurance owing to the memories I had regarding Gabby's dad. It was a diner environment and it allowed me to always spend time with Gabrielle in the evenings while I worked the day shifts. Plus everyone who came in was generally friendly as were the staff, of whom I made several friends.

"About three months into the job, I decided to go out with some co-workers for the night. It was at a club that I encountered a gentleman by the name of Michael."

"You mean, Mike, your husband?" Jamie intrigued.

"That's him," Imogen cheerfully responded. "We became good friends after that night, sharing many mutual interests and he became part of the social circle I had managed to amass during my four months in England. I actually enjoyed having a male friend amongst all my female ones, it balanced the dynamic out somewhat."

"Obviously it didn't stay that way."

"You don't really choose who you fall in love with," Imogen replied after a brief pause. "To say I hadn't felt some sort of attraction to Michael throughout our friendship would be a gigantic lie; I just couldn't help but feel immense guilt over having feelings for another man not even a year after Gabby's father's passing so I ignored them and simply tried to maintain the status quo."

"As you say, you don't choose who you fall in love with," Jamie said, almost in reflection of her mixed feelings towards her own close male friend. "Maybe it was a bit soon but surely he would've wanted you to move on and find happiness."

"That's what I had to convince myself of following one night out of excess drinks and me and Mike going back to his flat while the minder had Gabrielle for the night. The inevitable happened and we spent the next morning talking it all out; he already knew that Gabby's father had died though I kept the rest of the story from him and we agreed to take it slow."

"Does he know now everything that happened?"

"He does, though it wasn't an easy decision on my part. After a few weeks of dating, I unexpectedly became pregnant again with my and Mike's first child, Max. It felt like an awkward situation –

we were both overjoyed but at the same time, we did wonder how we were going to raise Gabrielle and Max together as step-siblings without them feeling alienated from each other for having two different dads. I did also worry about Gabrielle and Mike's future relationship being fraught by the fact he was not her biological father."

"So you let Gabrielle grow up believing Mike was her father instead," Jamie cut in.

"I absolutely hated the idea of Gabby not knowing who her real daddy was and her true heritage but I felt for my new family's sake, it was the better option going forward. It's something I've held a degree of remorse for ever since but seeing how tight a unit we came to be over the years with Gabrielle, Max and later, Shane, all viewing themselves as natural siblings, I couldn't help but feel a small sense of comfort in deciding to do what I did."

"You really don't have to justify anything to me, Imogen," Jamie said. "There's nothing I've heard from all that where you tried to put your own interests above Gabrielle's."

"Maybe not but I still caused her to live a partial lie her entire life," Imogen rebutted. "I always intended to tell her the truth after she reached adulthood and she was able to fend for herself but now having done so, I just feel like everything's been torn to pieces between her and her family. She refuses to answer my phone calls and hasn't spoken to Michael, Max and Shane either."

"She reacts to things badly. I've been on the end of that myself but she came round soon enough. She just needs time to process it all."

"How has she been at home?" Imogen asked.

"Withdrawn, particularly by her standards," Jamie grimaced, prompting Imogen to put her head in her hands.

"I just wish I could fix all this," she whimpered in despair.

"It's just going to take time," Jamie said, grabbing Imogen's hand. "You and Gabby helped me through my own tragedy and I'm a lot better now despite everything that has happened and the pain I still feel over what I went through. Gabrielle's a fighter, she won't let this destroy her or her family bond."

"I just hope your right."

"Well she's still got me to talk to even if she feels like she can't talk to you; I'll be gently pushing her in the right direction every chance I get until she's ready to face up to all this."

"Thank you," Imogen replied, absorbing the comfort of the moment.

Jamie bid Imogen goodbye as she left the house thirty minutes later, having spent the rest of the visit talking about her own recent (non-ability based) mishaps and happenings to move away from the unpleasantness of the prior subject. Having witnessed Jamie's despair from the previous year, it had been warming to Imogen to know the teenager's life had been gradually improving with new friends and outgoings. As much as Jamie felt the need to help repair Imogen's bond with her daughter, it was already seeming an uphill task given that Gabrielle was avoiding talking to her as it was without even bringing up the whole situation.

But now knowing exactly what was going on in her friend's head, Jamie knew she had to find some way to address the matter whether Gabrielle wanted her to or not. It was an awful burden for her to be carrying around and it would help talking it out with someone besides her mother first.

It had struck a nerve though finding out that Imogen and her husband had started off as good friends before progressing onto being romantically involved. Or more precisely, that it was fuelling more conflict in her mind over her and Jesse. Jamie proceeded to shove it to the back of her mind as always, much like every other suggestion that she and Jesse were meant to be.

Aside from dealing with Gabrielle, however, it did dawn on her that she was supposed to be trying to track down a potentially rogue, mind-controlling enhanced human as per her assignment. She had found it strange that the empathy/analysis combination had not passively detected anything like it had with the teleporter, but then she had had a previous encounter with him beforehand whereas the latest empowered criminal was completely unknown to her. The empathy power within her had since run its course from its passive use over the course of the morning anyway so using the analysis power alone to target the telepathic suspect was now her only means of accomplishing her task at hand.

She then activated it, using her knowledge of it to focus directly on trying to sense a telepathic ability in active use. Despite the concentrated effort, she felt absolutely nothing. Not an unexpected result considering the ability only detected other powers in active or even passive use, though preferably the former. At least she could say that she had tried.

Still though, it did interest her in being able to succeed in the endeavour if nothing but to be able to prove her worth to the operation. And to shove Layne's negative attitude towards her down his throat.

Jamie pulled out her phone and dialled Jesse's number.

"Hey, Jamie. I'm at work at the moment, what's up?"

"Was wondering if I could borrow more of Kayleigh's empathy power later when she's home from school?"

"You could probably get some of it now, she's off for half-term."

"Oh really? Is your aunt home too then?"

"No, she got called into work to cover for someone who took ill at the last minute. Luckily I managed to swap out half of today's shift so I'll be home in half an hour but we do trust her to mind herself in the meantime if it ever comes down to it."

"Should've just asked me to go round, you tart!" Jamie jokingly rebuked.

"Thought you were busy as part of your new job!" Jesse replied.

"Well that's why I need more of the ability, I'll go round and stay with her until you get back."

"Thanks. See you in a bit."

Jamie put her phone in her pocket and headed to the nearest secluded area she could find before taking to the air with flight and hazing. She didn't consider it too odd that Kayleigh was left alone to fend for herself for a few hours, seeing as she was quite mature for her young age. She herself had always gotten home from school at least two hours ahead of her parents' return from work at the same age and nothing ever went badly under those circumstances.

She did find it uncharacteristic of Jesse to not even ask if she could watch his sister until he got home though. Maybe he really did just think he would be distracting her from her new 'job'.

Meh. Kayleigh will always come before any dumb task.

She touched down in the usual forest area near Jesse's house before making her way over and knocking on the door while opening up the letterbox.

"Kayleigh sweetie, it's Jamie!" she called through the opening as she soon heard rapid footsteps bouncing down the staircase.

"Jamie!" Kayleigh exclaimed as she proceeded to squeeze Jamie's waist in an adoring manner upon opening the door. "What brings you here?"

"Well I will be giving your brother a clout when he shows up for not calling me up to watch over you," Jamie replied light-heartedly.

"Oh I've dealt with worse situations," Kayleigh bragged.

She's probably right sadly.

"Was also looking for a personal favour from you though," Jamie followed up.

"My powers?"

"If I could be cheeky?"

"Say no more," Kayleigh replied as she allowed Jamie to take her hand to begin absorbing some of her empathy ability.

"Thanks kiddo," Jamie said. "What were you doing anyway?"

"Just watching TV, though there's not much to watch during the daytime so I gave this female panel show a go. So far I've learnt how to ignore any so-called stigma of breastfeeding a baby in public and that I don't need a man to be happy."

Jamie couldn't help but laugh.

"Hey!"

Jamie shook as she turned around to see Jesse standing behind her.

"You two really do enjoy scaring the hell out of me, don't you," she bemoaned. "You're early."

"Yeah, the store manager allowed me out fifteen minutes early seeing as the floor was pretty dead heading into lunch. You been here long?"

"Literally just showed up. Suppose I should get on with my assignment instead of slacking off any further."

"Awwwww!" Kayleigh moaned.

"But I can come and spend a whole day with you sometime this week seeing as you're off school," Jamie quickly followed up.

"Tomorrow!" Kayleigh blurted out.

"Sure, anything you want," Jamie replied as she knelt down to give Kayleigh a hug before doing the same to Jesse. "Take care!"

"As always," Jesse said before closing the front door. Making her way to the forest to make another ascent, Jamie deemed it better to tell Jesse about the Gabrielle situation on another occasion when she wasn't so focused on her current task at hand.

Now with a full arsenal of abilities, Jamie began trying to sense any telepathic power she could using the analyser ability while leaving her borrowed empathy in a passive state. Still she detected nothing.

She then took back to the air upon reaching the forest area to begin sweeping the city for any potential telepathy use. Using four simultaneous abilities was challenging but just about effective. Had she not chosen to focus solely on detecting the one ability, it was probable she would have picked up a few active powers already.

I am going to need a serious recharge on every one of these abilities after this.

Though efficient, the speed of her flight movements was leaving her eyes watering and making it hard to maintain her concentration as well as seeing where she was going. Jamie then opted to descend to the nearest rooftop to quickly recuperate.

An unexpected jolt then went off in her head.

Gotcha!

The analysis ability was confirming the use of a telepathic/mind controlling power beneath her somewhere. It felt strong enough that it was being used within the vicinity directly around her but Jamie also noticed that her passive use of empathy was failing to connect with the individual using the power.

In response, she increased the output of the ability to its maximum, though still to no effect before deactivating it upon feeling just how depleted it was already getting from the extreme effort.

Frustrated, Jamie began quickly trying to seek out the source of the telepathy being used overhead. As she felt the power strengthening, she swooped down to the ground and began conducting her search at surface level. Whoever it was was fortuitously using the telepathic ability for a prolonged period of time, making it easier to track but Jamie knew it could cease at any given moment and as she, for whatever reason, could not lock on to the individual using it with empathy, she had to work fast.

In the distance, she could make out what appeared to be a small crowd gathering. A closer look revealed that some people were trying to break up a fight between two young men with several on-lookers amassing around them. The sensation from the telepathy being used was now overwhelming.

Which one of you lot is it then?

Out of all the people surrounding the fracas, Jamie caught sight of a young woman with raven-dark hair smirking at the brawl happening before her. Slowly approaching, Jamie could feel the analysis power peaking.

Got you now.

Before she made another step forward, Jamie remembered that her task only involved locating the person to confirm their use of a mind-controlling power and reporting back to base *without* engaging them. Begrudgingly, she held her position and pulled out her phone to contact Detective Brody.

Still baffled by the lack of effect the empathy ability was having on the person, Jamie decided to quickly apply the remainder of it within her on them once more into one powerful surge. As hard as she tried though, she continued to fail to connect with the telepath until the absorbed empathy finally ran out. This in spite of the fact her borrowed analysis ability was detecting the current power usage perfectly.

As she searched through her phone contacts to find Brody's number, Jamie again found herself in two minds over what to do – sure, she could call the enhanced human in but the individual could easily flee the scene before Brody and his team made it over and there was no guarantee that she wouldn't use her mind-controlling powers for more deadly purposes in the meantime. After all, it was highly likely she had been responsible for sending a young man to jump to his death previously; causing further fatalities doubtlessly wouldn't be beneath her.

And as much as she knew how egotistical it was, Jamie could really feel herself wanting to show up Layne by proving herself to the overall operation. It had worked for Rachel – it could also work for her too.

Jamie contemplated her next move as the telepath continued watching the brawl she was presumably causing with her powers. Her choices were to either strike her with a hard kinetic energy wave in the hope of an instant knockout or approach her from behind and attempt a power drain, thereby neutralising the threat of being brought under mind-control herself. Of course, if either failed then she would most likely be at the deviant's mercy.

Deciding on the absorption option, Jamie began slowly moving forward in the hope that her target's attention would remain on the chaos currently occurring in front of her.

Getting within three metres, Jamie engaged her base ability and prepared to launch herself at the telepath.

Suddenly, the young woman turned her head around, locking eyes with Jamie.

Now or never.

Caught off guard, Jamie quickly made her move without further hesitation. As she was about to grab her foe's neck, she felt the loss of feeling in her arms and legs before a numbing darkness completely overcame all her senses.

What's happening...?

Chapter 7

Marcella studied the teenage girl before her who was now completely entranced and standing motionless.

"So there *are* others out there," she mused to herself as the commotion going on behind her came to a stop.

"What's going on?" one of the two unwitting combatants asked in a daze while being held from behind by a man twice his build.

"What do you mean 'what's going on'? You were going at it blow for blow with that other guy!" the man responded while maintaining his grip.

"What?"

"Time to take our leave, my new friend," Marcella said to the zoned-out Jamie as they both departed the vicinity of the brawl.

After a brief walk, the two opted to take a seat on a bench in a small, grassy square.

"I must say, I'm quite impressed by your choice of wardrobe," Marcella complimented her unresponsive captive. "Very rebelling, though admittedly still far from the perfect ideal for my liking – Heavy metal may have a devil-ish image but it really is just theatrical with no theistic conviction. Well, aside from Norwegian Black metal I guess to a degree.

"I digress; it was lucky I overheard you thinking of attacking me in the background, although you did ruin the fight I was enjoying by breaking my concentration. So what's this business about absorbing my powers, is that what you can do?"

"Yes," the mind-controlled Jamie spoke in a monotone voice.

"And use them for yourself, I suppose?"

"Yes."

"An opportunist; a decent attitude to have," Marcella spoke aloud. "And what is your name?"

"Jamie."

"Well, Jamie, I could erase your memories of ever having met me and send you on your way, or I could even have you jump onto the nearest motorway but I doubt my master will like the prospect of wasting such a potentially useful asset as you. Have you any other powers?"

"Flight, power analysis and tracking, generating a haze and kinetic energy wave projection."

"I'm intrigued by that last one. Show me."

Still within a trance, Jamie stood up and swung an energy wave directly at the grass, unearthing a small piece of turf.

"Not bad, not bad," Marcella said. "We can make real good use of that power tracking ability of yours though; what say you activate that and we go scout some other recruits?"

Wordlessly, Jamie began engaging the analysis ability. Still in control of her victim's mind, Marcella used her telepathy to experience exactly what Jamie was in the midst of her power usage.

"Interesting….how about we just go with whoever's closest?" Marcella thought aloud while examining the analysis ability in progress via Jamie's mind. "Well the nearest one appears to be some lame x-ray vision power but still, it's a power nonetheless. We'll walk over to it so you can absorb it for our use, you understand?"

"Yes," Jamie affirmed before leading Marcella towards the source of the active ability still being detected in the near distance.

"Jesse!" Kayleigh called out from her bedroom.

"I'm literally only next door to you!" Jesse said as he entered his sister's room. "What's up?"

"Not much, just need some help with my homework."

"What do you need help with?"

"The bit in my geography work that asks what the three types of boundaries are in plate tectonics."

"Er…did you not learn what they were during your lessons?"

"Did *you* not learn about them while you were in school?" Kayleigh cheekily replied.

"Alright, smart alec," Jesse responded. "Too bad you didn't start your homework while Jamie was here earlier, she'd probably know."

"Well you do have her phone number."

"I guess she won't mind lending a hand," Jesse said, pulling his phone out and dialling Jamie's number. He could have easily searched for the answer online but he knew his sister would rather hear it come from her 'cool, older friend', Jamie. He hoped he wasn't interrupting her during her assignment in the process.

Marcella continued to monitor the x-ray vision enhanced human through Jamie's thoughts with the analysis ability still in full affect, the target getting closer with every step they walked meaning that whoever it was was remaining in one spot while using their powers. *Unfortunate for them, good for us.*

Her concentration was mildly broken briefly by the sound of a phone ringtone going off, realising it was coming from her 'partner'.

"Now who would be trying to call you?" she asked out loud, mentally commanding Jamie to pull her phone out from her pocket. However, the call attempt ended before she had a chance to answer it. Undeterred, Marcella took the phone and observed the name of the missed call.

Jesse :D.

"This someone of significance I'm guessing, based on the added emoticon in the name?"

"Yes," Jamie plainly stated.

"More than just a friend?"

"I don't know," Jamie replied in the same monotone voice, almost subconsciously confirming her mixed feelings regarding the matter.

"Maybe I can help you decide," Marcella followed up with a wicked grin on her face. "Call him back."

As commanded, Jamie unlocked the phone and immediately called Jesse's number before waiting for an answer.

"Hi Jamie."

"Hey babe!" Jamie responded in a slightly exaggerated happy tone being influenced by Marcella's mind-control. "You called?"

"Uh, yeah," Jesse replied, sounding perturbed by the manner of his friend's reply. *"Sorry if I'm interrupting you, it's just a quick one regarding Kay and her homework. You wouldn't happen to know what the three types of boundaries in plate tectonics are?"*

"Convergent, divergent and transform," Jamie answered.

"Thanks, I'll let the little one know and leave you to it."

"Hang on, Jesse," Jamie said, Marcella taking full control of her dialect. "I've got something to tell you."

"What is it?" Jesse replied.

"I've been thinking a lot about you lately; how dreamy your eyes are, how gorgeous your hair looks, how good you generally make me feel about myself."

"You alright, Jamie?" Jesse responded after a confused pause.

"You're all I ever think about every minute I'm awake, I can't really keep it to myself anymore. Ever since we first met, I've known you were that kindred spirit that I've always lacked in my life."

Silence befell the line, Jesse utterly bewildered at what he was hearing.

"You don't need to say anything – when I see you later I'll give you what I've wanted to do for so long now," Jamie said before hanging up the call immediately after.

"Delightful, now we have something to look forward to later once we're done here," Marcella smirked before telepathically forcing Jamie to re-engage the analysis ability. "Best hit the trail again in case our x-ray vision subject gets away."

Jesse felt dumbfounded as he looked at his phone. *What the hell was that all about?*

It was very clearly Jamie on the other end of the line, yet it didn't sound like anything she would say at all. Or not anything he would have ever expected from her anyway. Was she really deeply in love with him? Surely not, he assured himself that he would have noticed something by now. Sure, she was friendly with him but it had always been in a brother-sisterly manner.

As he continued to second-guess himself, Jesse thought back to what Jamie had said during the call: 'ever since we first met'. Their first meeting had been a short duel in an alley using their powers, not exactly a moment of fondness for either of them. Nor was their 'true' first meeting initially either on the rooftop.

It then dawned on him what kind of empowered being Jamie had been hunting – a *telepath.*

"Hey bro, did Jamie know what the answers were?" Kayleigh brightly asked as Jesse re-entered her room.

"Yeah. Um, can you try something for me quickly?"

"What's going on, Jess?" Kayleigh responded with a concerned look on her face.

"It's nothing to worry about."

"That's not what you feel like right now."

"Kay, don't use empathy on me without asking!" Jesse blurted out in annoyance before quickly composing himself. "But actually, that's what I need you to help me out with."

"What, my powers?"

"Do you think you could use your empathy to tell me where Jamie is?"

"Don't know, never tried. Why, what's wrong with Jamie?"

Jesse hesitated, trying to come up with a decent excuse on the spot to avoid upsetting his sister.

"I just want to surprise her, that's all," he finally spoke. "And it'll be interesting to see if you can actually do that with your ability."

"You can't lie to me, Jesse," Kayleigh angrily replied out of concern for Jamie, obviously having used her empathy on her brother once more.

"Kay! What did I just say about that?" Jesse bemoaned.

"What is wrong with Jamie?" she replied, ignoring the previous comment. Jesse knew he wasn't going to win the battle of wills.

"She could be in trouble," he reluctantly replied.

"How?"

"I don't know but I plan to find her to make sure she isn't. That's why I need to see if you can locate her, you know I wouldn't be asking if I could help it."

"I can always try I suppose. Jamie told me she felt the emotions of the guy she tracked down once using empathy but I don't know if that's the same as what you're asking of me. And I've only just managed to achieve feeling emotions without touch as it is, never mind using them to locate someone."

"I'll admit it's virtually a new concept but we've got nothing to lose by giving it a try," Jesse said while trying to avoid sounding desperate. Kayleigh gave a short pause.

"How would I begin to try and do it?"

"I suppose you would focus on using your empathy to locate Jamie's exact position," Jesse suggested.

Putting in a concentrated though unconfident effort, Kayleigh tried to channel her ability into somehow locating Jamie. After half a minute, it was obvious the young girl was struggling.

"I don't know what I'm doing!" Kayleigh wailed, trying to keep her emotions in check despite fretting over Jamie's wellbeing.

"Alright, let's try going about it with what we know," Jesse cut in with a comforting tone. "You're able to remotely sense how I'm feeling based on your will without physical contact, is that right?"

"Yeah," Kayleigh replied, calming herself down.

"Okay, so you just need to apply that to wanting to find Jamie. Summon the desire to want to know where she is."

"It's still a bit vague."

"Also, you could feel just how much Jamie means to you," Jesse went further. "Feel how much you want to find her and how much it would mean to you to know where she is."

Kayleigh sat in a cross-legged position with her head bowed and her eyes closed, trying as hard as she could to utilise what minor control she had over her powers to try and find Jamie. How, she still didn't exactly know but she was channelling all her love for Jamie into the effort. Jesse simply looked on in the vain hope that his sister was able to succeed in doing the near impossible.

"I'm starting to feel something," Kayleigh murmured, trying to maintain her concentration.

"Like what?" Jesse chimed in.

"Like a heartbeat, a different one to my own. It feels warm."

Jesse didn't know how to respond, though felt hopeful still that Kayleigh had latched on to Jamie.

"I think, I've picked up on something," Kayleigh exclaimed.

"What do you feel?" Jesse asked.

"I think I'm feeling Jamie's location, if it *is* her but not in a physical way. More like how close I currently am to her, or how far away she is from me."

"Well, it's something," Jesse replied, caught between amazement that his theory actually worked but also disappointment that it didn't unveil a specific place to find Jamie at.

"We could try catching up to her using this," Kayleigh suggested.

"No way are you coming with," Jesse sternly replied.

"Well how are you going to know how close you are to her without me around?" Kayleigh protested, though acknowledging that the situation must be serious enough for Jesse to dig this deep in trying to find Jamie.

"I don't know…..what if you tried focusing on both of us at the same time and tell me how close I am over the phone?"

"I can't keep breaking my concentration to constantly dial the phone."

"Then leave it on loudspeaker the whole time. You'll be here on your own anyway the whole time. Give it a quick try."

"It's asking a lot, Jesse," Kayleigh admitted.

"We got lucky once," Jesse shrugged. "Shall we go for twice?"

Kayleigh relented, just about remembering the feeling she got when locating Jamie but trying to focus on two different people was going to be difficult, even if one of them was directly next to her currently. Again, she tried focusing on how much Jesse meant to her, not hard considering he had been there for her since she was born.

"I've got you," Kayleigh said, to Jesse's delight. "But I don't know how well I can keep it going for, it's a lot to concentrate on you both."

"You're the brightest kid I know," Jesse replied. "I trust in your capabilities."

"Well get out there and find Jamie already!" Kayleigh remarked, pretending not to enjoy the compliment.

"Let me set up the phones quick," Jesse said as he called Kayleigh's mobile and put it on loudspeaker.

"Just don't speak into the line too much and break my concentration," Kayleigh said. "I'll give you regular updates if you're getting closer or further away from her."

"You're a star, sis," Jesse beamed as he headed downstairs.

*   *   *

"Ah, so it seems our target is a super-powered pervert," Marcella spoke as she and the entranced Jamie spied on the enhanced human they had tracked down currently using his x-ray vision to stare at any woman walking past him across the road from the bench he was sitting on. "Explains why we were able to easily trace him the whole way over if he's been spending his entire time doing this. I imagine he'll make great fodder for the master when his day comes. For now though, feel free to do to him what you were planning on doing to me."

Jamie moved forward, seemingly obeying Marcella's command accurately to the point she really was approaching the young man *exactly* how she had been going to attack Marcella from behind previously. Marcella herself was feeling quite curious to see how the process was going to work as she gleefully monitored her captive's very direct approach towards her prey.

Without warning, Jamie quickly caught the person's neck in the crook of her arm from behind and began draining the still active x-ray vision from him with her free hand grasping his face. Marcella found it to be an interesting technique while contemplating whether to have Jamie snap the young man's neck upon completion of the absorption, ultimately opting not to on the basis she didn't want such a valuable asset being locked up on murder charges and out of her access upon doing so.

Instead, Jamie allowed the voyeur to get up off the bench, only to then hurl a kinetic energy wave straight into his stomach. As he lay prone on the floor clutching his midsection, Marcella focused her mind-manipulation powers onto the young man while also keeping control of Jamie, using her ability to completely wipe the incident from his memory and leaving him disorientated.

"Might as well give you a taste of your own medicine while we're here," Marcella remarked as she commanded Jamie to test her newly gained x-ray vision on the unlucky individual, using her telepathy to see through Jamie's point of view. "No wonder you're a total creep with a penis that small. Oh well, good luck to you."

With that, Marcella approached Jamie and led her away from the scene before the enhanced voyeur recovered. "Let's pay a visit to lover boy then. You do know where he lives, of course?"

"Yes," Jamie answered.

"Then feel free to introduce us – who knows, he may enjoy having us both for company before we completely annihilate him."

"You're going in the right direction now!"

"Thanks, Kay!" Jesse yelled into the receiver against the noise of the wind blowing past in the middle of the air.

"Must say, not easy concentrating with that racket going on!"

"Sorry, babe! I'll try and slow it down a bit!"

"I can feel you moving faster than Jamie by a large margin so if you just keep heading forward, you'll come up to her soon."

"In that case, just keep focusing on your powers and let me know when I'm right near her."

"Okay."

Jesse maintained his flight pattern, suspenseful of the upcoming alert from Kayleigh. The problem was that he had no real strategy in approaching the situation – if Jamie was indeed under control by the telepath she had been trying to hunt down, he possessed little power to counteract that. Worse, he could be mentally enslaved too. For the time being, he decided to settle on simply finding her first before further contemplating a game plan.

"You're right near her now!" Kayleigh's voice emerged from the still-open phone line.

"Thanks!" Jesse replied. "I'm going down to get a closer look, can't see anything from this far up. If I spot her, I'll let you know."

Jesse began his descent towards the nearest rooftop, deactivating his hazing ability and taking a look over the ledge of the building he was currently standing on. His hope was that Jamie had her hood down so that her hair would make her easier to seek out, otherwise her three quarter-length cargo trousers and full black attire was the next best thing to keep an eye out for.

After a minute of looking, Jesse could feel himself getting frustrated. As helpful as the empathy ability had been in narrowing the search down, it hadn't exactly given a pinpoint location and there was little sign of Jamie's relatively recognisable appearance anywhere on the surrounding ground.

"Kay, are we definitely within the same place?" he spoke into the phone once more.

"That's what I'm picking up," Kayleigh responded. *"I can't tell the difference between you two anymore due to how close you are to each other but I can just about tell that one of you is still moving and the other is staying still which I'm guessing is you."*

"Okay, still looking over here," Jesse replied. At least the empathy ability itself was apparently working fine. He continued spying down on the street before him, trying to spot a black hoodie and pair of trousers at least from the few people that were walking around.

Out of the corner of his eye did he finally catch a glimpse of someone wearing Jamie's exact style of clothing walking along the pavement, with someone by her side no less. It had to be the telepath surely.

"Think I've found her, sis," he spoke down the phone receiver.

"Is she okay?" Kayleigh asked back.

"She looks alright, I'm going to go speak to her. I'll call you back in a bit."

After hanging up, Jesse plotted in his head how he was going to go up to the pair of them. He still didn't know exactly what was going on but Jamie's extremely uncharacteristic demeanour during their phone call was enough to convince him that she currently wasn't right in the mind and the presence of the dark-haired person next to her was likely the culprit.

Using his flight, Jesse descended down the back of the building and entered the main road from the back street, keeping a short distance between himself and the duo ahead. His plan would be to follow them until they entered a more secluded area away from the public which would allow him to engage his abilities to rescue Jamie if it came to it. With his very little offensive capabilities, both powers and physically, flying straight into the back of the telepath and knocking them out by surprise before they could react seemed the best option, especially if they were able to control Jamie and use her against him.

Suddenly, the two came to a halt. Jesse felt a shiver down his spine. *Have they detected the use of my powers?*

Instead of turning around, Jamie and the person continued onward after a few seconds. Jesse breathed deeply as his heartbeat began to slow back down again before continuing his slow pursuit.

To his fortune, Jesse watched as the two made their way into a forested pathway. He contemplated following them from the air again but opted against using any powers after his near-scare a few minutes earlier, at least for the time being in case Jamie was indeed using her analysis ability as he worried she could be.

The path continued on for what seemed half a mile with Jesse extending his gap from Jamie and the telepath by an even greater margin. He did begin to wonder what the telepath's exact plan was while the journey dragged on as they walked through the barren passage surrounded by decaying woodland either side. *Were they bringing Jamie out to kill her?*

Once more, the duo came to a halt. Jesse responded by stopping in his tracks, feeling a sense of unease at the lack of clarity of the situation.

No, Jesse. I haven't brought Jamie out here to kill her.

Jesse froze in fear upon hearing the voice speak to him within his head. Jamie and the raven-haired person then both turned around, Jesse seeing the blank stare in his friend's eyes.

"I have to say, smart idea staying grounded the whole time while following us to avoid using your powers and being detected –

except that I had already felt you using your flight a while ago through your buddy here and once I used my telepathy to get inside your head, I knew that you were following us without the need to turn around and see for myself."

Jesse grimaced, realising that the telepath had probably stopped randomly with Jamie earlier in the street in order to pick out his specific thoughts worrying about being caught in the act of following them.

"Allow me to introduce myself to you: my name is Marcella, and you may be wondering why I haven't enslaved you like I have your little friend here. Well don't worry, it's so we can play a little game."

Jesse stared down the young woman. *What game would that be?*

"As you can see, I have Jamie here under my control. We were actually on the way to you but somehow you managed to find us first. According to Jamie's knowledge of your abilities, you make quite the formidable opponent when you can bring yourself to do so. And also according to her, you've often successfully come to her aid when she's been in a tight spot. But how about when the person you're facing is *Jamie* herself?"

Jesse felt another cold sensation, though it wasn't a possibility that he hadn't been anticipating. Defending himself against Jamie had been the very first encounter between them so he knew how to counter her powers but now she would likely be without restraint while being manipulated by Marcella.

"And one more thing," Marcella added. "This bout will be survival of the fittest; whoever wins will earn the right to kill the one who loses."

Chapter 8

Great... Jesse thought to himself as he prepared for what would literally be the fight for his life. How he would even bring himself to hurt Jamie, even in self-defence would be difficult enough and despite the limited reserves of all of her borrowed powers, she was extremely adept at utilising them all while she had access to them.

Nonetheless, Jesse determined that his best bet would indeed be to draw the fight out as long as possible in order to cause Jamie's individual powers to eventually deplete through their continued use but that still left Marcella free to take over his mind instead if she then considered Jamie obsolete, to which he had no defence against.

Jesse then braced himself as the unwitting Jamie took a combative stance. He assumed she would be coming at him with either flight or Gabrielle's kinetic energy wave attacks, both of which would probably deal him a great amount of bodily harm if successfully executed. His defensive shielding would block virtually all of her attacks no matter what though to his advantage. The battle with her would-be rapist previously, however, had proved that the barrier's strength was not infinite as he would prefer to rely upon.

Jamie quickly flung a kinetic energy wave in Jesse's direction, who barely had the reaction time to deflect it with a barrier. Before he could prepare himself further, Jamie had taken to the air in what seemed to be an oncoming low and direct charge. Jesse activated his shielding again to absorb the impact, instead being taken by surprise as Jamie unexpectedly flew directly over his body and caught him in a chokehold from behind. Jesse tried to wrench her arm from around his neck, though finding little manoeuvrability to be able to do so.

Forgive me, Jamie.

Out of desperation, Jesse clamped his hand around one of Jamie's wrists and activated his burning ability, hoping the painful sensation would cause his friend to release her grip. However, after a few seconds he realised that the attempt was having no effect whatsoever; the telepath's mind control appeared to be blocking Jamie's ability to feel pain.

"Smart idea, Jesse," Marcella said out loud in the background. "Any other person would have felt searing agony from that, which you yourself will soon be subject to if you don't get a foothold in this duel."

Ignoring the taunt, Jesse took to the air with Jamie still clinging on. He then began spinning around in a circular motion as fast as he could, reckoning that Jamie's robotic-like mind state didn't extend to her physical prowess too as he hoped the force of his motion would cause her to lose her grip on the hold around his neck.

Trying to fight off the increasing light-headedness, Jesse finally felt Jamie's arm loosen enough to be able to pull it off with his own hands as she activated her borrowed flight ability once more to avoid hurtling to the floor.

Marcella watched on, marvelling at the young man's ingenuity and use of his various powers. She of course knew that Jesse would not in any circumstance want to kill his friend but that was an irrelevant matter now anyway; once she had seen enough of Jesse's own capabilities, as well as seeing him fight his close friend for her own amusement, she would simply place him under her control as well and utilise his powers for herself alongside Jamie's. *Unstoppable.*

Jamie aimed a mid-air kick at Jesse, only for him to block it with another shield. A flurry of physical blows then rained down upon the barrier which were vastly insufficient in providing enough force to break through it, a continued assault Jesse knew played into his hands – punching the barrier would likely be akin to hitting a brick wall which carried the possibility of Jamie injuring her limbs in the process of constantly striking it and thereby weakening her offensive capabilities. Considering she currently felt no pain, Jesse felt at peace allowing it to occur as he had the power to heal her body after he had broken the mind control. *As soon as I figure that part out anyway.*

Jamie then backed off and fully descended to the ground with Jesse following her down. He braced himself behind another barrier as he saw her raising her arm diagonally across her chest.

Gabrielle's ability, he thought to himself. After a few seconds, she unleashed the energy wave straight at the invisible shield. Jesse unexpectedly found himself being shunted a foot backwards by the force of the impact, though with the barrier still intact. Whether it was through Marcella's influence or her own innate thought process, Jesse realised that Jamie had discarded brute force in favour of trying to break through his defences instead with over-charged energy wave attacks.

But he knew that the extra exertion of her borrowed power from Gabrielle would cause it to run out faster, thus it was just a matter of how long he could maintain the shielding before she fully depleted her reserves.

That wasn't his main concern though; Marcella was still the mastermind of the assault and he knew he had to figure out a means of taking her out before the fight could come to an end, lest a premature defeat of Jamie cause Marcella to turn her mind control on him instead. Jesse prayed that her full focus was currently on controlling Jamie and not also listening to his thoughts at the same time.

Aware that Marcella was currently positioned behind him, Jesse began activating his water manipulation ability – although there was a lack of obvious available water source around them, the moisture in the ground among the surrounding trees would probably suffice for what he had planned.

As Jamie launched yet another energy wave directly at him, Jesse leapt up into the air to avoid it assisted by flight. The attack instead flew straight at Marcella who was surprised by Jesse's dodging of it, having lapsed in monitoring his thinking process due to her indulgence in enjoying the bout between the two.

Seeing Marcella narrowly jump out of the way to avoid being hit, Jesse telekinetically summoned the abundant ground moisture he had been focusing on amassing and brought it all forth towards the telepath in her moment of distraction.

Before she could properly react, Marcella witnessed a surge of muddy water coming at her from multiple directions, of which she was unable to prevent from completely engulfing her as she fell to the floor in a helpless and drenched state.

Behind him, Jesse heard the sound of something hitting the floor, turning his head to see Jamie on her hands and knees but still conscious, despite being heavily disorientated. As much as he wanted to check up on her, Jesse knew he had to continue his counter-offensive against Marcella immediately before he missed his opportunity.

Marcella staggered to her feet, barely able to see with all the sediment in her eyes. As she furiously tried to rub them clean with her fingers, she suddenly felt a strong grip around her neck that was quickly beginning to cut off her air supply. She tried to physically overpower her assailant to very little avail while trying to regain her senses and fight off the light-headed feeling rapidly consuming her.

Jesse held on with all he could, knowing from a mere moment beforehand just how debilitating being choked out was. Not that he felt good about doing so but it really was a matter of life or death and if he could bring Marcella into a state of unconsciousness, he could focus on rejuvenating Jamie with his healing ability and let her properly deal with their defeated foe afterwards.

Jesse then let out a piercing yell as his entire body became overwhelmed with pain, like every part of his nervous system was on fire. The agony too much to bear, he released his grip on Marcella before collapsing to the floor, allowing the subdued telepath to slowly recover and regain her composure.

Swiftly, Marcella delivered a hard kick straight into Jesse's midsection as he cried out in further anguish. Her attention then momentarily turned to the downed Jamie who was still on all fours in the background.

You can bear witness to the aftermath of this.

Enraged, Marcella continued the relentless barrage of kicks to Jesse whose body remained partially paralysed from the telepathic attack on his body's entire pain receptors, being left unable to defend himself.

"Don't worry, what I just made you feel a second ago will feel like pleasure once I send you down to my master in Hell for an eternity," Marcella growled as she unleashed another telepathic attack on Jesse's mind. This time, the embattled young man opened his eyes to realise he had gone blind, leaving him completely unaware of the next vicious kick connecting with the side of his head that promptly laid him out on the floor, still conscious but heavily injured and unable to see anything at all.

Although acknowledging she was about to throw away a useful accessory in favour of gaining vengeance, Marcella drew a concealed blade from her leather trousers and approached Jesse, her anger still welling within her. She then pressed the tip of the knife against Jesse's neck, enough to draw a small amount of blood as he groaned from the pain.

"To your credit, you just did what no-one has ever done before you," Marcella said as she pulled the blade away slightly. "May it be some small source of comfort as you writhe in hellfire until the end of days!"

As she went to plunge the dagger into Jesse's throat, Marcella again found herself being grabbed from behind out of nowhere, dropping the blade in the process. Jamie, acting on pure instinct, took her other hand and gripped it squarely across Marcella's forehead and began draining as much of her telepathy power as she could with her hapless foe struggling to wrench her off.

After a further few seconds, Jamie used her flight to physically drag Marcella across the path and flung her several feet away from the incapacitated Jesse who began to slowly come round following the telepathic hold on his mind being broken.

"I've changed my mind," a greatly agitated Marcella menacingly seethed just within earshot of her liberated captive as she got back up. "You'll be the one to send him down to the dark master, and you'll be fully aware of what you're doing this time too!"

As she attempted to invade Jamie's mind telepathically once more, Marcella became confused as she watched the teenager simply staring back at her nonchalantly.

"Surprised? I wouldn't be seeing as you know I can absorb powers," Jamie remarked aloud to Marcella. "Now that I have some of yours, you won't be controlling my mind again anytime soon."

"Then looks like your boyfriend will be the one to kill *you* instead," Marcella gleefully responded as she focused her powers on Jesse. Before she could fully integrate her will upon him, Jamie quickly surged towards her with flight and grasped her bare neck with both hands, deactivating the telepathy ability as she held Marcella down on the floor of the path.

"Wanna try that again?" she taunted as she floated up off the neutralised enhanced deviant, allowing her to get to her feet. Marcella tried once more to take control of Jesse but found that her attempts were failing to have an effect. She looked back at the triumphant Jamie with a dishevelled look of fear before turning to run in the opposite direction.

Jamie immediately swooped over to cut her off, planting a double-footed stomp square into Marcella's torso that sent her crashing back down to the floor.

"You can kill me but it makes no difference in the end," Marcella smirked. "By taking my life, you will only corrupt your own soul while mine takes its place beside the throne of Hell."

"I'm going to take an educated guess that you're some kind of devil worshipper?" Jamie calmly asked.

"You aren't worthy of your gifts, you insolent waste of flesh and bone," Marcella snapped, awaiting her inevitable fate.

"Maybe, maybe not but I do know that you won't be harming anyone else with yours from this point on," Jamie said as she activated the absorbed telepathy within her and used it to possess Marcella's mind, plunging her into a state of unconsciousness.

From there, she forcefully began to harness the remainder of the power and further applied it to the fallen telepath.

A moment later, Jamie collapsed to her knees from the effort, the entirely of her absorbed telepathy exhausted as Jesse ambled over to her.

"What did you do?" he asked curiously.

"Erased her memories of us as well as her Satanic fanaticism and knowledge of her own telepathic powers," Jamie said without looking up.

"Do you think you succeeded?"

"I hope so. I only had a rough idea of what I was doing but with my experience using Kay's empathy, I just winged it. At least while I have her in a slumber and her powers negated, she won't be a threat to anyone."

"Allow me to take care of those burn marks," Jesse said as Jamie looked at her arm, realising the pain emanating from the burned flesh now that her adrenaline rush was wearing off.

"I suppose a few things occurred while I was out of it?" Jamie said as Jesse healed her skin, absorbing some of the healing ability in the process and tending to Jesse's own visible head injuries.

"You could say that," Jesse remarked. "I don't know what she had you do prior to me finding you but she certainly had me fighting for my life when she sent you at me."

"Sorry," Jamie remorsefully replied.

"Don't be, you weren't in control of yourself at the time."

"Maybe, but I shouldn't have tried to engage her to begin with. I should've listened to Brody and just called it in when I found her."

"Probably but in the end, you managed to subdue her with little consequences."

"Well, none that I know of."

"Between you leaving my house and me locating you with her, you wouldn't have had long enough to cause much havoc on her behalf," Jesse attempted to reason.

"How *did* you end up finding me?" Jamie asked.

"I called you up to discuss a homework-related issue for Kay and you ended up coming out with all this talk about wanting me," Jesse answered with a slight smile.

"Oh, no...." Jamie replied, completely mortified as she buried her face in her hands in embarrassment.

"It's fine," Jesse laughed. "Had you not been made to say all that, I might not have known something was up. She practically did us a favour."

"Suppose," Jamie mumbled, slightly miffed at Jesse's response. "How did you track me down anyway?"

"It was Kayleigh and her empathy," Jesse answered, to Jamie's surprise. "I suggested she use it to try and sense where you were based on how much she wanted to find you."

"Clever," Jamie replied, somewhat comforted by the fact Kayleigh cared that much for her but also intrigued by her developing powers.

"Plus you also managed to give her the answer to her homework during that phone call so I'd say it all turned out well, even though I forgot to pass the answer on."

"Yeah..."

"Are you alright?" Jesse asked, feeling a diminished mood from Jamie.

"No, it's all good," Jamie responded, perking up. "I need to contact Detective Brody and left him know I've got our rogue telepath before she wakes up. Guess they'll know how to handle her."

"What do you reckon will happen to her?"

"The police's version of Ryan Sharp's dungeon I imagine."

"Really?"

"I don't agree with it but what else could they do with someone as dangerous as her? It's a lousy thing to do locking a person up and putting them in a semi-permanent state of sedation but the alternative would be a lot worse, as we both found out today."

"At least it's being used for good intent this time round," Jesse attempted to lighten the mood.

"You'd best head back to yours, I don't want them discovering you and putting you in the same position as me," Jamie said. "I'll catch up with you later."

"Okay," Jesse said. As he took off into the air with haze surrounding him, Jamie looked on with slight disappointment. It didn't feel good that the person she had underlying feelings for had simply laughed off the fact she had told him she wanted to be with him, albeit in a mind-controlled state. She knew she was just being paranoid but she couldn't help but feel that maybe she wasn't good enough for him anyway, especially following the laughing response.

Oh well.

But enough dwelling; she had managed to succeed in her task and then some. It was time to at least revel in any accolades she had coming her way for having apprehended an empowered murder suspect despite only being sent out to locate them. And see the look on Layne's face with any luck.

"There she is, the new star of the operation!" Rachel said aloud as Jamie approached the staff tearoom at the precinct. "Knew you could do it."

"Thanks," Jamie modestly replied. "Was a bit of a fluke though, mind."

"Got the result though and that's what matters in this business. Well, catching the criminals with powers anyway. You spoke to Brody yet?"

"Not since he met me in the field to pick up that telepath I brought down. He seemed to be in a decent mood at the time."

"I can imagine he would be with you shutting down that tricky customer. Oh, talk of the devil…"

Jamie turned around to see Brody walking up to the tearoom. *Not the phrase I would use after dealing with that telepathic Satanist, Rachel…*

"Ah, the person of the hour," Brody said. "Mind if we debrief in my office?"

"Sure," Jamie said as she followed Brody, Rachel giving her a double thumbs-up gesture and a smile on the way out.

"Well you certainly made a good impression, I must admit," Brody stated as he and Jamie took their seats either side of his desk.

"Quite the outstanding effort on your part to be able to take down someone with such malicious abilities as that Marcella individual."

"I kind of get the feeling that's not all you want to talk to me about," Jamie interjected, picking up on Brody's tone of voice.

"Don't take this as criticism; I don't know what led up to your apprehension of her but did you actively try to engage her rather than simply locating her as instructed?"

"I'd be lying if I said I didn't," Jamie answered honestly.

"Okay. Again, I'm not criticising you and I may even be coming across as slightly patronising considering the fact you previously took down Ryan Sharp single-handedly but I do have to empathise the importance of keeping yourself safe when you're working on a task with us, Jamie," Brody said, trying his best not to dampen Jamie's enthusiasm. "Anything could've happened with that suspect, as that unfortunate young man who took a swan dive off his apartment found out the other day. That's not something I want happening to you."

"I know, it won't happen again," Jamie replied indifferently, already feeling deflated despite Brody's efforts to avoid making the talk sound like a reprimand.

"Was it Layne getting inside your head?"

Jamie glumly gave an acknowledging nod.

"I don't need to tell you that we all need to leave our egos at the door when it comes to a job like this," Brody said. "Regrettably Layne doesn't and it's made all the more worse that he is one of the leading figures in this operation. This is where you need to prove that you can be better than him."

"How did he react to the collar?" Jamie asked.

"Not as you would have wanted him to," Brody replied. "He more or less dismissed it as you proving you're untrustworthy for going beyond your orders."

"Fabulous(!)" Jamie remarked.

"Well that was all the negatives; let's actually end this conversation on a high note. First of all, an extremely problematic individual with deadly powers is now off the streets, thanks to you. Secondly, if Rachel didn't already blab it to you, my superiors are very happy with how successful you were today despite going off script to a degree as it shows you can handle yourself in the heat of an unpredictable situation."

Yeah, only with Jesse's help, Jamie lamented.

"And to top it off, Layne is most likely silently seething over your accomplishment today even if he refuses to admit it out loud. So go home and rest, you've earned it."

"Thanks," Jamie replied, trying to sound grateful but still feeling very weary over everything. Rachel would have to forgive her for not stopping by on the way out as she just wasn't in the mood for a chat, especially not about work.

"Hard to believe Gabby's actually from Northern Ireland," Jesse spoke, still amazed at everything he had just heard.

"I know, her prominent English accent would never give you that impression," Jamie said. "I suppose finding out you've been living a lie the majority of your life was never going to go down easy. I do feel sorry for her mother too though for having to go through all that to begin with."

"Makes sense now why she's been so despondent lately, what an awful burden to be carrying around with you."

"Think it may be about time that I give her a chance to open up about it," Jamie said.

"You think she'll appreciate the fact you went to her mother to find out?" Jesse warned.

"Probably not but this needs to be addressed. My best friend is suffering in silence and I hate that she's miserable with no-one she feels she can turn to over what she's going through."

"Well if there's any fallout over it, you always have me and the nipper for company."

"Appreciated as always," Jamie replied warmly as a knock on Jesse's door was heard.

"Can I come in yet?" Kayleigh called out. "Or are you two still snogging?"

"Yeah, you're good(!)" Jesse called back with an acidic tone. The door opened up with Kayleigh bolting straight towards Jamie and tackling her onto the bed into a hug.

"Affectionate today, aren't we?" Jamie said.

"Glad you're alright," Kayleigh replied, to Jamie's confusion as she worriedly looked towards Jesse.

"Yeah, it was a false alarm it turned out but all's well that ends well," Jesse said with a reassuring notion to Jamie who quickly caught on.

"What happened to you anyway?" Kayleigh asked. Jamie felt uncomfortable trying to come up with a lie as her analysis ability had started to sense Kayleigh secretly using her empathy ability to try and detect any deceit, yet it was possible to say something that at least bordered on the truth to get round that conundrum.

"I had a problem with an ability I had come into contact with and it was messing around with my head," Jamie thought fast, choosing her words carefully. "But Jesse managed to help me out with it."

"What ability was that?" Kayleigh responded, her powers indicating Jamie was (somewhat) telling the truth.

"A dangerous one that was putting a lot of people at risk. Just remember that these powers aren't anything to be mucked around with when you're using yours," Jamie replied with an exaggerated stare at Kayleigh, hinting she was aware that the youth was using her empathy on her.

"Oh Kay, really?!" Jesse reacted in an irritated tone upon realising what was going on, much to Jamie's surprise. "What did I tell you earlier about doing that without someone's knowledge?"

"I'm not hurting anyone!" Kayleigh protested.

"It's invading people's privacy and it's just downright rude. Thought you knew better than that," Jesse continued the dressing down.

"Sorrrr-reeee then," Kayleigh sulked as she stormed off into her own room, slamming the door behind her.

"I'm guessing I missed something earlier on," Jamie muttered awkwardly.

"Yeah," Jesse grumbled. "I'll find it hard to trust her if she keeps abusing those powers of hers like that."

"Still, it's nice to see her acting her own age with that little temper tantrum," Jamie smiled. "Kinda cute."

"She'll shake it off by morning, she's stubborn but knows when she's in the wrong. Especially when I have to tell her off about anything."

"Just like Gabby with me," Jamie joked. "On that note, I best prepare for that much-needed talk back home."

"You sure about it?" Jesse asked.

"Better sooner than later," Jamie replied as she got up off the bed. "I think we've let this play out for long enough as it is anyway."

"Hope it all goes well," Jesse said as Jamie left the room and hovered down the staircase to put her shoes on to depart, reasoning that it was best to say goodbye to Kayleigh another time when she was done stewing in her room.

"Gabby!" Jamie called out, expecting to find her friend somewhere in the house seeing as her car was parked outside, indicating she was home from work already. When she failed to respond, Jamie then went to call her mobile, only to find that Gabrielle had already attempted to call her while she had been travelling back home and had left her a voicemail instead.

"Hey, babes! Just gone out with some of the work lot to a cocktail bar, I won't be back 'til much later so I'll sort my own dinner out. See you soon!"

Jamie sighed as she settled into the couch and put her game console on. After the day she had had and her plan to mediate with Gabrielle now up in smoke, taking the chance to unwind seemed the best thing to do for the next few hours.

By ten o'clock, Jamie had settled into bed but remained awake while awaiting Gabrielle's return. The chance to have any conversation with her was all but gone by that point but she still wanted to see her friend arrive home safe as they always made sure of one another during any late night out.

As the time neared half past ten, Jamie finally heard the sound of the front door opening as she continued to lie awake, which was immediately followed by the door slamming obnoxiously hard and then a loud thud. She quickly got out of bed and made a beeline for the staircase, looking down to see a dishevelled Gabrielle lying on the floor.

"Gabby!" Jamie called out before levitating down the stairs and kneeling beside Gabrielle who was slowly trying to get up.

"Heeey, Jamie baby!" Gabrielle said, clearly inebriated.

"Gabbs, are you alright? Did your friends drop you off?" Jamie asked worriedly.

"Yeeahhh, they're such a nice bunch of people," Gabrielle slurred her words. "Hey, have I ever told you you're the most gorgeous person in the world?"

"Come on, I'm getting you to bed," Jamie said, ignoring the drunken compliment as she helped Gabrielle to her feet who was barely able to stand of her own accord. "Hope you had a good time tonight."

"Oh yeah, it was terrrrific!" Gabrielle replied as the pair slowly staggered up the staircase. "It really felt nice to let myself go after everything that's gone down."

"Oh really?" Jamie said, trying to feign ignorance as they made it onto the second floor. "What exactly has that been anyway?"

Suddenly, Gabrielle stopped walking forward and collapsed onto her knees, dragging Jamie down with her before bursting into tears and crying loudly.

At a loss at how else to deal with the situation, Jamie simply held her hysterical friend in her arms in an attempt to comfort her, knowing deep down that there was only going to be one way to try and resolve her inner conflict and it was going to happen the following morning, whether Gabrielle was ready to talk about it or not.

Chapter 9

Jamie awakened beside Gabrielle in the latter's double bed, having spent the whole night comforting her friend and making sure she wasn't violently ill from the alcohol consumption. She was probably going to be extremely hungover and barely in the mood for talking about anything relating to her personal issues but the previous night's events had been the last straw – Jamie was determined to bring it all out into the open to start trying to resolve the matter as best as she could.

As she went downstairs to prepare a coffee, she could hear Gabrielle starting to stir in the background.

Please don't hate me for this.

Boiling some water in the kettle, Jamie fretted over the best way to reveal the fact that she knew what was going on in Gabrielle's head, predicting a hostile response for breaching her privacy regardless but how less hostile being down to exactly how she delivered it.

Returning upstairs with beverages in hand, she peered back into Gabrielle's bedroom to see she was still ebbing in and out of her slumber.

"Gabby," Jamie gently called out, receiving a groan in response. "I've brought you coffee."

Gabrielle slowly opened her eyes, trying to snap out of her disorientated state.

"Urgh, my head is killing me," she said groggily. "Can you get my painkillers out of my bag?"

"Sure," Jamie replied, setting the coffee down on the bedside table and pulling out a packet of paracetamol from the nearby handbag lying on the floor. Gabrielle sat up in her bed and quickly swallowed two of the pills with a small amount of her coffee.

"What did you get up to last night then?" Jamie asked.

"When it all comes back to me, I'll let you know," Gabrielle responded, brushing her hair from her face. "Think I had too many cocktails."

"Quite possibly," Jamie jokingly agreed. "Did you mean to get that plastered?"

"Well not *that* hammered but maybe a little bit off my head for the sake of having a fun night out."

"You sure that's all it was?"

Gabrielle gave a weary look back at Jamie.

"I really don't want to discuss it, Jame," she dismissively answered while looking down at the cup in her hands.

"I know you don't want to but maybe it's what you *need* instead," Jamie replied. "This is obviously not a run-of-the-mill issue going

133

on here and whatever it is has been making you miserable for the last few days now. It will probably help to talk it out rather than keeping it bottled up."

"I will get over it in my own time," Gabrielle responded in a mildly irritated tone.

"I know you like to be fiercely independent but I really do think this is something you need to get out of your system before it consumes you like my depression did with me all those months back. Take it from someone who knows what it's like to go through something as traumatic as what you're dealing with."

Gabrielle gave a hard look at Jamie that slowly became more of a glare with Jamie realising she had just caught herself out but despite her fear of her friend's reaction, sought to hold her nerve.

"How?" Gabrielle asked in a blunt and agitated manner. "Did you use your powers to find out?"

"I visited your mum," Jamie answered calmly as her anxiety increased. "And she told me what you had fallen out with her over."

"You had no right," Gabrielle fired back. "That is so out of order, Jamie. I can't believe you would go behind my back like that, I should be able to trust you."

"No, Gabby," Jamie replied in an equally stern voice, choosing to throw her cautious stance to the wind. "Going behind your back and betraying your trust was when I borrowed your powers and used them to fight empowered criminals without telling you. This, on the other hand, is me doing what I had to do to try and help you in your time of need, just like you were there for me when I was completely overwhelmed following my mother's death."

"It's not the same as what you went through, Jamie!" Gabrielle responded combatively. "When your parents died, as awful as that was, at least you knew exactly who they were and what you were. I've spent my whole life believing one thing and finding out that it's a complete and total lie! And I'm just supposed to act like nothing is wrong with the fact I was led to believe an imposter was my real dad?!"

"That's your father you're talking about, Gabby," Jamie sullenly cut in.

"But he's not," Gabrielle ranted. "My father was senselessly blown up in a conflict he had nothing to do with nearly eighteen years ago and my mother just moved on like he mattered nothing!"

"Gabbs!" Jamie yelled over her apoplectic friend. "You have the right to be angry but don't dismiss your family over it. Your mum explained to me what she went through and her decision to move to England and it wasn't easy for her but she did it to give you a chance at a normal life. To protect you from what happened to your biological dad."

Gabrielle continued to stare angrily back at Jamie but could feel herself losing a hold on her bitterness as she saw her friend's eyes starting to well.

"Nobody chooses who they fall in love with but it happened to your mum with your adoptive dad and regardless of everything that occurred before that, you've grown up with a loving family with two parents, biological or otherwise, who have raised you and your two brothers well and believe me when I say that I envy the fact that you still have that compared to me."

Gabrielle completely lowered her resentful expression as she let Jamie's words sink in.

"Don't throw all that away," Jamie said mournfully as she saw a single tear streaming down Gabrielle's cheek. The two girls sat in silence for a few seconds before Gabrielle looked back up.

"I don't mean to make you feel that way," she quietly spoke, her anger now completely gone.

"It's not about me, Gabby," Jamie despondently replied. "I will always have you in that regard. The last thing I want to see you do though is end up feeling as hopeless as I once did by walking away from the people who love you as much as I do, if not more."

Gabrielle sighed as she bowed her head with Jamie clambering into the bed beside her.

"How do I even begin to process all of this?" she said dejectedly. "How do I act like everything's the same as it was before? I can't just forget the fact that I'm not what I thought I was and my father isn't the man who I assumed to be my real dad."

"It doesn't really matter if he's not bound to you by blood, Gabbs," Jamie consoled. "A father is ultimately someone who takes care of their children or even someone else's and loves them no matter what. Michael has always been that person as long as he has known you and you've never seen him as anything less than that."

"Until the other day anyway," Gabrielle remarked with regret.

"Can you imagine how hurt he and your mum are feeling about all this too right now, feeling like they're losing their daughter?"

Gabrielle finally broke down with Jamie allowing her to cry into her chest in a sombre embrace on the bed. Though she felt bad about driving home her points so hard, she was glad that Gabrielle had decided to open up about her inner turmoil at long last as she continued to express her outpouring of emotion for the next several minutes.

"What are you going to do?" Jamie eventually asked Gabrielle who remained curled up beside her.

"...Guess I need to speak to mum," Gabrielle replied with some reluctance. "I still don't know how we're going to move forward after all this."

"You've always been the rational one out of the two of us. I know you'll resolve it one way or another."

"I can only hope so," Gabrielle said as she turned her head to the wall. "Did your phone just go off in your room?"

"Could be Brody I suppose, if not Jesse. Probably should check to make sure," Jamie said as she got up off the bed and walked into her room, seeing the light from her phone screen dissipating as she walked in. Sure enough, a message had been left by Detective Brody which she proceeded to open and read.

Right now, Brody?!

Disgruntled, Jamie walked back into Gabrielle's room who was now sitting up in her bed.

"You alright?" she asked.

"Brody's asking me to come in as they've got another case involving more of our mob that they want me to be a part of."

"Anything tough?"

"Will find out when I get there I imagine. Probably nothing too bad, he's been adamant about not throwing me in the deep end too much. Are you going to go visit your mum today?"

"Yeah, better to do it as soon as given the situation. I should be alright going alone if you want to go do your thing."

"Wouldn't it be better me coming to support you?" Jamie asked.

"It will probably be best if we just sort it out on our own," Gabrielle replied. "Not that I don't want you there, it's just something that we need to clear up between us that will probably go smoother without anyone else around."

"Let me know how you get on," Jamie said as she took Gabrielle's hand and kissed her on the forehead. "Love you."

"Love you too, babes," Gabrielle replied. "Thanks for being there for me."

"Just returning the favour," Jamie smiled as she went off to get changed.

Jamie walked through the precinct towards Brody's office, feeling slightly annoyed that it hadn't even been a full day since her last task had concluded and she was already being pushed forward into undertaking another one. The fact they were doing so though did make her consider the possibility that they already saw her as a valuable commodity in fighting enhanced human-based crime, a position she would gladly flaunt before Layne whenever she needed to.

"Jamie, welcome," Brody said as Jamie entered his office. "I hope all is well."

"Well, mostly," she replied. "A small issue at home but otherwise all good. What have you got for me this time then?"

"Something that I hope will be right up your alley," Brody said while activating a video on his open laptop.

If only you knew just how many incidents had gone down regarding me and alleys…

"This is security footage from last night at a jeweller's shop – pay attention to the left side of the screen."

Jamie stared at the monitor not really knowing what to expect. Out of nowhere, she saw a hooded figure walking through the wall that then put their arm straight through the solid glass shelving unit without damaging it to obtain a necklace before leaving the same way they had come in.

"Seen that kind of power before?" Brody asked.

"Can't say I have," Jamie replied. "And I'm guessing you haven't either seeing as you're asking me."

"It's definitely not something that I and the department have dealt with before. I don't even know what to classify it as."

"I suppose 'phasing' would be the closest thing to describing it," Jamie said. "What did the shop owner say when they saw this footage?"

"Probably thought they were going mad," Brody replied. "But they reported it to us nonetheless and we sent over the lawyers with some legal forms to prevent them from broadcasting the footage on the internet or the evening news."

"That your main method of covering things up?"

"Well Rachel's abilities in hacking into the web definitely is the far greater tool at our disposal but paying off people and having them sign non-disclosure agreements is also an effective approach. It's not just corrupt businessmen who opt to do that(!)"

"So what do you require of me?" Jamie asked.

"Specifically, the same as before which is to locate them and call them in, *without* engaging them this time preferably."

"Duly noted," Jamie snidely spoke, though with a slight humorous tone in acknowledgement of her prior *faux pas*.

"Detective Brody," Layne's voice trumpeted as he walked straight into the office without knocking. "I see that you're prepping Miss Avonoit for her latest assignment. I do hope that she will remember to follow her directives properly this time."

"Yes," Jamie icily said in response.

"I don't believe I was talking to you," Layne responded. Jamie shot a venomous glare as she eyed Brody motioning her with his eyes to let it go. "I actually dropped by, Larry, to see if you had anyone spare today to accompany me on a rape investigation – one of my guys called in sick this morning with a case of man-flu. Probably just woke up after a bender the previous night and couldn't be asked to come in if you ask me though."

"Yes, I've got Officer Delaney free," Brody answered. "She's just catching up on some paperwork if you want to swing by her desk."

"Good man," Layne replied as he turned to leave. "Of course if women would stop dressing like tarts when they're out and practically giving an open invite to all these rapists, I wouldn't even have a case to bother investigating."

That's it!

"Or maybe we should be teaching MEN to not view women as sex objects and learn to accept that 'no' means no!" Jamie raised her voice to the surprise of both men.

"What did you say, Avonoit?" Layne fired back as he turned around.

"Jamie..." Brody attempted to quell the outburst.

"How can you seriously blame a victim for getting raped when you're a detective?" Jamie continued in her irate state. "Your attitude is absolutely disgusting for a person in your position!"

"Seems like you forget your place in this hierarchy, young lady," Layne pretentiously replied while approaching Jamie. "You see, *I'm* the one in charge of what goes on around here and I am more than willing to send you down with your mate, Ryan Sharp, if you as much dare to speak to me like that again, alright? Now if I were you, I would focus more on your own job and keep your opinions to yourself."

"And if I were *you*," Jamie retorted. "I would learn how to respect wom–"

"Alright, enough!" Brody interrupted before turning to Layne. "Detective Layne, would you mind leaving the room so I can have a word with Miss Avonoit about talking down to her superiors?"

Layne, grated but nonetheless appeased by Brody's intervening stance against such insolence, proceeded to leave the room without any hassle though lingered outside momentarily to watch the subsequent dressing down through the unobstructed windows of the office.

"What have I personally said to you about undermining the department and anyone working within it?" Brody spoke several decibels above his regular levels to Jamie, who was staring back at him with a look as though she was about to erupt with anger.

"Why are you taking his side?!" Jamie responded. "Did you not hear that sexist drivel he came out with?"

"Do as you are told in future and leave your personal feelings out of the workplace!" Brody continued his tirade while looking out of the corner of his eye towards the window. "We have certain rules in this place for a good reason and you are expected to adhere to them as a member of.......right, he's gone."

Confused, Jamie looked out the office window to see an empty corridor, quickly realising that Brody was putting on a show to satisfy Layne who had likely been loitering around to watch the admonishment.

"Okay, so obviously everything I just said there was a load of bull," Brody said in a normal tone. "And you're not wrong about Layne and his woeful comments a minute ago but you do have to understand, Jamie, that that man holds your future in his hands and it is not a smart idea deliberately trying to wind him up."

"Then why don't *you* say something next time?" Jamie shot back, still annoyed.

"Because I've worked my way up to this prestigious position over the years by adhering to the politics of this precinct and the arseholes who fill the top spots in the hierarchy whether I agree with what they think or not and believe me when I say that I use the power entitled to me for the greater good. Rest assured, I play the game for the benefit of others including yourself and I do so by keeping my mouth shut and staying on the good side of the people in charge around here, lest I choose to go the other route and see myself shoved right back down to patrolling the streets."

Jamie maintained her gaze towards Brody, slowly calming herself down knowing he wasn't deserving of being on the end of her rage.

"I'm sorry," she said.

"I know, and I don't blame you for lashing out," Brody sympathised. "A man of Layne's position indeed really should not be holding those kind of views towards victims of violent crime. It is what it is, however, but rather than letting yourself get worked up by those degrading comments, put your energy into more productive means like trying to hunt down that mystery 'phaser' who burgled the jeweller's. You're in our superiors' good books with that last bust and I imagine they will be considering you an essential part of the taskforce if you maintain that success rate."

Jamie, still brimming with frustration, decided to leave the conversation on what had ended up being an amicable note and headed straight out the office door, albeit without saying a word to Brody on her way out. Trying her best to see the positives in her forced arrangement was becoming a task in of itself having to deal with Layne's antagonistic attitude, even if he did only pop up on small occasions. Too bad she had used up Marcella's telepathy powers or she might be able to alter Layne's backwards manner of thinking and antipathy towards her.

Then again, not having the means to act on such temptation to control someone against their will was probably a good thing, owing to her most recent experience.

"Jamie! Where you going?" Rachel called out as she walked over from her desk at a hurried pace.

"Just out of here at least," Jamie replied acidly.

"Layne again?"

"Yeah."

"Why don't you tell me about it over lunch?"

"It's only ten o'clock," Jamie pointed out.

"*Brunch* then, I'm buying," Rachel said as she looped her arm around Jamie's and led the aggrieved teenager down the corridor towards the staircase.

Gabrielle sat in the front seat of her car while parked across the road from her family home. She already knew her mother would be in, it was just whether she could bring herself to approach the house to initiate any attempt at reconciliation. Every ounce of stubbornness within her was telling her to just drive back home and let her mother be the first to reach out but the situation really wasn't going to benefit from any foolish pride.

Hesitantly, she exited the vehicle and made her way towards the front garden, trying as hard as she could to maintain some composure. She was glad she had chosen to forego putting her make-up on as she knew an outpouring of emotion was going to involuntarily and inevitably come forth, not that she had ever needed to look glamorous around her parents or siblings anyway. It was one of the things she could warmly look upon about her family at that moment in time.

Standing before the front door, Gabrielle thought about using her door key before instead deciding to ring the bell, almost symbolically as a stranger to the household. She held her breath as she anticipated the door opening, watching as it then swung open.

"Gabby?" Imogen spoke upon seeing her daughter standing before her.

"Hi, mum," Gabrielle lowly replied, already feeling a lump in her throat. "You free to talk?"

"Of course," Imogen answered in an astonished tone while moving aside to let Gabrielle walk in. "I wasn't expecting you."

"I can come back if you're busy?" Gabrielle said, hoping for an affirmative response to avoid the predicted talk.

"No, no, I was just cleaning the house, I've got time for you," Imogen quickly replied, notably speaking in her adoptive English accent not knowing if her natural Irish one would sour the mood. Gabrielle took a few seconds to brace herself as her mother took a seat beside her on the couch.

"I'm sorry," Gabrielle muttered. "For ignoring you the last few days."

"Oh, Gabby," Imogen responded. "Don't be sorry, I dropped a massive bombshell on you that perhaps I shouldn't have. I thought now that you were all grown up that I could at least tell you of your true origins and be honest with you rather than you finding out for yourself and resenting me for keeping it from you."

"I could never resent you, mum," Gabrielle refuted, still feeling on an emotional edge. "I just didn't know how to accept it, and to be honest I still don't. That doesn't mean I don't want anything to do with you or dad. You've given me everything in this life and you have nothing but my love and respect no matter what my true heritage is."

"Oh, sweetheart, you don't know how much it means to me to hear you say that," Imogen said as she gave her daughter a tearful hug.

Oh, brilliant…

With that, Gabrielle succumbed to the tears that she herself had been desperately trying to contain as the two gripped each other tightly in their emotional state. Eventually, they began to calm down and released themselves from one another.

"I know things may never be the same as they were before," Imogen said while wiping her eyes. "But we will always be here to help you through how you're feeling about everything."

"Can I ask you something?" Gabrielle asked sombrely.

"Anything," Imogen replied.

"What was he like? You know, my birth father. Am I anything like him at all?"

Imogen sat still on her side of the couch for a moment in deep thought, then gave a smile as she prepared to revisit her tumultuous past once more.

*   *   *

"I'm guessing you didn't originally plan to go out of the office this early today?" Jamie asked as she and Rachel settled down at a table in the nearby diner.

"Caught me out, didn't ya?" Rachel responded brightly. "I *might've* received a text shortly after your chat with Brody and that idiot Layne asking me to take you out to calm you down. I figured it must've been a bad one based on that. So, what did the moron come out with this time?"

"He barged in asking Brody for someone to aid him in a rape investigation and implied women brought it on themselves for dressing 'like sluts'."

"Uh, huh," Rachel calmly replied, lowering her usual bubbly demeanour into an agitated-looking scowl.

"I mean, how can you be a cop with that thought process anyway? It just diminishes the impact of sexual assault on the victims making it sound like they bring it on themselves."

"Did you know that I was once in an abusive relationship when I was 21 years old?" Rachel chimed in.

"No," Jamie responded.

"Well until now, no-one else apart from my inner circle and my then-arsehole boyfriend did, as well as a certain police officer a little while later. He was charming when I first met him and I quickly grew attached but after a while he developed a real nasty side that he had a habit of expressing in my company, or perhaps he had it all along and just waited until I was completely under his thrall before showing it."

"What kind of things did he do?" Jamie asked, intrigued.

"Initially just snapping at me over the dumbest things like wanting to watch something he didn't like or wanting him to cook dinner for a change instead of me always doing it as well as full blown rows over what to eat, if you'll believe that. And then we graduated onto stuff like him demanding more sex from me and trying to get it even when I would say I wasn't in the mood for it which just led to more petulant outbursts."

"How did you put up with it?"

"I just did," Rachel replied. "I kept assuring myself that things would get better but they never did, yet I was still very much in love and I thought the heartbreak I'd feel from walking away from him would be far worse than the crap I was dealing with in the relationship.

"Then after another few weeks, he got aggressive in his approach one night trying to get in my pants and I shoved him off me. Next thing I know, he responds with a right hook to my face and catches me square in the eye."

"What?" Jamie said in shock.

"I immediately began putting my clothes back on with him apologising and begging me to stay in the background but I was so afraid of him after that that I fled to my nearest friend's house after calling them up and stayed there until the following morning when they managed to convince me to report him to the police."

"Did they arrest him?"

"I went alone to the station and asked the male officer behind the desk that I wanted to report an act of domestic violence. Keep in mind I had an obvious black eye by this point that I hadn't bothered to put make-up over. You wanna guess what his response was?"

"Go on."

"'So what did you do to make him do *that* to you then?'"

Jamie's jaw dropped slightly in disbelief at what she had just heard, staring motionlessly back at a still-calm Rachel with a wide-eyed stare.

"You're telling me a police officer actually said that to you?"

"Yeah."

"How did you react?"

"I didn't. I just turned around and walked back out the door without saying anything. I was just so mad at being accused by a cop of all people of instigating the assault on me that I lost all interest in doing anything about it. Well, anything legal anyway."

"What did you do?"

"It was soon after that incident that I discovered I was able to muck around with computers and such. By this point I was living with the same friend who had sheltered me that night but my now ex-boyfriend was trying to stir up rubbish about me being crap in bed and that I had caused the black eye myself by falling into the kitchen counter while pointing out that he hadn't been arrested or cautioned over it so I was obviously lying about him hitting me. I could've ignored it but I wasn't prepared to just let my reputation be trashed by a lying woman-beater. And of course, what was to say he wouldn't do it to someone else?"

"Highly likely he would've if he felt he could get away with it like he did with you," Jamie replied in agreement.

"Possibly. I figured he should probably be in jail for assaulting me anyway so I did think to myself how I could get him in trouble for something else to make up for getting off scot-free with me. I kept it relatively simple as my knowledge of computing was quite low at the time; I waited until he was home and used my powers to remotely access his laptop and created an e-mail account with an obviously bogus name. Then I sent my own e-mail a series of messages laced with threats and misogynistic insults from the fake account via my ex's computer."

"What happened as a result?"

"I opened up the messages in my e-mail on my own laptop and reported them to the police via phone to avoid having to deal with any morons face to face this time on grounds of harassment and malicious communications; my ex was arrested and pretty much didn't have a leg to stand on as they were sent from his own computer with no-one else in the house at the time for him to accuse of fabricating the e-mails. He ended up being sent down for six months, of which he served three before being released."

"Brutal," Jamie responded in an impressed tone.

"His own stupid comments about me that he had sent to his friends using his phone were also used as evidence of his 'misogynistic yearnings'," Rachel sniggered. "It may sound harsh what I did but doesn't change the fact he should've got a similar sentence for assaulting me just because he couldn't take no for an answer."

"True, I suppose."

"Wasn't all good though – I haven't really been able to commit to a relationship since because of what I went through. In a way, he's still exerting his dominance over me from a mental standpoint."

"How long has that been going on for?"

"I'm 25 now. Nobody said healing was an easy process but I do wonder if I'm ever going to be able to trust anyone again following that nightmare."

"I know your pain," Jamie said.

"Rough experience yourself?"

"The worst," Jamie reluctantly admitted. "A super-powered psychopath attempted to rape me in an alley."

"Huh?" Rachel replied, a confused yet concerned look on her face emerging.

"He didn't succeed though, I managed to fight him off when my powers manifested for the first time."

"Oh sweetie," Rachel said softly as she reached across the table and held Jamie's hand in her own. "I'm so sorry you went through that."

"It's fine, he can't bother me anymore."

"He locked up with the other empowered criminals?"

"No, he's dead."

Rachel's eyes widened.

"I didn't kill him, don't worry," Jamie assured her. "I did witness it though, it wasn't as satisfying as I thought it would be but I do take some comfort that he can't hurt anyone else now."

"Who did it?"

"His brother, funnily enough. Yet another victim of his cruelty it turned out. Guess blood isn't always thicker than water in some cases."

"Has that had any lasting effects then?" Rachel asked.

"Probably. I've never had a relationship before then and I haven't really been seriously considering it since either…….mostly."

"Ah, who's the guy?" Rachel gleefully enquired. "Or gal?"

"I don't know," Jamie squirmed. "I do fancy this guy but I don't know if it'd be right. I mean we're good friends as it is and I'm not sure I want to ruin what we already have risking trying to take it further."

"Nah, that's reasonable," Rachel replied. "Don't force it; if it's meant to be, it will come organically. Sounds like you care about him a lot though."

"Yeah, he's helped me through some bad times, both emotionally and with our powers."

"So he's another one of us then. Guessing he's not involved with the operation?"

"No, I've done my best to keep him away from that. Goodness knows he's got enough on his plate as it is without being pressganged into serving Layne and his sociopathic attitude too."

"Might sign that moron up to some feminist newsletters later," Rachel joked. "But laughs aside, his ignorant attitude regarding women and sexual assault should disqualify him from rape investigations and even being a police officer, period. Victim blaming like that just adds to the problem; we shouldn't be expected to adjust ourselves to feel safe walking the streets when it's the men who try to sexually harass and assault us who should be the focus."

"Amen. But doesn't look like that's going to happen anytime soon. I guess we were the lucky ones in the fact we survived our ordeals when many other women and girls probably can't say the same."

"Well we're not in medieval times anymore but despite the long way we still have to go, change does come eventually."

"Seeing as I'm only nineteen, any tips for when I enter my twenties?" Jamie asked.

"From what I've learned – don't be afraid to pay the bill when on a date or at least your half of it so you don't 'owe them anything' later, always keep an eye on your drink in a bar or club and your keys can always be utilised as a makeshift weapon if it ever comes to it. Though I imagine that's not an issue in your case."

"Well being able to hurl energy waves at people is certainly more effective," Jamie smirked.

"Touché. I also wouldn't give Layne the satisfaction of knowing he's gotten to you in the future as you can bet he thrives off winding people he doesn't like up."

"Comments like the one he made earlier are a bit hard to ignore, mind you."

"I understand, and I respect the fact you're willing to stand up for yourself in that aspect. Some day Layne will make one of his boneheaded remarks to or in front of the wrong person and maybe the department will get in someone to run the show who has more of a decent personality."

"Seems he reserves most of his bile for us empowered folk," Jamie stated.

"I have snooped through some of his personal messages before using my powers but I never found a specific reason behind his perceived dislike of us. I don't really want to invade the man's privacy any more than I already have though. Compared to what I did to my ex, I don't consider it fair on him to keep doing so."

"Would've thought he deserved it if you're asking me," Jamie remarked.

"Layne may be an unbearable, pig-headed, ignorant prat most of his time spent awake but I don't consider him a heartless monster. I like to think people like him can get over their hang-ups, and although he's failed to show any signs of change as of yet, I feel he has a right to a private life at the very least."

"Generous of you," Jamie said. "I don't know if I could trust myself to do the same."

"At this point in my life, I don't want to be shrouded in negativity. Not to say that *you* are if that's the route you choose to take with your powers but I only want to feed off everyone's positive vibes. Of course I'm not against giving Layne a kick up the backside with my powers every now and then to keep him in line. After all, even I have my limits with the amount of rubbish I'm willing to put up with."

"No objections there," Jamie laughed, enjoying the moment. Rachel was a welcome addition to her small but growing circle of friends and allies and one she felt she shared a lot of personal experiences with, particularly being sexually harassed and assaulted by unscrupulous or outright depraved individuals. She was also grateful to have someone close to vent to about her unpleasant interactions with the likes of Layne and his sexist ideology.

Ironically Jamie could acknowledge that her choice to wear oversized clothes was in part to avoid being sexually assaulted while venturing outside, though she knew Layne's words of women dressing more conservatively to avoid being raped were complete nonsense – it was her own personal decision to want to dress that way and regardless, it really was about keeping the focus on the rapists instead of suggesting preventative measures for women, as Rachel had pointed out.

Nonetheless, she was thankful for having a means to defend herself in the form of her abilities compared to the majority of the normal population who didn't.

In her living room, Jamie awaited the return of Gabrielle by watching a series of documentaries regarding the modern history of the island of Ireland to gain a better understanding of the conflict that had caused Imogen to want to flee her home to begin with. Much like Imogen, she took the overall view that it featured some horrific moments regardless of which side committed them including the bomb blast that had killed Gabrielle's biological father. She couldn't help but still feel glad that Gabrielle had ended up coming to England as a result, however, not knowing what she would be now without her friendship.

In the midst of everything, she had had to take a moment to call Jesse to apologise to Kayleigh for not being able to show up to the house as she said she would be the previous day, owing to Gabrielle's situation and emotional needs taking precedent. To her relief, Kayleigh had taken it stride albeit while making Jamie promise to play her at any board game of her choice when she was next scheduled to visit. Not that she had any complaints upholding that promise.

Upon the sound of a car, presumably Gabrielle's, pulling up outside the house, Jamie quickly changed the programming to something else in case the sight of the footage could trigger her friend. Gabrielle had already texted her in advance to let her know that the talk had gone well and that she was in a better mood but it still wasn't worth taking the chance.

"Hey, Gabby," Jamie said as Gabrielle entered the house.

"Waiting for me?" Gabrielle asked.

"Maayyyyybee," Jamie replied with a mischievous smile.

"Soppy sod. Did that trip to the secret department go alright?"

"Well it ended well, that's all I'll say about it," Jamie said. "But never mind me, how did it all go down with your mum exactly?"

"I'm glad we had a talk about it all," Gabrielle replied in a satisfied voice. "I don't think I could've gone on feeling like an emotional wreck much longer and I don't blame mum for keeping it all from me. She was right to wait until I was older and able to process it better and it must have been hell for her all those years to have kept that all to herself, and to suppress her heritage all the while too."

"So where do you go from here?"

"I still need to chat with my dad, I couldn't face having another extended emotional breakdown upon him coming home from work so I'll probably go see him tomorrow or something to clear the air. Mum's going to let him know everything's okay and I'm not going to view him any less than how I've done so my whole life."

"And your brothers? Are they going to be told about it?"

"We decided it's best that they don't know. Maybe we're just continuing the web of deceit but they're still young and it's not really anything that affects them in the long run. I still see them as my full brothers as opposed to step-siblings and that's never going to change. Just as you're always going to be my sister from another mister!"

"Now who's being the soppy one?" Jamie joked back. "I suppose the only question left really is what do you do with the knowledge of your biological father?"

"Mum told me a bit about him," Gabrielle responded. "She said I got my eyes from him and that he was completely devoted to me. He would always get up in the middle of the night to try and put me back to sleep when I woke up crying, always taking the opportunity to entertain me, trying to coax me into saying 'daddy' as my first word….."

"Babes…" Jamie said as she walked over to comfort Gabrielle as she began to lose her composure once more.

"It's fine," she replied, wiping her eyes. "I got most of it out my system round mum's anyway, just some lingering emotion. Do wish I could've got to know him though."

"I know, hun," Jamie replied gently. "Just always remember that even though he's not related to you by blood, you still have a world-class dad back at your family home."

"Yeah. Hope he'll be alright until I get my chance to have a sit-down with him. Couldn't have been easy on him to think I had completely cast him aside the last few days. Oh yeah, I also told mum she could talk in her natural Irish accent around me when the boys are out of the house."

"That'll be nice for her," Jamie mused. "It'll be just like when me and my mum used to speak French to each other when it was just us on our own, keeping a part of her culture with her in the foreign country she adopted."

"Definitely going to take getting used to after hearing her speak with an English accent my whole life. Might even go out there with her during the summer hols, though she said it rains a lot so I should pack a raincoat."

"Think you have enough experience with that over here as it is," Jamie laughed, happy to see her friend back to her usual self once more even if it did make her miss her own deceased parents in talking it out. And it was good to have finally returned the favour after all that Gabrielle had done to help her throughout her depressed stupor the previous year.

The following morning appeared to continue the return to normality within the Avonoit house; Gabrielle was already at work while Jamie sat watching the morning news after having been woken up by her friend digging her fingernails into her ribs. What would have previously annoyed her was instead a welcome reminder of their usual morning hi-jinks.

Jamie pondered how to spend her day – she knew Jesse had the day off as did Kayleigh who was still on her half-term holidays so spending time with them was always an option. She also realised that she hadn't spoken to Sissy since their last encounter so it was probably an idea to contact her at some point to either simply catch up or even jam on their instruments. And after dealing with Layne the previous day, the last thing on her mind was going out trying to hunt down another enhanced criminal.

"Breaking news just coming in," the newscaster on the television announced. Jamie immediately perked up, curious to know what was going on.

"Reports are that a shooting incident has occurred at Lanford Secondary School in London which is currently still ongoing. The identities of the perpetrators are unknown but gunfire and the sound of explosions have been heard coming from the vicinity of the building. We now go live with our correspondent on the scene."

Jamie continued to watch the screen in disbelief and amazement that such an incident was occurring, especially in England where shootings were rare compared to other countries with less stringent gun restrictions. She took her phone out of her pocket and opened up the sat nav app before typing in the name of the school – the location of it was only ten miles from her home.

She also noticed that it was within close proximity of where Jesse lived.

Was that the secondary school you went to?

Her phone then began ringing; it was Detective Brody trying to get through.

"Hello," Jamie answered.

"Jamie, I'm going to need you to listen very carefully," Brody spoke with an unusually serious tone. *"I need you to locate Lanford Secondary School on your phone and head over there as soon as you can to meet me and the rest of the taskforce."*

"What do you mean?" Jamie asked with a sense of worry coming over her. "Brody, I'm watching the news right now and there's a shooting going on there. Why do I need to be there?"

"Because we have detected ability-based activity going on at that very location and my superiors have made the call – they want you as part of the counter-offensive to neutralise the culprits in order to retake the school."

Chapter 10

"Are you kidding me, Brody?" Jamie responded incredulously at what she had just heard. "You want to send me in to a volatile situation where I risk getting shot or blown up?! I don't even have the proper training for anything like that!"

"Jamie, believe me when I tell you I've tried everything within my power to stop this from going ahead," an exasperated Brody replied. *"I do not want you going anywhere near that scene but as it's now officially our business with people in possession of powers involved, the higher-ups want the best possible approach to it and despite my objections, they've deemed you as that ideal method."*

"A victim of my own success," Jamie angrily muttered down the phone. "And how do you know someone with abilities are involved anyway?"

"Dawn picked up an active power in use."

"Of course she did(!)"

"Jamie, I know you're angry but I need to brief you on the situation," Brody attempted to reason. *"The power that was detected is a 'combustible energy' power, which would explain the*

reports of explosions being heard on the scene. I will send a police escort to pick you up in order to get you here as soon as possible to plan out how we're going to enter the building in order to take out the perps."

"Don't worry, I can make my own way there a lot faster," Jamie stubbornly replied, although in the knowledge that flight would indeed be the fastest method of travelling to the school unhindered.

"Are you sure?" Brody asked.

"Positive."

"Okay, let me know when you get here. When you see the police cordon upon arrival, just ask for either me or Layne."

"Got it," Jamie replied while hanging up the phone in annoyance. Once she managed to let her anger subside, the gravity of her predicament began to seep in. But if she was going into such a dangerous environment, she was going to need all the aid she could get as she opened up the contacts list on her phone.

"Hi, Jamie," Jesse said upon answering the call.

"Hey, Jess," Jamie replied. "You free to meet up quickly?"

"Only quickly? Thought you might be coming round for a bit at some point."

"That was the plan but I've just been conscripted out of nowhere into a pretty dire task by 'the operation' involving that school that's currently being reported on the live news."

"You mean that dump, Lanford?" Jesse replied. *"They want you to be involved in that shooting crisis? Why on earth would they do that?"*

"The suspect is packing an ability so now it's landed on my lap, whether I want to or not."

"Jamie, you can't go in there! It's dangerous!"

"Not helping, Jesse," Jamie responded, unappreciating the inadvertent reminder. "But you *can* be of help by lending me a load of your powers so I can subdue this lunatic with as much ease as possible if you're down for that."

"I can be even more help if I'm there with you," Jesse replied.

"Absolutely no way, I can't let them snare you into this B.S. department too, Jesse," Jamie said.

"They don't even have to know I'm there. I can sneak in away from everyone's attention and I know that place inside out seeing as I was a student there."

"So it really is the crappy secondary school you went to," Jamie said. "I don't disagree with you but they have that Dawn bitch detecting power usage though, even if they can't see you."

"Yeah but that doesn't identify the user of the powers so as long as I stay out of their sight, I should be good."

"But you still have Kayleigh to rely on you," Jamie persisted in trying to keep her friend out of harm's way.

"And we both still have you*, Jamie. We'll get you through this as a team like we've done so many times already and plus, we can share my healing powers to make sure nothing happens to us."*

Jamie hesitated with her response, knowing that Jesse made a lot of valid and logical points. And he was also right in the fact they could keep each other safe in being able to heal each other, even if she really didn't want to risk having him there regardless. But knowing him, he would probably try to tag along anyway.

"Alright, but you absolutely cannot be seen by any police officers or a member of the operation, nor a member of the public either for that matter."

"Hazing will be my friend today then," Jesse remarked.

"Okay, I'll meet you in the usual forest area in the park near your house and we'll sort out transferring and boosting your powers," Jamie instructed, hoping she wasn't making a huge mistake.

"I'm sure the sunglasses aren't necessary," Jamie said upon seeing Jesse approach the forested part of the park that they normally chose to disguise their flight ascents and descents wearing a pair of shades.

"Can't identify me without a face to see," Jesse countered in a friendly manner. "What powers do you need from me then?"

"Flight, shielding, hazing and healing," Jamie responded, holding her hand out to initiate the transfers.

"Let's do them one at a time," Jesse said, taking Jamie's hand and subsequently allowing each power to be absorbed while she began boosted his powers back to their maximum levels.

"Alright, got everything I need and you're at max power; let's make a move over to the school," Jamie said. "And get rid of those shades for goodness sake!"

"If we fly there together, they might not recognise both our flight and hazing powers as being used by two different people."

"I don't think Dawn will fall for that but if she knows what's good for her, she won't blab about another set of powers being on site. Although she could mistake it for another empowered perp though, saying that."

"Regardless, they have to be able to identify me anyway," Jesse replied.

"True. Let's head over there then."

Taking to the air with hazing, the duo made a short journey of the mile and a half trip with the police cordon and accompanying crowd of onlookers obvious even from the altitude they were elevated at. Jamie began activating her borrowed analysis ability, immediately detecting the use of Dawn's own version of it being used below as well as a brief activation of the reported 'combustive energy' power as well.

"Right, Dawn's ability is active down there so make sure you're not noticed as best as you can," Jamie spoke to Jesse through the cloud of haze.

"I'll be going in through the back as I imagine you'll be going through the front as part of the operation's directive," Jesse stated. "I'll make my way to the front of the building whichever way the coast is clear as there's multiple staircases that access it."

"Okay, please take care of yourself and call me if anything goes wrong," Jamie said as Jesse made his descent towards the back field of the school grounds. She then made her own way down, choosing to find the nearest secluded place she could land without drawing the attention of anyone, particularly the numerous news vans and cameras that were about reporting the situation live before heading over to the police cordon.

"Stay back, Miss," one of the officers spoke to her as she neared.

"I'm here for Detective Brody and that idiot Layne," Jamie stated.

"*You're* the contact?" the officer blurted out, clearly unimpressed with the sight of the young, black-clad teenager before him.

"Got a problem with that?" Jamie quipped back in an identical tone.

"I'll let them know," he said before walking off. Jamie noted the lack of gunshot noise in the background at that current moment as well as her analysis ability failing to pick up any further abilities besides Jesse's active flight and hazing nearby.

"Jamie, come on in," Brody said as he arrived to the edge of the cordon with a distinctly smug Layne behind him in the near distance. His words were met with a cold look from Jamie who proceeded to step under the police tape.

"Good morning, Miss Avonoit," Layne said, much to Jamie's irritation. "Hope you're ready to put your incredible attributes that proved so effective in apprehending the mind controller to effective use to help solve this crisis."

"This your means of revenge then, Layne? Trying to get me killed to satisfy that fragile ego of yours?" Jamie immediately fired back. "Starting to think you're more than just the sexist creep I gave you credit for!"

"This is not the time!" Brody tried to impose himself.

"I hope you've got that all out of your system, because here's what is going to happen," Layne nonchalantly replied. "You're going in with a squad of five to search the building and take down the suspects. Your aim is to provide the squad with cover to protect them against the powers of the perpetrators and even any gunfire if you can muster it while neutralising the empowered individuals."

"You sure you also don't want me to clean their boots before we go in?" Jamie sarcastically remarked.

"Oh there'll be plenty of time for that after you achieve your objective," Layne replied, followed by a malicious grin. "Time for Detective Brody to introduce you to your colleagues."

As Layne departed, Jamie glared at him with intense animosity. Rachel could not have been more wrong in her opinion of his alleged lack of true malignancy.

"I really am sorry, Jamie," Brody attempted to speak before Jamie cut him off.

"Just show me the people I'm going in with, Brody," she apathetically retorted.

"I will. If you need to top up on your analysis ability first though, I can take you to Dawn who's on site."

Jamie scowled upon hearing Dawn's name being uttered but admitted to herself that replenishing the analysis power within her was necessary, especially with keeping track of everything going on inside.

"Fine, let's go," she pessimistically answered as Brody, clearly feeling uncomfortable with the tense atmosphere, led her over to a parked police van a short distance away in the school car park.

"Dawn, Jamie needs to absorb more of your ability before she goes inside," Brody said upon opening the door to the van.

"Yeah, sure," Dawn replied with a shudder at the sight of the clearly agitated Jamie.

"So couldn't kill me in your mate's basement, you got to point out that there's empowered psychos inside a school being shot up to get rid of me, huh?" Jamie snidely lambasted her while holding her hand out.

"That's not fair, I didn't know they were doing all that when I sensed their powers going off," Dawn protested.

"Dawn, the power transfer," Brody cut in as Jamie continued to hold her hand out. Dawn slowly grasped it with her own, allowing Jamie to immediately absorb the entirety of her ability while boosting it back to regular levels.

"Done," Jamie scoffed while sharply turning around and walking away from the van. Brody gave a courteous nod to an aggrieved Dawn before trying to catch up with his infuriated star asset.

"Alright Jamie, these guys are the best we have in the department and I've given them clear instructions to put your safety above everything else when going inside," Brody attempted to smooth things over as he walked along Jamie towards an unmarked van nearer to the school building.

"Funny, that's not how Layne put it," Jamie replied with indifference. Brody then walked in front of her in response.

"I know you're angry and you have every right to be," Brody spoke with a sterner tone. "But I'm not the one you should be angry at. Hold it against Layne all you like because he definitely deserves some of it but I'm doing my best to try and protect you and you need to be thinking with a level head in there for your own sake. Do you understand what I'm saying to you?"

"Ryan Sharp would've had his way with this city had I not done anything," Jamie calmly said. "And I ended up forced into this arrangement simply for doing the right thing. I think I understand clearly, Brody(!)"

Exasperated, Brody simply continued leading Jamie towards the squad who had just exited the van with their firearms at the ready.

"Guys, this is Jamie Avonoit," Brody introduced the team to the hooded, black-clothed teenager standing before them with a decadent look on her face. "This is the individual who single-handedly apprehended Ryan Sharp and prevented the destruction of London at his hands, just so you know exactly how important she is to the cause and how imperative it is that you treat her life exactly as you would treat your own."

"I would say it's quite the honour," the lead squad member directed at Jamie who was surprised by the welcoming attitude. "You don't have to worry – we'll have every inch of you guarded tightly as we make our way round those corridors. We hear you can detect the enemy's location via their powers?"

"Yes, while they are in active use," Jamie replied, in a friendlier tone than she had afforded Brody.

"That's good to know. My name is Bennett by the way and may I introduce you also to Allen, Veron, Hernendez and Spricer. Now that we've gotten acquainted, I'll quickly brief you on what the game plan is."

"Okay," said Jamie.

"We will approach the building via the east wall and make our way along to the fire exit situated near the far corner of that side. From there, we will form a close formation around you and slowly try and hunt down those lunatics in there. Can we rely on your power detection to relay to us where they are at all times?"

"I'll let you know if I pick anything up," Jamie confirmed.

"Alright then, let's get moving then. The longer we delay, the less chance everyone trapped inside has of getting out alive. Hernendez, pass Miss Avonoit her bullet-proof vest."

"Here you are, Miss," Hernendez said as he handed over a black, padded vest to the teenager. "I believe it's in your colour."

"Thanks," Jamie smiled at the attempt at friendly humour as she put the vest on. "Just call me Jamie by the way."

"No problem," he responded.

"Okay, Brody: we'll be in communication with you and Layne at all times," Bennett spoke to Brody. "Anything happens in there, you'll know of it as we go along."

"Gotcha," Brody replied. "Good luck to you all in there."

As the squad readied themselves to move, Brody cast one final apologetic but confident look towards Jamie, who acknowledged it with a simple nod of her head knowing that the weary detective was merely caught between a rock and a hard place in sending her into such a dangerous situation.

"Go, go, go!" Bennett barked as he and three of the squad members sped forwards towards the side of the building with Hernendez following up with Jamie.

The sound of gunfire had been silent for nearly five minutes as had any explosive noises. The only powers that Jamie could detect were Dawn's own nearby use of power analysis as well as Jesse's flight and hazing quite close by as the sextet arrived at the fire exit by the far right corner of the school building.

"All clear so far," Bennett spoke aloud. "Any activity going on, Jamie?"

"I'm not picking anything up at the moment," Jamie replied, regarding the non-Jesse power usage at the least.

"Okay, everyone be vigilant," Bennett said as he took a key from his vest pocket and inserted it into the fire exit door, unlocking it as everyone slowly made their way inside.

The corridor upon entry was eerily quiet, the suspense unnerving Jamie despite the presence of the squad members who were now surrounding her in a pentagram-like formation covering every available direction around.

"Jamie, quietly notify us if any ability-related activity pops up," Bennett whispered.

"Will do," Jamie replied in an equally low tone of voice.

"This way," Bennett then instructed his team as they began moving down towards the further end of the corridor, Jamie still only detecting Jesse's flight and hazing throughout the tense walk. Being able to communicate with him even via text was being made impossible among the presence of the squad, leaving her to only hope that he wouldn't run into the culprits before she did and avoid being seen by the task operatives accompanying her as well.

Turning the corner, the group began making their way down one of the longest corridors on the ground floor with classrooms either side of them barricaded from the inside by terrified school kids and their teachers, seemingly oblivious to their presence.

As they neared the end of the corridor, a loud bang erupted from the adjacent hallway, causing the squad to halt their advance and train their weapons on all sides surrounding Jamie once more.

"Jamie, anything?" Bennett loudly whispered.

"Still no," Jamie replied. "They're not using their powers if that's them."

"Could be a student," Bennett muttered aloud. "Everyone keep alert."

The squad crept forward cautiously. Jamie then felt a sensation go off in her head, detecting the use of another ability aside from Jesse's flight and hazing very nearby.

'Burning'?

Jamie was baffled by the power analysis' reading, apparently indicating that Jesse was utilising his absorbed burning power for some reason. *Are you in trouble, Jess?*

Suddenly her thoughts were disrupted by the sound of a loud scream coming from around the corner of the corridor. The squad immediately stood still while all aiming their weapons towards the sound of the noise, which was then followed by the sound of an obnoxious laugh.

Bennett then raised his hand and motioned to move forward with his index and middle fingers with the other operatives and Jamie responding as such.

"Shut up, whore!"

Whoever was on the other side of the corner was extremely close. Jamie could tell at least a teenage boy and girl there judging by the voice tones but still wasn't sure why Jesse was being detected there too. Yet for some reason his flight and hazing abilities were still being sensed from what felt like slightly further away than where the two individuals behind the commotion were situated.

Does this mean that it's someone else with the same burning ability around there instead?

"Please, let me go!" the female voice cried out.

"Come on Wes, here's what you've been waiting for!" the obnoxious male voice yelled out once more.

"Don't, please!"

Jamie began to feel an anxiety attack upon hearing the scene going on, reminding her of an all too-familiar nightmare that she herself endured several months ago and once more only a few weeks prior. The screaming echoed around the hallway and was impossible to ignore as she reluctantly maintained her position.

Meanwhile, Bennett was holding a mirror down on the ground slightly facing around the corner in order to see what was exactly happening while trying to remain hidden. After a few seconds, he raised his hand and produced three fingers to indicate how many perpetrators there were as the group held firm waiting for their opportunity to move in.

Amidst the screams and pleading tormenting her, Jamie suddenly thought back to the ability her analysis power had picked up mere seconds ago; it was the first power Jesse claimed to ever absorb and it was on the very school grounds where he had gained it.

It's you…

Jamie was then brought out of her reflection by another loud scream followed by more desperate cries for help. Being forced to listen to the teenage girl's anguish and suffering was bad enough but standing by and allowing it to just happen was too much to bear.

Sorry, Bennett, Jamie thought to herself as she activated her borrowed flight ability.

"Come on Wes, here's what you've been waiting for!" David yelled out through his balaclava to the tall teenage boy behind him as he let go of the terrified female student on the floor.

"Don't, please!" she cried while recoiling from the burn mark on her wrist that had somehow been painfully imprinted onto her by the individual currently brandishing a gun with his hand grip alone. As the taller person also clad in an identity-hiding balaclava behind him moved towards her, she let out another piercing scream in the vain hope that anyone nearby would come and save her.

"Don't shy away too much back there, Justin!" David spoke to the younger boy accompanying them who was watching on visibly scared from several metres behind him. "There's plenty for all!"

Out of nowhere, he then caught sight of someone quickly swooping round the corner and landing on the floor in front of a set of lockers before raising their arm against their chest.

"What the hell..."

Without a second's hesitation, Jamie unleashed a kinetic energy wave straight in the direction of the person brandishing a gun in their hand. The balaclava-wearing miscreant had no time to raise their weapon and return fire before the attack struck them square in the torso and sent them flying backwards several feet, being separated from their gun as they hit the ground hard.

Jamie then looked to the left of the corridor at the sight of the female student being manhandled by another individual in a balaclava that also completely obscured their facial features, with another co-hort huddled up in the background appearing to take no part in the mayhem.

The taller miscreant then turned his attention onto her and aimed an outstretched palm right in her direction. Jamie's analysis power then re-activated.

Combustive energy blast…

Jamie immediately switched from planning an offensive to activating her borrowed shielding ability, hoping that it could absorb the full force of the combustion attack. She watched as the masked assailant then shot an intensely white, misshapen ball of energy straight at the floor in front of her.

Despite the indirect hit, the invisible shield completely shattered from the resulting blast with the shockwave throwing Jamie backwards into the wall of lockers behind her, banging against them hard before crumpling to the corridor floor in considerable agony.

"Jamie!" Bennett instinctively yelled out as he witnessed the teenager bouncing off the row of lockers following the explosion. Before he had time to react himself, a second explosion emerged from point blank range against the corner of the wall, obliterating it and launching another shockwave that sent the entire squad flying backwards down the hallway.

Jamie looked to her left, her ears ringing as she saw the unconscious bodies of all five operatives strewn all over the corridor. She then looked up at her foe slowly making his way towards her.

"Another one of us, eh?" Wes remarked as he approached the downed, hooded individual by the lockers. "Well you're not stopping us."

Before he could attempt another attack, Jamie watched as the masked miscreant was grabbed from behind and flown straight into the lockers behind her with a loud thud.

Jamie turned her head to see Jesse then quickly drag the maniacal empowered teen's dazed body using flight back across the hallway towards his other two accomplices.

"Wes!" the younger individual yelled through his own poorly-fitting balaclava as he witnessed his stricken partner laid out completely disorientated on the floor.

"Nice timing," Jamie remarked as Jesse landed beside her.

"Nice checking your phone(!)" Jesse replied.

"Sorry, had close company watching me," Jamie said. "Can you heal me?"

"Ah, Jesse. We finally cross paths once more."

Jesse turned around, realising whom the voice belonged to in spite of their masked appearance. Jamie also looked up from her position on the ground to see the individual with the gun standing while aiming it in their direction.

"I was hoping we would meet again sometime," David said with a vicious smirk on his face.

"Funny, I hoped that we wouldn't," Jesse glared back at him.

"Is he the one you got your burning ability from?" Jamie asked, slowly rising to her feet using flight despite the pain in her upper body from the collision with the lockers.

"He is," Jesse replied. "He's the one who made my life hell in this shithole."

"You haven't seen anything yet," David rebutted.

Jamie suddenly felt her analysis power go off in her head, indicating an ability that she didn't recognise was becoming active.

Combustion aura?

Jamie looked at the downed Wes who seemed like he was barely aware of where he was, let alone preparing another combustive energy blast. She then looked at the young boy cowering by the wall with an increasingly intense look through the eye and mouth holes in the balaclava covering his head.

"This the level you're stooping to now, David?" Jesse fired back. "Gunning down innocent school kids?"

"Please, Jesse," David responded. "I've always been on this level!"

Jesse activated his shielding ability as David prepared to pull the trigger on his gun.

"Watch out!" Jamie yelled while instinctively placing her hand on the back of Jesse's neck and using her manipulation power to amp up the shield to its full potential.

David, upon realising the hooded girl was looking not at him but towards his right, glanced to his side to see Justin on the verge of letting out a scream.

"NO!" he exclaimed before quickly diving to the floor and covering his head just as a huge, semi-spherical shockwave burst forth from Justin's body.

Chapter 11

Justin opened his eyes, feeling a tingling sensation in every part of his body as he examined his surroundings – the ceiling had completely caved in around him with the rubble forming a partial wall between himself and the boy and girl who had been standing next to the lockers. Near to him was the stirring body of David who had managed to avoid the shockwave itself by keeping low but appeared to have been rattled by it nonetheless.

"Wes?"

Justin turned around to see his brother trying to pick himself up off the floor, having also managed to miss being hit by the expanding combustive aura due to the sheer luck of having already been knocked down beforehand. His attempt at standing on his feet, however, came to nothing as he quickly collapsed soon after.

"Wes, what's wrong?" Justin asked in a panic as he approached his fallen sibling.

"Feel...sick," Wes replied groggily. He then vomited shortly after speaking and threw himself away to the side to avoid landing in the mess. He looked up at the badly damaged ceiling, seeing several flashing circles.

"I think I'm concussed, Justin," he said aimlessly in his disorientated state. "We need to get out of here."

"Can you move?" Justin asked.

"I'll need...your help. Let me rest my hands on your shoulders for balance and we'll find a way out together."

"Okay," Justin replied as he helped Wes up onto his feet and allowed him to prop himself up against his body as they slowly began to move towards the other end of the corridor.

David gradually got up from the floor, seeing the brothers ambling away down the hallway. Their attempt to leave did not bother him as they had played their part in the scheme to perfection. Now all that remained was to finish things up as originally planned.

Seeing the door next to him having been completely blown off its hinges, he decided to enter the empty classroom to check on the remaining arsenal in his rucksack.

Jamie snapped back into full consciousness, having been thrown once more along with Jesse into the set of lockers upon the shockwave exploding against his shielding ability. The fact that she had maximised its defensive capabilities just seconds before impact had probably been the only reason they had survived the full effects of the powerful blast. Whether he had meant to do it or not, the young boy's ability was far stronger than the other empowered individual's own version of it.

Jamie then saw the female student half-buried under the wall of rubble with her upper body lying motionless. She attempted to use her healing ability on her, only to realise she was already beyond saving when it failed to work.

"Jamie…" Jesse groggily moaned in the background. Jamie staggered over to him, barely able to walk properly from her injuries.

"It's alright, Jess," she said while placing her hand on his forehead and activating the healing ability once more, this time managing to succeed as Jesse regained his full health. He then returned the favour by rejuvenating Jamie with his own power.

"What happened back there?" he asked.

"A combustive energy attack by that kid," Jamie replied. "My analysis power picked up on it just before it emerged. I had no idea it was going to be that destructive."

"A miracle we survived considering the damage it caused."

"She wasn't so lucky," Jamie grimaced, motioning towards the deceased teenage girl amongst the debris.

"Oh, man," Jesse replied in horror as he looked away, instead seeing several other unconscious bodies laid out in the adjacent corridor. "What about them?"

Bennett! Jamie thought as she swooped over to check on the operatives, finding all of them merely knocked out based on their pulse readings.

"They're all okay," she said.

"Aren't we going to heal all of them?" Jesse asked, confused as to why Jamie had not already done so.

"Not yet, they'll just end up being caught in the crossfire. They're way out of their depth with this one."

"And we're not?"

"I can't let those scumbags continue on with this, Jess."

"I agree they need to be stopped but getting anywhere near them is going to be a problem."

"Maybe not; the elder of those two brothers – I'm assuming they are based on their near identical powers anyway – looked pretty out of it when you slammed him into the lockers so the main threat is the younger one and I get the feeling he doesn't even want to be here taking part in all this."

"But can you actually manage to shut down their powers without getting hurt though?" Jesse asked, almost hoping to talk Jamie out of her plans.

"I managed to quell one younger brother's uncontrolled ability once simply through dialogue alone in spite of his manipulative older brother's negative influence," Jamie replied, remembering her experience with her would-be rapist's sibling, Scott. "Maybe I can get through to this kid too."

As she finished speaking, another explosion rocked the building though failed to cause any further damage to the hallway they were both standing in.

"Doesn't sound like they'll be hard to find," Jesse remarked. "Doubt David will allow you to speak to them though, especially with those weapons he's packing."

"Then my best bet is to separate them from him if possible," Jamie replied.

"You're really gonna try this, aren't ya?" said Jesse.

"For the sake of everyone else in here who isn't already dead," Jamie answered, grimly looking down at the body of the student nearby once more.

"Well, looks like we've got some super-human tossers to scope out then," Jesse replied, resigned to the fact Jamie was not going to accept simply leaving the chaotic scene behind.

"Is this ground floor just one big corridor effectively?"

"Yeah."

"We can try and head them off by going round the other side then," Jamie said. "We can fly faster than they can run."

"Let's be cautious though," Jesse warned. "Our shields clearly cannot withstand the force of their attacks, even if they might protect us from any bullets."

"If it comes to it, I'll have to try and get in with a kinetic energy wave before they can try and hit us with their combustive blasts. It might be a problem tracking them if none of them are using their powers though."

"Can you feel anything right now?"

Jamie activated her analysis ability but sensed absolutely nothing going on around them except a distant feel of Dawn's own analysis power still active back outside.

"Nope, no abilities working at the moment," Jamie reported with disappointment. She stared with grievance at the wall of rubble blocking their path that had enabled the trio's escape in the first place.

"Huh?" she said aloud.

"What?" Jesse asked.

"I just saw the other side of the corridor through the blockage."

"How so?"

"I don't know, it was like I had x-ray vision or something," Jamie replied, utterly confused at the development as she attempted to see through the barricade again. "Yeah, it's definitely something that's allowing me to do it."

"Surely you would remember picking something like that up?"

"Or maybe I don't," Jamie sussed, thinking of Marcella. "Maybe I gained it while I was under mind-control?"

"Possibly, if you honestly can't recall absorbing it at any point," Jesse accepted. "Coming in handy for us now either way."

"Too right – let's see if I can find them with it now."

Jamie activated the x-ray vision again, trying to be as efficient as possible not knowing how much of a supply she had stored within her body. Through the collapsed ceiling, she could make out a figure in the room nearest the piled rubble.

"I can see David," she said. "He's sorting through his gun cache in one of the rooms next to the blockage.

"And the brothers?"

"Can't see them anywhere near but that's a plus at least knowing that their ringleader is away from them."

"So what's the plan?"

"Try and find the brothers first and hope David stays away long enough for me to chat to the younger one."

"As reluctant as I am to suggest this, why don't I keep David away from you while you're doing that?" Jesse asked, much to Jamie's surprise.

"You want to split up?"

"No but it may yield a better chance to end this with more ease."

"He's packing a lot of firepower there, Jesse," Jamie stated.

"So am I," Jesse replied, holding up his palm which began to glow with warmth from his burning ability.

"If you think you can stop him."

"I know I can," he said with a degree of smug confidence.

"Then let's get going," Jamie said with both of them taking flight without bothering to activate their hazing abilities knowing that no student currently trapped in the building would in their right mind want to be venturing out into the corridors with the sound of explosions going off every other minute to witness them.

As they turned the final corner, Jamie descended and checked out the surround classrooms with her x-ray vision.

"I see them," she said aloud. "They're up against the far wall in that classroom to our right. It looks like the older one has passed out."

"Even better," Jesse said.

"Yeah. Are you going to really take on David then?"

"Suppose it would be symbolic if I did," he quipped. "You don't have to worry about me; if anything goes down, we're within earshot of each other and our respective healing powers."

"Good luck," Jamie said as Jesse continued on down the hallway with flight. Summoning courage, she carefully pulled down the door handle.

"Stay away!" Justin yelled.

"It's alright," Jamie calmly spoke, sensing the combustive aura power activating. "'Justin', did I hear earlier?"

"Yeah," the youth spoke through his loose head covering.

"I can tell you don't really want to be doing this."

"It's not my fault!" he blubbered. "Wes said I needed to help him and David stop some horrible people with my powers."

"What horrible people were they talking about?"

"All the people who made their lives miserable in the school. Wes said they needed to pay for everything they had done to the innocent!"

"Justin, do you think shooting people with guns is the right thing to do?" Jamie attempted to reason.

"No," the boy snivelled with a shake of his head.

"At least you know that," Jamie followed up. "You've been coerced into joining in something which you should have had no part in to begin with. And you're right; it's not your fault. David is an evil person who's just using you to get what he wants."

"I didn't mean to blow up the hallway," Justin pleaded. "I can't stop it from happening, it just does it on its own."

"You're talking about your ability?"

"My what?"

"Your power – the part of you that causes those explosive shockwaves. I have one too."

"You can do the same as me?" Justin asked in a more calm tone.

"Not exactly; my ability allows me to manipulate other powers," Jamie explained. "Part of that lets me deactivate powers by hand contact. If you want, I can turn your ability off for a while so that it can't accidentally cause any further damage to anything."

Justin cowered further up against his unconscious brother, interpreting the offer as a threat. Jamie sighed impatiently but quickly recomposed herself.

"Justin, if I wanted to hurt you I would have done it the second I walked into the room," she reasoned. "Trust me when I say I just want to help you control your powers."

"Will it hurt?" the youth asked.

"Deactivating your ability? No. If anything, you should be able to feel less afraid of it once I've shut it off."

"….Okay," Justin acquiesced. Jamie held out her hand and motioned for the boy to take hold of it with his own. As soon as Justin gripped her hand, Jamie activated her base power and began to negate the unpredictable ability completely.

"It's done," Jamie remarked, releasing Justin's hand.

"It won't go off again now?" Justin asked.

"Not for the next several hours at least. Are you able to control it normally though?"

"It only came on once before today; Wes started yelling at me while we were walking in the forest and I just wanted him to stop. Then it happened out of nowhere and caused a few trees to fall down around us."

"So when you're stressed then?" Jamie inquired.

"I guess so."

"That's unfortunate, but not impossible to remedy if you take yourself away in your head to a happier place when you feel like getting upset."

"Wes doesn't normally get like that with me, he was just wound up from school when he lost his temper in the forest," Justin said. "He says he's fed up of the abuse he gets for not being able to get a girlfriend and just in general."

"On that note, I think it's time I had a word with your brother," Jamie replied, turning her attention to the older sibling still slumped against the wall.

"Don't hurt him!" Justin pleaded, grabbing onto Jamie's arm.

"On the contrary, I'm going to heal him," Jamie replied. "But your brother may well try to attack me again like he did earlier when I revive him so I'm going to have to try and drain his powers too whether he wants me to or not. No matter what happens though, I won't bring any harm to him in the process."

"You promise?"

"I've been honest with you so far, haven't I?" Jamie smiled, leading the weary Justin to let go of her arm. Slotting her body in between Wes' and the wall, Jamie wrapped her legs around him from behind to anchor him down while preparing to restore him to full health. She took a deep breath, hoping she could deactivate his combustive energy powers before he could turn them on her a second time.

*   *   *

Jesse peered past the ruined doorframe, spying on David as he began packing his remaining ammunition back into his rucksack upon reloading his handgun. Even with the balaclava on his head, the sight of his past tormentor still got to him. The last time they were face to face, Jesse knew he had been fortunate to walk away victorious.

There'll be no luck involved on this occasion.

Jesse levitated back into the air to mute his approach towards the pre-occupied David, hoping to lock him in a chokehold from behind to render him unconscious before he could make use of his firearms.

As he floated forward, a loud noise then echoed from out in the corridor as another chunk of the destroyed ceiling hit the floor.

"You again?" David spoke as he turned around to see Jesse levitating mere feet away from him, pointing his gun straight in his direction. "I see you have other tricks up your sleeve too. Where'd you learn to fly anyway?"

"About the same time I got your burning hand ability," Jesse replied with impudence while descending back down to the floor, still being held at gunpoint.

"That's a day that hasn't left me," David reminisced ruefully. "Things fell apart for me after that; I didn't really command the same level of fear when it came out that I had my arse handed to me by the lowly Jesse Webster. Not that I ever cared about school anyway but if you'll excuse the pun, you really burned me with what you managed to do to me. I suppose my luck must be turning now that I have you right where I want you."

"Is shooting up the place of your humiliation not enough for you then?" Jesse asked with contempt.

"This was quite the euphoric experience, don't get me wrong but I do also like squaring my debts and I've owed you a severe measure of vengeance for the past three years now. This moment here has just made the whole thing complete."

"And those two with their explosive powers – you coerce them into your little scheme under the guise of getting revenge on those who have wronged them too?"

"Ha! Coming across Wes was absolute sheer chance but what an accomplice he's turned out to be," David bragged. "And it was so easy getting into his head, him being the unlucky virgin an' all. All I had to do was convince him that all the girls here were laughing at him behind his back and he was more than willing to help me take this place to the cleaners. Justin and his powers tagging along were an added bonus even if he hasn't been as willing as his brother to join in the mayhem but who's complaining?"

"I imagine the families of those you've killed today probably are," Jesse scornfully rebuked. "I always knew you were sick in the mind but I never thought you'd resort to something this deranged."

"Same ol' bleeding heart Jesse," David sneered. "I'd say you'll realise someday that playing nice gets you nowhere in this world but your time on this planet has come to its end."

As David fired off his gun, Jesse quickly put up a shield to block the bullet. To his relief, the shield took the kinetic force of the shot and deflected the round towards the other side of the room as David reacted by ducking to the floor.

"What did you do?!" he yelled while preparing to raise his weapon once more, only for Jesse to charge towards him feet-first using the power of his flight ability before he was able to fire another shot off. David took the double-booted kick straight to the face, dropping his firearm as he fell to the floor.

"Here's a reminder of the last time I beat your arse," Jesse said as he activated his burning ability and grabbed the back of David's neck, a yell of agony erupting from the beleaguered sociopath before Jesse delivered an uncharacteristically malicious kick to his head. The final blow was enough to see David failing to get back to his feet, remaining unconscious on the floor as Jesse looked down at him with disgust.

Jamie removed Wes' balaclava and placed her hand on his now-bare cheek while activating her healing ability. Sure enough, her analysis power began picking up activity from the slowly recovering enhanced teenager as he became aware of his surroundings.

Though not complete with the healing process, Jamie instead began utilising her power manipulation ability to begin shutting off Wes' combustion energy reserves.

"What's going on?" Wes blurted out as he realised a pair of legs were wrapped around his torso and pinning his arms down with someone holding his head in place. "Get off me!"

Jamie felt the combustion energy ability spike as she began using both hands to shut it off within Wes who was struggling furiously to shake her off. Her dead weight and his semi-weakened state was proving near-impossible for him to succeed in that endeavour, however, as he felt a sensation akin to an extreme cold feeling flowing through his body as his powers were simultaneously negated and drained out of him into his attacker's body. Justin watched on in fear, unsure whether to help his brother or trust the hooded girl.

Feeling Wes' supply of power completely nullified, Jamie levitated herself out of the space between his body and the wall. Angrily, Wes stood up and aimed a blast at the girl before him, only to see nothing happen.

"It's not going to work now, Wes," Jamie said while standing motionlessly before the confused teenager.

"What did you do to me?" he raged.

"I turned your powers off," Jamie replied as Wes lunged himself at her, only to be met with a kinetic energy wave to the chest which knocked him back down to the classroom floor.

"Wes!" Justin cried. "You said you wouldn't hurt him!"

"On the grounds he didn't stupidly try and attack me first," Jamie remarked while keeping her gaze on the stricken Wes. "Stay down or I'll level you with another one."

"Stupid bitch," Wes responded. "You're just like all the others."

"Yeah, I've heard you have a problem with the women in this place, and in general," Jamie quipped. "So this is what you do in response to not being able to get laid then? Trash everything and help some lunatic shoot a load of people?"

"Shut up!" Wes screamed as he attempted to pick himself back up. True to her word, Jamie hit him with another kinetic energy wave that slammed him into the wall, leaving him too injured to attempt to get up again.

"I guess you're what some circles would label an 'involuntary celibate', or an *InCel* for short," Jamie spoke. "That's someone who believes that they're entitled to sex from women and holds misogynistic feelings towards them as a result of not getting any. That how you see me, right?"

"You know nothing about me," Wes replied.

"I know *that* much," Jamie refuted. "I'm not that much older than you for the record so I know the crappy things that go on in school. You think girls don't come under pressure to have sex too? Yeah, I'll admit I haven't had sex myself down to personal choice rather than an inability to get it but then the flip side as a woman is that I get sexually harassed, objectified and even being forced upon by guys who won't take 'no' for an answer."

"I would rather be in your position any day if it meant getting the attention you get," Wes snapped back.

"If you had gone through the experiences I have, you wouldn't be saying that," Jamie replied. "And maybe you should start clueing yourself up instead of going along with this toxic masculine notion that sex is the ultimate goal 'cause there's a lot more to life than that."

"I don't really care about your feminist agenda," Wes flippantly answered back, leading an irritated Jamie to raise her arm once more across her chest.

"Don't!" Justin yelled, running in front of his prone brother. "You said you wouldn't hurt him!"

Jamie hesitated, remembering her promise to Justin and begrudgingly lowered her arm.

"As per the reason I'm inside this school building right now," she spoke to the brothers. "I'm supposed to be calling in the pair of you to the police as dangerous empowered beings."

Justin began to feel panic overcome him as he leant against Wes still down on the floor.

"And what would become of us then, if they know what we can do?" Wes asked, feeling the same anxiety starting to hit him.

"Probably imprison you both in an underground basement while sedating you indefinitely owing to the destructive nature of your abilities."

"No!" Justin screamed, wrapping his arms around Wes who had an equally terrified look on his face.

Jamie looked on with a significant amount of conflict going on in her head. She really did not have the heart to go through with what she was supposed to do, yet she barely saw an alternative solution. She certainly did not want to be thrown into perpetual confinement herself for deliberately letting the culprits of a mass school shooting escape, especially with Layne all but ready and waiting to make sure it would happen.

Suddenly, a piercing gunshot was heard going off in the background from down the opposite end of the hallway.

Jesse! Jamie thought in a panic. Then she calmed herself down in realisation.

David....

"Here's what is going to happen," Jamie said to the brothers. "I'm leaving this room and by the time I get back, you're not going to be here. Because if you are, I'm shopping you in to the police who are waiting outside and expecting a collar for this mayhem."

"What happens when they ask why you haven't got the people responsible for all this?" Wes asked, though feeling an overwhelming sense of relief at the same time.

"Oh they'll be getting somebody," Jamie replied as she walked towards the door. "If I were you, I'd walk out the main entrance claiming to have been students caught up in the chaos. If you're lucky, they won't recognise you as the perpetrators owing to you having worn those dumb ski masks throughout this rampage."

"Thank you," Justin said.

"But if I catch you doing anything like this again, I won't be so forgiving next time" Jamie said towards Wes as she left the room.

Still injured from the kinetic energy attacks, Wes slowly hauled himself to his feet with Justin's help as they made their way down the opposite end of the corridor towards the exit.

Jamie flew straight down the decimated corridor and towards the last room on the left just before the collapsed ceiling blockade.

"Jesse!" she called out softly as she entered the classroom, forgetting that she still had x-ray vision to check through the wall beforehand.

"I'm alright, Jamie," Jesse responded. Jamie walked in to see the unconscious body of David lying on the floor with Jesse unscathed.

"I heard his gun go off."

"My shield managed to block it. At least those bullets don't explode upon impact. Speaking of which, what happened with the brothers?"

Jamie looked awkwardly at the floor before deciding to answer.

"I disabled their abilities, then gave the older one a bollocking on his stupid attitude towards girls. Then I left the room."

"They got away?" Jesse asked incredulously.

"Probably," Jamie replied with a hint of regret.

"Jamie, they're responsible for all this chaos," Jesse said with an elevated tone. "That girl in the corridor is dead because of them among probably many others."

"I know, Jesse," Jamie responded irritably. "And truth be told, they both deserve to be thrown down in the police's basement where they can't hurt anyone else. But I couldn't do it. At least not the boy."

Jesse stared back wordlessly, though realising the difficult position Jamie had found herself in.

"I also got flashbacks of what happened with that Scott kid dying a couple of weeks back over his idiotic rapist brother putting him through hell. It's obviously a different situation but I bore a lot of guilt over his death due to our fight causing him to push his ability to extreme levels that overwhelmed his body; in this case, I'd be condemning this boy to an indefinite imprisonment while being placed in a coma owing to his destructive powers just because of his old brother manipulating him. And unlike his brother, at least he held remorse for what he had done."

"Not that I don't sympathise with your thought process but what happens if they do something like this again?" Jesse asked.

"I like to think that the fear I put into them of where they'll end up will stop them from ever wanting to do so," Jamie answered while looking down at David. "Suppose I still have the ringleader to hand over to Brody and Layne to my credit."

"Too bad we can't just pin everything on him," Jesse remarked. "But he *is* ultimately responsible for what happened here today; convincing that Wes teen that all the girls in the school thought he was a loser for not having had sex. Probably would never have managed to achieve all this devastation without that combustion ability effectively at his disposal."

"Sadly I don't think he's going to be letting go of that stupid attitude any time soon either based on our little 'talk' just before we parted company. And that's on me if he turns into another super-powered rapist like that Jason psychopath."

"No, actually it isn't," Jesse argued. "We're all responsible for our own actions and that applies to him too. One would like to think that being spared the fate that would've awaited him upon you defeating him will be enough to change his attitude moving onwards."

"Not really the same as realising that women don't owe him their bodies," Jamie replied. "And he won't be the last person to have those pathetic thoughts either. Rest assured though I'll be on him in an instant as promised if I ever detect his ability in active use again in the future."

"Hopefully he got the message then," Jesse spoke. "Unlike our friend on the floor who has no limit to his depravity."

"He'll be lucky to ever see the light of day again," said Jamie. "You'd best go out the back way again while I call Brody to come collect him."

"Okay," Jesse replied as he made his way over to the door. Jamie then grabbed his hand as he attempted to pass.

"Thank you," she said.

"You should never have been put in this position to begin with," Jesse replied, gripping Jamie's hand back supportively. "And together, we make an unstoppable team anyway."

"I like to think so," Jamie smiled, releasing Jesse's hand. "Now head off before anyone sees you."

"I'll speak to you soon," Jesse said as he quickly set off down the hallway, the sound of his footsteps instantly disappearing as he took flight.

Jamie then pulled out her mobile phone which miraculously had avoided being damaged amidst the chaos, seeing that she had missed a few texts from Jesse and several missed calls from Brody while in its silent mode.

"Jamie!" Brody spoke on the other end of the line. *"What happened? Is everything alright? We lost contact with Bennett."*

"He's fine, as are the others," Jamie responded. "I have your culprit ready and waiting for your arrival."

"Is the building secure then?"

"Yeah, it's safe to come in," Jamie said, knowing Wes and Justin's powers had been completely nullified even if they were to encounter the police forces on their way out of the school. "Lot of structure damage where I am though, you will have to be careful."

"Understood. We will be seeing you shortly."

Jamie hung up the phone, choosing to stay put with the unconscious David until Brody arrived. She reflected on Jesse pointing out that they made a good crime-fighting duo, noting the irony that he shared Gabrielle's desire for her to avoid engaging empowered individuals. Of course, that was prior to being required to do so whether she wanted to or not but she couldn't deny that the unofficial partnership had been proficient since the start of her arrangement of working for the police.

She wondered though if she was going to continue to be constantly thrown into wretched situations like the one she had just endured with the expectation of solving any given predicament no matter the threat to her wellbeing, and if it was actually Layne's intent to see her seriously injured or worse in the process.

Only time would tell, Jamie thought to herself as she heard the sound of rapidly approaching footsteps coming from the hallway.

Chapter 12

Jamie sat in Brody's office, expecting him and Layne to arrive for a task review regarding her engagement with the perpetrators of the school shooting any moment. Knowing the latter's involvement would no doubt feature numerous criticisms, she would somehow simply have to hold her tongue and accept whatever Layne was going to level against her. As Brody had previously mentioned, to argue back was to be a losing effort and would only be giving him the satisfaction of knowing he had gotten to her.

And Brody – she could not really decide whether she was justified in talking down to him earlier prior to being sent into the school. Of course the decision to involve her in the first place was apparently out of his hands but she couldn't but help feel slighted by the fact she had been thrown into a potentially deadly environment when he himself had highlighted the importance of keeping her safe out in the field.

Then there were the brothers; they presumably remained at large and their powers would be restored to normal by the following day. Justin had little control over his and Wes had proved himself capable of malicious and homicidal intent as an empowered being which was hardly reassuring in the face of being personally responsible for having let him walk free. At least David, the true mastermind behind the attack, had been apprehended and being held for his crimes.

The door to the office then opened with the two detectives entering one after the other. Jamie sat still in her chair trying to look unconcerned.

"Miss Jamie Avonoit," Layne spoke. "Time to go over your performance today."

Jamie tried desperately to maintain a neutral expression, even though it was probably obvious to Layne that she was staring daggers at him at that moment.

"So you managed to bring down one David Oliver today, who was found in possession of a cache of guns and according to you, also possesses the ability to generate a burning sensation from his hands."

Jamie looked back in anticipation.

"That would otherwise be a successful capture of a dangerous lunatic with powers," Layne rambled on before darkening his tone. "Except that the other two individuals responsible for all the destruction of the school got away. So why did you allow them to escape your grasp?"

"I didn't just 'allow them to escape', Layne," Jamie snapped back, even though she knew that was a blatant lie.

"Well someone of your capabilities, I would certainly have expected better," Layne continued, Brody giving a tired look beside him. "And your failure to protect the squad of operatives you were assigned to work with and protect just about sums up your afternoon really. Dare I remind you that you're here to get results for the department and not screw up every chance you get?"

"And where were *you* when all this was going on, Layne?" Jamie fired back, having had enough already. "Too busy hiding out the front while I was getting slammed into lockers and nearly blown up?"

"Can we please take a step back from all this for a minute?" Brody attempted to interject.

"Your mouth will yet get you into trouble, Miss Avonoit," Layne responded, ignoring his colleague. "You're a liability who's going to get someone killed with your incompetence and carelessness so consider this an official warning – the only thing keeping you out of the cells is your ability to apprehend super-powered criminals like yourself and today you failed miserably at that so I would start shaping up if I were you and start taking this assignment seriously. Am I making myself clear?"

Jamie failed to respond, silently seething through her clench teeth hidden behind her closed lips.

"Am I making, myself, clear?" Layne repeated in an even more vicious tone.

"Yes," Jamie begrudgingly answered.

"Now, do you have an accurate description of Oliver's partners during the attack?"

Jamie hesitated, not wanting to risk being imprisoned for failing to have an answer but also not wanting Justin to be targeted by the police over something that wasn't entirely his fault owing to his brother's manipulation.

"They both wore ski masks that hid their faces, I don't know what they looked like," Jamie decided to respond.

"Great(!) So what did they physically look like beside their heads then?" Layne continued.

"One was tall, possibly six foot two inches at least," Jamie answered, describing Wes. "The other I couldn't tell as he was crouched down during the fight with the other one."

"Anything else on top of that?" Layne went on, acting as though he was in the middle of a suspect interrogation.

"That's all I've got for you other than the fact they both had explosive abilities but I imagine Dawn analysed those from outside."

"Well thank you for that inspired aid to our investigation, Miss Avonoit," Layne sarcastically replied. "Moving on, I'm aware that Brody has filled you in on another case regarding a suspect that can move through walls to commit robberies. Use it as an opportunity to prove that you're not as useless as you present yourself as. You've got until the end of the week to bring the person in or I might consider returning you to your residency in Ryan Sharp's dungeon."

With that, Layne abruptly left the room and walked down the corridor, not even bothering to stick around to see what Brody had to say. Jamie continued to quietly sit in fury at the desk, keeping her head fixed downwards.

"I hope you know that that's total rubbish," Brody attempted to calm her down.

"Whatever, Brody," Jamie solemnly replied, a lone tear falling down her cheek in the midst of her anger. "I do what I'm told to do which is to go apprehend arseholes with powers and all I get in return is a load of grief from some stuck-up jerk whether I'm successful or not. He can shove his warning up his backside where it belongs because I went in there and did the job I wasn't even qualified for that he was too craven to do himself!"

"That's fair enough, Jamie…."

"And was allowing me to go in there what you call 'staying safe', Brody?" Jamie followed up in a low and incredulous tone. Brody stared back with admitted embarrassment for a few seconds before choosing to respond.

"You're right to want to vent – what you were made to do today was a disgrace and I will be using what influence I have with my and Layne's superiors to make sure you're not thrown into a potentially lethal environment like that ever again. As for the incident itself, allow me to tell you the positives of your work today that Layne 'conveniently' failed to mention; you managed to defeat and neutralise a dangerous, empowered mass murderer single-handedly despite the other two suspects escaping which is still quite the achievement considering the odds were against you. Also, Bennett and his squad may very well owe you their lives as they were all completely vulnerable while unconscious with a gun-toting lunatic lurking about."

Jamie simply stared back with indifference, accepting the praise though feeling too vexed to want to care.

"And I should also point out that you have managed to succeed in both your first two assignments and seen the detention of two homicidal individuals that would've otherwise be still free to kill again without your intervention."

"I know you're trying, Brody," Jamie sighed. "But if I'm being honest with you, I don't really feel a lot of personal pride over any of that. What I should be doing right now is enjoying the social life I only recently managed to attain for myself after months of depression and loneliness, not going out and hunting down renegade super-powered scum which I had already been doing prior to this forced arraignment to little or no relief of that miserable state. I don't deserve to be here acting as Layne and your superiors' lackey and I do so as an unwilling participant. Can you kindly point out where in all that I'm supposed to be happy about all this? Because I'm not seeing it quite frankly."

"I can't argue with any of that, if *I'm* being honest," Brody replied. "In your position, I'd feel demoralised too at the thought of simply being used for my abilities rather than being respected as a valued partner of the operation. But I will say that it is only Layne that sees you as that; you have the respect of a lot of the precinct for your actions today that saw countless lives being saved by your intervention in a situation that most of the officers here wouldn't even dream of wanting to involve themselves in. And as you bluntly mentioned, Layne himself wasn't exactly rushing towards the scene while being happy to send you in untrained for such a crisis. I hope if nothing else you will take on all of this and recognise yourself as an important member of this department, even if it isn't being widely spoken aloud."

"You referred to David as a *mass* murderer a second ago," Jamie abruptly changed the subject. "How many people did he kill in that school building?"

"We haven't confirmed the total fatality rate yet..." Brody attempted to avoid answering.

"Then how about the ones you *have* confirmed?"

Brody pursed his lips before opening them to speak.

"Twenty nine confirmed deaths."

"Oh, man..." Jamie replied while hunching over the desk.

"And many, many more who survived, thanks to you," Brody said while putting his hand on the crestfallen teenager's shoulder.

"You mind if I go now?" Jamie asked, failing to take comfort in the gesture.

"Of course," Brody conceded his efforts were in vain. "Try to take in what I've said though and not let Layne's obvious bias against you get you down."

"I'll let you know if I find that phasing thief in the meantime," Jamie said as she left the office.

Walking along the corridor, she went to see Rachel at her desk but was left further disappointed to see that she wasn't there, possibly on a day off. Without a further reason (or desire) to stick around, Jamie made her way towards the staircase.

As she walked down the stairs, she locked eyes with Dawn who was coming from the other direction. Jamie slowly approached the intimidated enhanced human before standing within a foot away from her.

"I don't want any trouble," Dawn said quickly.

"I'm not in the mood anyway," Jamie replied. "But I do want to know one thing: what powers did you pick up on during that episode back there?"

"You mean did I sense Jesse's powers alongside your own being used?" Dawn asked, catching on to the point of the enquiry. "Then yes."

"I see," Jamie responded, feeling further disenchanted.

"And no, I didn't reveal his presence to Brody or Layne."

Jamie gave a peculiar look back at Dawn in reaction to the admission.

"Why?"

"I reckoned I owed you both that much for everything I put you through before."

Feeling gratitude but with zero desire to express it to her one-time foe, Jamie simply walked on down the staircase, leaving Dawn to continue upwards without a further word exchanged.

Upon leaving the building, Jamie checked her phone to see she had had a text message come through.

Hi Jamie. Going skatepark with the crew if your up for it around 4 =) xxxx

Aside from the grammatical error in 'your', Jamie was glad to hear from Cecelia, having already planned to contact her anyway at some point. Hanging out with the punk mob again would be a welcome relief to the aggravation that working for the police's special operation had been bringing on her.

Still though, she owed Jesse the courtesy of a visit following their antics earlier on, acknowledging that he had once again come to her aid when she had been in a tight spot. Not being able to openly credit him for his help felt wrong but she knew it was better off that way anyway with Layne probably going out of his way to make his life a living hell too. Whatever Layne's reason for his apparent dislike of her and empowered beings as a whole, she didn't feel like she was going to be finding it out anytime soon.

"Well it's nice to see you on less chaotic terms," Jesse joked as he opened the front door to Jamie.

"I can imagine," she replied, barely able to hide the weariness in her voice.

"Earlier still fresh in your mind?" Jesse asked.

"Only half as much as what just went down in Brody's office with Layne," Jamie said while taking her shoes off at the bottom of the stairs as Jesse closed the door.

"Bad, I'm guessing?"

"Nuclear, but he's nothing but a total prat anyway. Just focusing on the fact the brothers got away, even though I was too polite to point out that his stupid arse also let them walk right out the building from his safe spot on the outside. Well, if that's what they managed to do in the end anyway."

"Don't let him bother you too much," Jesse replied. "It's on his head if two of the culprits got away if he's the leader of the operation."

"Maybe that's the reason he decided to lash out at me over it, or at least one reason."

"Who knows? Sounds like a proper pillock regardless," Jesse said while walking into the living room. "Let's unwind a bit and forget about everything that went down, it'll only drive us nuts to keep thinking about it."

"Wherever you get those chill pills from, send some my way," Jamie laughed as she followed. "Where's the lil' 'un?"

"She's out round a friend's house. She'll be back around half 3 when they drop her off."

"Anything special?"

"Nah, just hanging out round their house. Kid stuff I guess," Jesse said as the pair sat down on the sofa.

"Fair enough," Jamie replied. "Was hoping to grab more of her ability while I was here, and get a few much needed hugs in of course. Actually going out to the skate park for 4 so doubt I'll get much of a chance to hang out with her by the time she comes home, even though I still owe her a day of my undivided attention for bailing on her last time."

"Well she needs to do some revision anyway, her SATS exams are getting near."

"Revision during term break? What kind of monster are you?" Jamie joked.

"The kind who wants her to do better than her big brother did at her age," Jesse semi-joked back.

"It's not like you didn't have a good reason for your education suffering," Jamie pointed out in a more serious tone.

"True but she's naturally smarter than me anyhow and I know she has a good chance of going places when she grows up as long as she applies herself."

"Funny, I think the same thing," Jamie smiled.

"Are you honestly doing okay though? Was a bit rough earlier."

"I don't think it's all caught up with me yet really," Jamie answered. "Think my loathing for Layne's obnoxious attitude just completely overtook the shock of dealing with David and the brothers' mayhem."

"I'm just glad he's locked up where he belongs," Jesse reflected. "With any luck, for good. Powers or otherwise, he's too diabolical to be allowed to roam free."

"It does make me wonder if they're actually developing a way to remove or permanently deactivate abilities in the meantime," Jamie mused. "And if they are, if they're anywhere close to achieving it. Already know it's possible to implant them of course, courtesy of Ryan Sharp."

"For all we know, they're taking Sharp's research and creating a load of super-powered soldiers for the army or something."

"Hope not. I did point out to Brody mind that I'm only being forced into this dumb one-sided arrangement with the police because I chose to face the maniac down instead of letting him have his way with the city. Think I know what I'll do next time."

"Would you though?"

Jamie pondered the notion for a moment.

"…No, probably would end up still saving all those ingrates," she replied.

"Well you have one very grateful person right here who is glad you did," Jesse replied in recognition of the deadly predicament Sharp has placed him in in order to lure Jamie out into the open to begin with.

"Soppy tart," Jamie smiled. "What we watching them? Another direly bad horror flick?"

"If you don't mind laughing at all the flaws in it," Jesse responded.

Dire was right, Jamie thought to herself an hour into the film as she sat with her head on the armrest and her legs laying across Jesse's lap with his hands placed upon them. She wondered had she had the empathy ability inside her at that moment that she would pick up on whether Jesse was enjoying having her partially lying on him or if the oblivious boy still held no particular feelings whatsoever towards her. It would feel nice if he lightly teased or tickled her right there but clearly he was just enjoying the film, or at least laughing at how bad it was just like all the other ones they had ever watched.

Meh.

"Have to give you credit," Jamie spoke, breaking from her daydreaming. "Your taste in piss-poor films is definitely an uplift for someone in a bad mood."

"Thought the 'so bad, it's good' variety would be the better choice over any mass-killing horror flick considering what we went through earlier," Jesse replied, giving an assuring smile. "You feeling a bit better then?"

"Somewhat. As much as I'm making it sound like I blame Layne and the school shooting itself for my bad mood, it did also kill me a bit to know of the preliminary death toll a minute later from Brody. I really could have broke down right there in front of him upon hearing that."

"What stopped you?" Jesse asked.

"Just stubbornness I guess," Jamie admitted. "I've never liked getting upset in front of people, even Gabrielle though goodness knows she's seen me do it enough in the last few months alone."

"And there I thought it was just a crappy male thing to hide one's emotions," Jesse replied.

"Not really much different from the 'InCel' rubbish that Wes prat was indulging in when he decided to help attack the school – 'men must hide their feelings' and 'women are a bunch of slags who men are entitled to bang'. Please. The sooner we toss those toxic attitudes, the better we'll all be for it."

"But would you feel comfortable crying in front of just about anyone?"

"Probably not but I don't feel that based on my gender as much as my personality. Suppose as a woman it would supposedly be accepted for me to get upset publicly and not be seen as weakness, which in itself is an inherently sexist notion. It's not like men don't feel negativity themselves that they should be able to express however they want without being expected to just 'man up'."

"I agree, even though I have always felt the need to hold my emotions back based on that myself," Jesse said. "Think I also learned to suppress my negative feelings owing to the turbulence of my teenage years out of self-preservation."

"Have you never really cried much over all that happened to you?" Jamie asked.

"Maybe occasionally but I always convinced myself that it would only be making things worse for myself and that I would end up succumbing to despair. The other side of things was the fact that I had Kayleigh to be there for and breaking down in front of her wouldn't have exactly projected the image of a strong older brother figure I guess."

"And to think I expressed my misery by the bucket loads when my mum died and I then turned to recklessness and violence with my powers as a way to distract myself, whereas you kept it all bottled up and still became the wonderful and caring person you are now."

"Everyone has their dark side though," Jesse replied. "I think I definitely expressed some of that when I decided to kick David in the head to end his rampage when it was just me and him in the classroom one-on-one."

"Perhaps," Jamie remarked, considering the idea highly ironic coming from Jesse given the vision she had previously seen of him ominously preparing to attack her in a deserted and derelict London.

"But don't sell yourself short either though; you're still one of the most caring people I've ever met too. And in spite of that alleged stubbornness you have, one of the earliest memories I have of you was you breaking down in tears up on the rooftop."

"That was more of an involuntary reaction, saying that," Jamie argued. "But I appreciate the kind words though. Maybe I should make you watch a sad film to get you to cry too(!)"

"Yeah, good luck with putting any of that bile on near me," Jesse laughed.

"Such a guy," Jamie jested as the front door was then heard opening.

"I'm hooooommmme!" the unmistakable voice of Kayleigh yelled out as the door slammed shut.

"Oh, I didn't hear, *Slammer*," Jesse sarcastically spoke aloud.

"Jamie!" Kayleigh exclaimed upon entering the living room and seeing purple hair lying on the sofa armrest. "How's it going?"

"Hey, babes," Jamie responded. "Have fun round your friend's house?"

"Yeah. What have you been up to?"

"Just laughing at the lame film your brother put on."

"I'm sure I can make you laugh too," Kayleigh said before moving to the other end of the sofa and raking her fingers across Jamie's bare soles, causing her to lightly scream while recoiling her legs.

"Think that was more of a yell than a laugh," Jesse quipped with a smirk.

"How about now?" Kayleigh mischievously asked as she jumped onto the sofa, hooking Jamie's ankles under her arm and continuing the tickling assault on her feet.

"KAY, NO!" Jamie cried out before succumbing to a fit of laughter as Jesse simply looked on in amusement. Jamie then leaned forward, grabbing Kayleigh from behind and pulling her body up against hers towards the other end of the couch.

"See how you like it!" she taunted before digging her fingers in the young girl's sides.

"Jesse, HELP!" Kayleigh squealed with Jesse watching the play fight between the two girls with muted adoration. After a few seconds, Jamie backed off and kept Kayleigh in a reverse hug against her, of which she lovingly accepted.

"Gotta be able to take what you give out," Jamie mockingly said.

"Was worth seeing your reaction," Kayleigh replied through her exhaustion.

"By the waaayyyy......could I pinch some of your empathy power again?"

"Sure!" Kayleigh replied, holding her hands up with her fingers spread out. "Whenever you're ready."

Jamie then interlocked her own hands with Kayleigh's before absorbing her ability in full to provide an effective combination with the analysis power before restoring it to normal.

"All done," Jamie said as she kissed the top of Kayleigh's head while keeping their hands entwined. "Thanks, munchkin."

"No problem, *sis*," Kayleigh responded.

"Just realised – should we be having this on with you here?" Jamie asked, upon hearing an expletive being spoken by one of the characters in the film.

"I heard swearing all the time around the guy mum was having us live with, I'm used to it," Kayleigh nonchalantly replied, invoking an awkward silence from both Jesse and Jamie. "Sorry, didn't mean to bring that up."

"Don't worry, sweetness," Jesse replied, turning the television off. "Fancy dominoes?"

"Yeah!" Kayleigh answered, releasing Jamie's hands as she sat up to face her directly. "You playin'?"

"Weeeelllll…" Jamie slowly responded, mindful of the time. "Sure; I should still have enough time to get where I'm going by 4."

"You're going? Awww," Kayleigh bemoaned. "Where to?"

"The park to see the punk girl I'm friends with."

"If she keeps stealing you away, I might have to have some words with her," Kayleigh half-joked.

"She'll just end up falling in love with you like everyone else does," Jamie replied while running her hand through Kayleigh's hair in affection. "Until then though, let's get a game going before I have to leave."

Kayleigh rushed off the sofa to retrieve the dominoes.

"Okay, so I have a new drinking game," Sissy announced to Jamie on top of the half-pipe platform in the skate park. "Every time Jez down there manages to wipe out on his board, we take a swig."

216

"Sissy, he's fallen off the thing like three times in the last minute!" Jamie laughed.

"Well that'll just make things more interesting, won't it?" Sissy joked while watching Jez taking another tumble. "Oh, make that four. Drink!"

Jamie took another sip, trying hard to somewhat enjoy the beer she was drinking but her taste buds had still yet to adapt to it.

"Starting to think you may be more of a cider person," Sissy said while holding out her pear cider can upon noticing Jamie struggling with the lager she was currently trying to swallow.

"Soon find out when Jez takes another spill," Jamie remarked.

"Nah, screw that. Just give it a quick go, see what you think."

Jamie then drank a small amount from the can, only to quickly spit it back out seconds later.

"Urgh, that tastes awful, Sissy!"

"Okay, I was wrong," Sissy laughed while taking her drink back. "You'll find something you like eventually."

"At least beer doesn't taste *that* vile!"

"Each to their own, love. And here's your opportunity to rinse that taste out," Sissy said as she watched Jez once again fail to maintain control of his skateboard. "Drink!"

Jamie wasted no time getting the lager down her throat, noting though that it didn't taste as bad as when she first drank beer which was some progress at least. She certainly saw herself only being a social drinker at best.

"Also wanted to ask – you up for watching Ryan's band playing on Friday at the venue?"

"Can do," Jamie replied. "Not doing anything that evening so should be all good."

"Feel free to bring anyone you want of course. The more the merrier."

"Could always see if my best mate wants to come."

"The fella?" Sissy asked, referring to Jesse.

"Nah, my housemate," Jamie replied. "I'll probably bring him sometime though but let's make it a girl's night for now."

"Yeah, among all the guys(!)" Sissy retorted. "It will be nice to meet her, especially if she's as awesome as you."

"She's not a rocker so it will be interesting how she does but she's normally good with anyone."

"She hot?"

"Insanely," Jamie answered with a prideful smile.

"Better get ready to slam anyone who makes an unwarranted move on her then," Sissy cracked her knuckles.

"Ha! She doesn't take shit from anyone anyway," Jamie replied. "If anything, I'd be on alert to protect them from *her*."

"Gotta stick together an' all," Sissy smiled, holding out her clenched fist for Jamie to fist-bump in solidarity. *Sadly, you couldn't be more right,* Jamie thought, reflecting on Layne and Wes' derogatory views on women as well as the police officer's response to Rachel trying to report a domestic violence incident.

"Was going to ask a cheeky request of you," Jamie asked.

"Lay it on me."

"Could I possibly get some of your electrical powers?"

"You actually want them now?" Sissy said, surprised by the admission considering their initial meeting where Jamie had refused to keep her absorbed share of the electrical manipulation ability.

"Only as a last resort, in case I ever need it," Jamie confirmed.

"I don't mind, as long as you're happy with it," Sissy responded. "What do you need me to do?"

"Just hold your hand out and activate your powers without actually using them. I'll then drain an amount into my body. Won't hurt or anything."

"If it was supposed to last time, I was thrashing about too much to notice," Sissy joked as she allowed Jamie to take her hand and absorb some of her powers.

"Done. Do you want me to restore it to full power quick too or just let it replenish naturally?"

"Nah, I've not been using it much lately anyway. Took on what you said about risking hurting or even killing someone with it."

"Reasonable," Jamie replied. "Before we get too drunk from Jez making a tart of himself, wanna show me some of your skills down there?"

"Well my boarding is better than my bass playing anyway," Sissy said while getting to her feet. "Slowly improving on that front though. Speaking of which, you want to come jam round mine again before we head out to the gig on Friday?"

"Sounds great," Jamie replied, actually looking forward to catching up on doing something other than working for the police's clandestine operation. *As long as Layne doesn't randomly throw me into another surprise situation anyway…*

*   *   *

"I'm home, Gabbs!" Jamie bellowed out upon walking through the front door of the house.

"Loike I didn't notice from all the hollarin'," Gabrielle sarcastically spoke back, garnering a weird look from Jamie in response.

"What did you say?" she said.

"Doesn't suit me, I'm guessing?" Gabrielle replied in her regular natural English accent.

"Maybe with practice but you don't need to adapt an Irish accent for the sake of it, sweets. Only reason I ever spoke with a French accent is because it would sound off speaking the language without it. I've grown up in England my whole life so makes sense for me to speak as such."

"Well yeah, but it would be nice to connect with my Irish roots," Gabrielle responded. "Plus it would be great for my mum to communicate with someone in her natural accent too seeing as she's had to put on a different one for so many years."

"I get that," Jamie replied, fondly remembering all the past conversations with her own mother in her homeland dialect. "If you want to connect somewhat, maybe you could try drinking stout in the meantime."

"Think we'll work our way up to that one, thanks!" Gabrielle laughed, preferring her wine to more beer-related drinks.

After dinner, the duo decided to spend the rest of the evening sitting in front of the television watching whatever they felt was worth giving a go, albeit better quality programming than Jesse's choice of lacklustre B-movies. Out of curiosity though, Gabrielle later forced Jamie to find a version of such of film online to see for herself, only to immediately lose interest after ten minutes after failing to find it entertaining even in a 'laughably bad' sense.

At around ten o'clock, Gabrielle decided to retire to bed with an early start to work in the morning in mind, giving the completely wide-awake Jamie a kiss on the cheek as she went to climb the staircase to her bedroom.

"Before I forget," Jamie said upon remembering. "My friend from the skate park has invited us to her friend's band's show at their local venue for Friday night."

"Am I likely to enjoy the music they play?" Gabrielle wearily asked.

"If I'm honest with you, not in the slightest," Jamie replied bluntly.

"Ah, screw it. We haven't had a night out in ages, I'm in."

"Really?" Jamie said, almost dumbfounded but nonetheless delighted. "I'm not kidding, it's music even *I* don't listen to."

"I'll just bring some earplugs and have enough drinks to want to dance through it," Gabrielle smiled. "Will it be full of idiots though?"

"Possibly but my friend is fiercely protective and has a large crew of skater punks to back her up so between them and our respective powers, I don't think we're going to have a problem."

"Then it's a date," Gabrielle replied cheerily as she made her way upstairs. "Night, Jamie."

"Night, love!" Jamie called back as she settled back into the television program they had been watching beforehand. As long as Gabrielle was determined to make herself enjoy the night regardless of the potential tuneless din she would be forced to endure by her regular standards of music, she herself could focus on having fun too without hindrance.

That of course, would be all well and good as long as she indeed didn't get an unwanted call demanding her involvement in something super-human crime-related leading up to the evening.

Jamie then remembered Layne's warning of getting her latest task wrapped up before the end of the week, which still left her a few days to go to track down the phasing thief. Not that she cared too much for his threats regardless but such was her antipathy towards him now following their last encounter that she could only imagine getting one over him again by showing him up as the idiot he was by delivering the latest perp to the department in record time.

Jamie activated her analysis power and tried to focus specifically on detecting a phasing ability. She knew she was letting her ego cloud her judgment again but she also reasoned it would also avoid the assignment clashing with her night out with Sissy and Gabrielle.

Nothing.

Jamie continued watching the television, opting to let her analysis ability passively operate indiscriminately in conjunction with her borrowed empathy powers to enhance one another. It still impressed her how Kayleigh had pluckily managed to use her empathy to effectively act as a form of clairvoyance to locate her while she was under the mind control of Marcella's telepathy, and in spite of barely having a proper handle on her own ability herself. Even she herself had only managed to make it work previously on Nate with the assistance of the analysis power working in unison with it. If anything it showed just how strong emotions were in utilising the empathy ability, something that Jamie knew she could work to her advantage with her greater experience and adaptability.

Trying something radical to narrow the field, she then used empathy to focus the analysis sensing to pick up only on abilities that she was 'interested in', or specifically any phasing power without putting a name to it seeing as she only identified the power she witnessed in the security footage as 'phasing' without being able to analyse it officially as such.

The whole process of course was just wishful thinking; it would take an active use of such a power to even be detected anyway but at the point of day where darkness had set in and most places were currently shut for the night, it was realistically the most likely time to pick up on any criminal activity going on.

At around half ten, Jamie was beginning to feel bored as she tried to maintain her interest in staying up by flicking through the TV channels in an attempt to watch something worthwhile.

Several more minutes later, the analysis ability finally managed to detect something through the empathy filter. Jamie concentrated to find out exactly what had been sensed based on her specifics.

Enhanced speed?

The analysis/empathy combination appeared to have failed to work properly. *How on earth does super speed cause you to walk through walls?* Jamie thought to herself in annoyance. She deactivated both abilities and re-engaged them in a makeshift 'hard reset' of the two powers.

However, the exact same enhanced speed ability was detected again.

You kidding me?!

Jamie then decided to use her empathy ability to lock on to the individual using the enhanced speed power, curious as to what it was being used for. She could soon feel the thoughts of the person it belonged to, albeit without actually knowing what the thoughts were precisely. It felt like such a complicated process she was going through but Jamie felt the need the find out to satisfy her wondering why the power in particular kept being sensed based on her specific power targeting.

No use of powers...Jamie thought, which was obvious as the analysis ability would have picked it up in tandem with the empathy ability. *You're excited over something.....like you're about to gain something you crave.....but what?*

Jamie almost felt like giving up, finding the effort far too vague but instead persevered in the hope of discovering something after sitting through the last half an hour waiting for something to come up and feeling the need to have something to show for her efforts.

Not beer or drugs....she continued.

Money?.....Money!

The process had begun to feel like some bizarre, out-of-body experience guessing game but getting the right 'answer' caused a pleasant sensation that one would feel when they were correct in something. Jamie tried a more direct approach with her next assumption.

Are you stealing it?......

Jamie then got what she needed to know. Even though it wasn't the phasing empowered criminal, it was still someone of interest to the police operation. Maybe it would be enough for Brody's superiors to realise her actual capabilities and not trust the rubbish Layne probably passed on to them.

Oh great, I'm worried what people I've never met think of me now!

Nonetheless, another successful collar might bring her one step closer to being released from the arrangement at a faster rate, she began to deduce as she got up of the sofa and put her shoes and jacket on in the hallway before taking off into the night sky.

Chapter 13

Jamie again struggled to maintain a direct focus on her empathy power while trying to concentrate on flight and hazing at the same time, much like when she was tracking the teleporter, Nate. However, the empathic psychic connection to the enhanced speed thief was still strong enough to tell that she was very close to their current location. So close in fact that she could feel their presence directly beneath her several hundred feet back down to the ground, necessitating a descent to the nearest flat rooftop.

Scoping the surroundings, Jamie could see a bank right next to the building she was currently atop with her empathy indicating that the enhanced speed burglar was still inside. However, she was still confused as to how the crook was managing to access the place with presumably speed powers alone. Being too fast for the cameras to pick up was one thing but actually being able to get through solid doors to even be inside the branch was another.

Rooftop access? Fire exit? Electronic key access codes?

Clearly whoever it was had some insider knowledge of the bank they were plundering as to get past the complex vault system anyway without taking any hostages to force them to open it on their behalf. The more Jamie thought about it, it felt as though something really wasn't adding up in her head. For the time being, all she could do was await their appearance back on the outside to be able to intercept them.

Her mind wandered to the prospect of Brody and Layne's operation, or whoever was directly overseeing the criminal empowered beings project, actually utilising Ryan Sharp's research to reverse-engineer a method of removing or deactivating the genetic coding within those affected to strip them of their powers. Or if they had managed to come up with something of their own. It seemed unfeasible to keep all the captured individuals detained down in the underground cells forever, especially those who were under near permanent sedation like Sharp himself, to prevent them wreaking havoc with their abilities. Then again, at least the sedated ones wouldn't be aware of their woeful predicament the rest of their natural lives.

Jamie then wondered why her dad had never been involved in such research, if he had been aware of super-human abilities to begin with anyway. After all, he had played a part in helping expand gene therapy to the point it could cure many deadly genetic diseases previously untreatable. It was probably his findings that had led Sharp to wanting to create his ghoulish enhanced human research project to begin with, a fact that she still resented despite knowing her father would never have taken an active part in the abduction of innocent people.

The analysis ability then snapped her out of her deep thought, indicating enhanced speed once again being used. Jamie kept an eye out on the building hoping to see a figure emerge despite the velocity they would most likely be moving at. She knew her flying power was fast enough to somewhat keep up and was virtually unobstructed by anything compared to a surface pursuit which would allow her to cover a lot more ground.

Jamie then caught the sight of what seemed like a leg emerging from the side of the bank.

What on earth….?

Jamie kept her eyes peeled on the figure passing through the wall, soon seeing the rest of their body come into frame until she could see a hooded person with a large rucksack in tow, presumably full of swag.

And yet the analysis ability was detecting enhanced speed the entire time despite obvious evidence to the contrary?

As chuffed as she was to have found the person she was supposed to be looking for as part of her assignment, the incorrect ability reading was absolutely mind-boggling.

Ignoring the problem for the moment, Jamie continued her gaze on the bank thief as they carefully walked down the street as if nothing was out of the ordinary. Eventually they joined up with another hooded individual at the end of the road before turning the corner into another road.

Jamie took to the air to follow their path, having no issue tracking them wherever they went as long as her empathic connection to the enhanced speed thief was maintained.

"All clear, Issy?"

"Yeah," Isabelle replied as she led Olivia through the gap in the railings into the park. "I still don't like the fact we're going in here in the dark to change into our secondary clothes. What if there's a rapist or murderer in here waiting for a victim or two to show up?"

"I'd like to see them be able to get anything in before you deck them with your speed, Iss. My powers told me the park was the best and most logical place to change into our secondary clothes as it's out of sight of any cameras as well as the roads leading up to it."

"And out of sight of anyone to see us in our underwear," Isabelle pointed out. "This *is* the last heist we do though, right?"

"For a long time anyway," Olivia replied. "You should've grabbed enough cash to hold us over for a while."

"I think I got enough," Isabelle said while changing her hoodie and t-shirt over. "Shit, it's cold!"

"Hurry up then and you won't be," Olivia said as she hurriedly pulled a pair of jeans up to her waistline. "There – now we just look like a pair of girls out on the town."

"So what are we doing with all this then? What if we get caught walking down the streets with all this?"

"We're not keeping the clothes; we'll put each bit of clothing in different bins as we walk home and obviously we'll take a different route than the one we came to avoid suspicion."

"What if we're stopped on the street by police?"

"They won't be looking already for crying out loud, Issy. You never tripped an alarm or anything so they won't figure out anything until the morning."

"How do you know all this?" Isabelle asked, letting a mild panic set in.

"Trust me, the power doesn't lie," Olivia claimed, completely bluffing her way through the questioning. The last thing she needed was for her friend to start losing her cool, especially after the planned theft had already taken place and there was now no going back.

"Are we really going to just sit here for half an hour waiting around, Liv? I don't even have my phone to kill the time with."

"Because we can be tracked with our phones on us, duh! Iss, I've thought of every angle for this so just trust me and don't start to lose your nerve."

"It's hard when you just committed a bank robbery, Liv. Or more specifically, I did."

"And like the last place, no-one's ever going to believe someone can walk through walls so chill out for the next half hour. Try thinking about where we're going to go on holiday with all this cash?"

"The club scene on one of those Spanish islands would be cool," Isabelle replied in a more optimistic tone.

"There you go. Now tell me everything you want to do while we're out there," Olivia said while re-engaging her ability out of caution to stay ahead of anything untoward that could interrupt the flow of their plans. She was aware by now that not every problem had a viable solution if she ended up backing herself into a corner and was always subject to any unplanned interference but so far, the current scheme had gone off without a hitch.

While she listened to Isabelle think aloud, Olivia's ability then indicated to her that her next best move was to completely lie flat on the ground as quickly as possible.

"Down, Iss!" she immediately said, grabbing her confused friend and pulling her down to the grass on pure instinct. Next thing they felt was a gust of air from above pass over them.

"What's going on?" Isabelle asked in an unnerved state.

"Keep calm and follow what I say," Olivia responded with her ability now instructing her to get back to her feet. As she helped Isabelle up, the duo looked forward to see a dark figure landing onto the lawn before them several feet away.

"Who's that?!" Isabelle reacted hysterically in fear of the unknown individual.

"Iss, be strong and remember they're nothing compared to you," Olivia said, trying to maintain a calm state herself for the benefit of her panicky friend despite the fact she was beginning to feel extremely uneasy with the current development herself.

Jamie looked back at the two young women before her, one of whom clearly the speedster she had been tracking based on the empathy ability despite the pair of them no longer wearing the same clothes from when they had committed the theft from the bank. Her same powers were also picking up on the very obvious fear emanating from both of them, which would prove a huge advantage in determining her strategy during the inevitable standoff.

What was problematic, however, was the 'problem-solving' power that the other girl was in possession of according to the analysis ability, of which seemed to be the reason the pair had hit the floor seconds prior to avoid the low swoop that she had attempted to make on them despite the lack of obvious sound alerting them to her movements in the air. Nonetheless, the enhanced speed power had the real offensive capabilities and there was no way the duo were going to back down without a fight after their robbery.

"Liv seriously, who is that?!" Isabelle began working herself up further, leading to Olivia to grab her hand.

"Calm things down, Iss," she spoke. "Whoever they are, they're can't hurt us. Not with *your* power."

Overhearing the comment, Jamie immediately levitated two feet into the air, feeling the intimidation within the person named 'Iss' growing even more.

"Do what you do, Issy," Olivia encouraged. "If they take us down or steal the gear, everything we worked towards is down the drain. Got it?"

Isabelle silently nodded in assurance while preparing to make a move on the hooded person. Her first instinct would be to flee with the loot but seeing as she was incapable of transporting Olivia with her too, she knew she had the upper hand in any bout as long as the opponent couldn't catch her. Wearing them down would be enough to enable a retreat.

Jamie could now feel the enhanced speed ability being activated. Getting close enough to make contact with 'Issy' could prove a challenge but she was still able to anticipate her movements using empathy in order to deliver an effective counter-strategy.

Out of nowhere, Isabelle shot forward with a quick burst of speed and jumped straight into Jamie before she was able to move out of the way, taking a shoulder barge straight to the mid-section with both teenagers hitting the ground.

Maybe not...

Jamie attempted to catch her breath as she felt her opponent about to launch into her from behind, failing again to successfully avoid the charge as the girl slammed into the middle of her spine.

Fighting off the pain, Jamie used flight to haul herself into the air and out of reach, retaliating with a surprise kinetic energy wave that missed its target as Isabelle dodged away from it.

"What was that?" Isabelle asked Olivia.

"Haven't a clue but the power's telling me to simply continue dodging to beat it," Olivia replied. Isabelle then awaited the next attack to emerge.

Overhearing the brief exchange as well as analysing the problem-solving ability once more, Jamie realised that the power did not identify her kinetic energy waves like her analysis ability would but merely formulate a way to overcome them. Based on the other girl's remarks, it appeared to figure out that her absorbed version of Gabrielle's power was only in limited supply and could be defeated by simply allowing the supply to run out.

But of course I have other methods of attack than that.

Nonetheless rattled by Issy's quick manoeuvrability, Jamie swooped down to attempt a feint charge which was easily avoided again by the speed of the girl, only to quickly turn around and launch another kinetic energy wave in her new position which very narrowly missed landing a direct hit owing to the lack of time to properly aim, much to Jamie's irritation.

"Issy, counter-strike while dodging!" Olivia called out.

Acknowledging how much the problem-solving ability operating in the background was thwarting her strategy, Jamie then aimed a kinetic energy wave instead at Issy's friend which made enough of a blow to knock the girl down to the floor in pain.

Carelessly lowering her guard in the process, however, Jamie herself was then knocked down by a hard, running charge into her from the side as she crashed along the lawn.

"Leave her alone!" Isabelle stated as she rushed over to her friend's assailant and began stomping away at their prone body on the floor. Jamie attempted to cover up but the enhanced speed was only boosting the force of the stomps to create greater impact.

Thinking quickly, she made a grab for the next stomp that came down and pulled Issy's ankle away using flight, causing the angered empowered thief to land flat on her backside.

"Liv, are you alright?" Isabelle asked in a low voice upon realising the person fighting them was back several feet up in the air.

"I'm fine, whatever hit me is just stinging a bit," Olivia replied, joining Isabelle in looking upwards before whispering loudly. "(What do you think they want with us?)"

"(I don't know!)" Isabelle responded back. "(Feels like they're going for *us* though and not the score.)"

"(Then it looks like we need to fight to win!)"

Jamie stared down at the duo, contemplating her next move. Keeping Issy's friend from concentrating on her problem-solving powers had been effective despite carelessly leaving herself open for attack in the process. Overall, slowing Issy down was the priority seeing as she was too quick to hit with blunt force or projectile attacks.

Then Jamie remembered that she had Cecelia's electrical ability within her. But using it while risking causing deadly harm still terrified her, having not had the chance to properly practice with it at any point. Being able to paralyse Issy's muscles via electricity appeared to be the best bet at that moment in time though to neutralise her speed. If she could accurately control the amperage while delivering what would in effect amount to a taser strike, it would get her close enough to drain the enhanced speed from her body. Plus, her lingering absorbed healing power would be available to undo any physical damage done to the girl.

"(Keep your eyes on them, Issy. They're up to something,)" Olivia whispered once more to Isabelle, becoming more and more unnerved herself at trying to predict their attacker's next move. The problem-solving ability was giving nothing on the current dilemma as they were too low down on the ground to do anything and the person above was simply biding their time doing nothing. Something had to give.

Then suddenly, the hooded aggressor swooped downwards towards Isabelle.

"Watch out, Iss!" Olivia yelled as her friend instinctively dodged to avoid the flying attack before attempting a return running barge on the person upon them landing on the lawn.

As Isabelle was about to strike, she appeared to stumble upon yelling out in pain and went crashing to the floor without making contact.

Jamie looked on at the downed Issy, lamenting that the current she had used was clearly far too small or the air in the distance between them had acted as too great an insulating force to produce the involuntary muscle contractions she had been aiming for but she had succeeded in momentarily disabling the young thief's enhanced speed for the moment at the least as she planned her next advance.

"Iss, what happened?" Olivia called out.

"I just got zapped by something, Liv!" Isabelle called out in literal and emotional shock as she turned around to face the culprit seemingly responsible.

"Issy, my power's saying to find a source of water to short-circuit them!" Olivia exclaimed.

Good luck finding that now! Jamie thought as she quickly flew straight at Issy while activating another jolt of electricity. Before the youth could even move away, the electrical attack made its connection with her body and caused an instant paralysing effect on her limbs. Jamie then subsequently grabbed her face with her bare hand while the enhanced speed ability was still in an active state.

"Get away from her!" Olivia roared while arming herself with the nearest fallen stick off the floor and making a senseless beeline towards Isabelle and the assailant.

In the midst of her energy absorption, Jamie flew herself and Issy out of the way of the stampeding Liv who missed with her wild swing of the stick and subsequently fell to the floor in a heap.

Using both hands, Jamie finished draining the enhanced speed ability fully from her victim's body before additionally using her healing power to undo any potential damage the electricity may have caused to Issy's internal organs.

"Wh-what did you do to me?!" Isabelle erupted in a mix of confusion and outrage. In her blind anger, she attempted to sprint straight at her attacker, only to find herself running at a normal pace.

Undeterred, Jamie caught the 'lunge' out with a shoulder barge of her own assisted by her newly acquired enhanced speed to send Isabelle sprawling backwards. The disempowered youth looked over to Olivia in desperation.

"What's it saying to do, Liv?" she cried out amidst the pain she was feeling, hoping her friend's ability would be able to come up with a solution to their current losing position.

"Flee!" Olivia called out while attempting to run past the unknown powerhouse figure without the bag of stolen bank money, only to be cut off with an enhanced speed-assisted elbow strike that completely knocked her off her feet.

Without turning around to see the fate that had befallen her partner in crime, Isabelle similarly tried to mount an escape. A moment later, the person who had apparently stole her powers landed right in front of her from up in the air to block off her way out of the park. She let out a terrified scream as she was then struck by the same energy wave attack that had been aimed at her earlier on, the force of which completely levelled her as she fell to the floor.

Jamie surveyed the scene with both her adversaries laid out on the lawn and the two rucksacks containing the money and their clothes lying by the bushes. She almost felt sorry for the two youths; not that they hadn't done anything deserving of their apprehension but the fear that she had felt from them via her empathy power had not been a pleasant sensation at all, right down to the final moments of the bout where the fear had become entwined with hopelessness and despair of their impending defeat, close to what she had endured for weeks on end as part of her grief and resulting depression.

On top of that, they were likely to now spend an indeterminate amount of time locked up in ability-proof cells until they could be deemed safe for release, whenever that turned out to be.

But a bust was a bust. Jamie pulled her phone out her pocket and reluctantly called Brody, whether he was expecting a call so late in the night or not.

"Hello, Jamie?"

"Evening, Brody," Jamie said. "You available?"

"I was actually on my way to bed, is everything alright?"

"I've got your 'phasing' thief laid out in a park with a load of stolen bank cash at this very moment," Jamie replied, trying not to sound too smug.

238

"Really?" Brody reacted with surprise. *"How did you find them?"*

"I have my methods," Jamie cryptically but confidently answered. "I don't know how long they'll be out for, are you going to send anyone over to come pick them up?"

"Well, it's a bit awkward because Layne is the one working the late shift tonight regarding the ability-based criminal operation."

Oh, brilliant. Jamie thought to herself.

"I can call him and offer to come out instead though if you'd like."

Jamie gave it some brief consideration, then deciding to reply.

"It's fine, just send him over to my location. The second he comes and does his part of the job, the sooner I can head home for the night."

"You sure?"

"Not entirely but thanks for asking anyway," Jamie responded. "I'll text a screenshot of my location on the GPRS app on my phone over to you so Layne knows where to come. Do me a favour and let me know when he's heading over though."

"I will. And well done for succeeding in the assignment so quickly."

"No worries," she replied before hanging up and sending her position on the digital map over. It actually surprised her that Brody didn't comment on the fact that she had again engaged the individuals she was supposed to be simply trying to locate but given his generous tone over the phone call, it appeared as though he was cutting her some slack based on the dressing down she had received the other day following the school shooting engagement. Or perhaps it was because he felt bad sending Layne of all people over to deal with her.

Whatever the reason, Jamie took up a spot on the lawn and began watching over her defeated opponents as she awaited the arrival of a certain insufferable detective to arrive on the scene to take them into custody.

"Alright, according to Brody that Avonoit brat is within the park about two hundred yards away from the entrance gate with our perp. So get the chain on the gate snapped and we'll drive right up to where they're situated."

Layne maintained a minor scowling expression as the team of police officers began opening up the locked gates to the main entrance to the park. Despite the objective of the task force to neutralise and detain rogue empowered beings for the benefit of society, it pained him no less to have to bear witness personally to Jamie 'hardcore femi-nazi' Avonoit having managed to bring down the super-powered thief who could walk through solid matter and in just over a day of being given the assignment, almost hoping she had gotten the wrong person just to be able to further put her down as the useless and unruly criminal she herself was.

Either way, your days of freedom will be coming to an end eventually, Miss Avon-noiyte.

The van then began making its way through the almost pitch-black park, illuminated only by the night lamps scattered either side of the pathway. Layne hoped that he would find something that

Avonoit had messed up on to justify delivering another admonishment to her despite her supposed achievement which also had the added benefit of being in front of his colleagues too.

"Sir, we've found them," one of the officers reported to Layne.

Right, let's get this over with…

Jamie caught sight of the approaching lights of an unmarked van coming in her direction. Although feeling magnanimous in her success, there really was no preparing herself for dealing with such an unreasonable jerk who just happened to hold her life in his hands. But that didn't mean she was just going to let him walk all over her either.

She watched as Layne stepped out of the vehicle, feeling her blood boil simply upon the sight of the man.

"So, where's the suspect then?" Layne spoke to her with a tone that insinuated he wasn't expecting to be impressed.

"Here *they* are," Jamie corrected him, motioning towards the bushes behind her. "The bag with their clothes they wore during the heist is also there along with the bag full of the stolen money, as I told Brody to pass on to you."

"Right," Layne replied, ignoring the thinly disguised barb. "And how are you sure these two were behind the theft, or even have powers for that matter?"

"You mean besides the bag of loot next to them or the fact that I just battled them with their abilities on show?" Jamie snidely answered.

"I'm not in the mood for your childish games, Avonoit," Layne snarled, getting up close to the teenager. "When I ask you a question, I expect a civil answer."

"Then perhaps try asking it without the attitude, Layne," Jamie replied, choosing to stand her ground. "But if you want specifics; this young lady here was the one who actually committed the theft using super speed and the other one next to her was in on the whole thing too."

"Well what are you doing apprehending a girl with super speed when the thief you're looking for can walk through walls?" Layne spoke with a degree of satisfaction as though he had managed to catch her out.

"What I did was catch the person who I caught with my own eyes walking through the side of the bank with a bag full of cash who then met up with her mate and who then both came to this park to change out of the clothes they were wearing during the heist and who are now laid out on the floor owing to my intervention. If you have any doubts about that, I suggest checking up on the bank's security footage to confirm that the clothes in the bag there are the same ones worn by the super speed girl while she was stealing the money."

"If this turns out to be another screw up on your part, Miss Avonoit, you can look forward to finally being thrown into confinement where you belong," Layne threatened with a half smile on his face. "Because this operation has no place for underachieving dregs who just waste everybody's time."

"Then why do they still have *you* in charge when you obviously can't get the job done without relying on the very same empowered scum you hate so much?" Jamie flippantly replied, quickly taking off into the night sky before an infuriated Layne had a chance to respond.

"Right, get those two into the van already so we can get out of here," Layne indignantly barked at the surrounding officers as he approached one of them standing by the back door to the vehicle. "Have I said something amusing, son?"

"No, sir," the officer replied.

"Then wipe that smirk off your face before I wipe it off for you," the incensed detective said as he walked to the side door of the van.

Jamie landed back at her house, having only spent five minutes travelling back from the park with flight. She again gave a passing thought back to the fact that she had left Issy and Liv to be rounded up and imprisoned for what could end up being the rest of their lives for all she knew in what was a bad reminder of what she herself had twice been subject to, albeit unlawfully by Ryan Sharp. Facing down petty empowered criminals had been somewhat less mentally conflicting when she had merely left them in her dust after defeating and laying them out rather than being picked up by the police afterwards.

How wise it had been to taunt Layne, and in front of other members of the task force no less, would soon be revealed in the upcoming days no doubt or whenever Brody requested her presence next. Goodness knows her empathy ability had felt enough venom radiating from him upon her final comment just before abruptly flying off to have earned some extreme retaliation but if Brody were truly repentant about the school shooting fiasco and failing to properly watch out for her during it, then he would have no issue with shielding her from Layne's wrath when it came.

Layne's personal vendetta could not change the fact, however, that she had managed to achieve her objective in record time and with enough evidence to be vindicated in doing so. To get to the level of personal immunity that Rachel enjoyed as an invaluable and irreplaceable member of the operation appeared to realistically be the only way she was truly going to be able to make the most of playing her part in the proceedings with Layne and anyone else like him around.

Of course, having cleared her schedule of any and all ability-based police activities to take care of, the real mission was still to come – having Gabrielle somehow enjoy her night out at the rock venue with her and Sissy.

Jamie suddenly found hunting down Issy and Liv far less challenging.

Chapter 14

"See ya, Jamie!" Gabrielle called out from downstairs as she headed to her car to go to work. Jamie managed to force herself to wake up enough to respond.

"Love you, babe!" she yelled back in spite of her half-awake state, having just about managed to get a full night's sleep following her antics the prior evening, though opted to fall back into her slumber anyway for good measure.

Upon waking a second time two hours later, she grabbed her phone from the side table to see if there was any morning correspondence from Brody over her departing shenanigans with Layne or in general.

Yup.

She read the text from Brody that had arrived only in the last ten minutes which simply stated to 'call back when available to talk', then subsequently dialled his contact number. The tone of the message had been ambivalent but knowing Brody by now, Jamie figured he would at least try and sugar coat any bad news that was coming her way.

Knowing Layne by now also, the talk probably wouldn't be without his influence in it either.

"Morning, Jamie."

"Hi, Brody. You wanted to chat?"

"Yes, mainly about what you got up to last night."

Here we go...

"Lay it on me," Jamie replied, trying to sound interested while expecting to hear Layne's wrath being passed down through Brody.

"Well firstly, congratulations on that extremely impressive job last night," Brody began. *"Even I didn't expect you to be as quick as you were and although you did engage the suspects again, admittedly you were the best person for the job to take them down so good work on that."*

"Thanks," Jamie responded, slightly surprised.

"And allow me to inform you that my superiors were extremely impressed upon finding out about the apprehension of not one but two criminal empowered beings in the process during the meeting this morning."

"Curious, Brody," Jamie cut in. "How did they find out about that? Through Layne?"

"Actually, yes," he answered.

"Then why were they impressed?" Jamie asked, not particularly surprised that Layne hadn't even waited until the next working day to file a report on her. "I imagine he did everything he could to annihilate me."

"Well that's the funny story I'm about to relay to you," Brody replied, almost sounding like he was looking forward to what he was going to say next. Jamie listened on with anticipation.

"Layne did indeed report the arrest and went as far to completely try and slate you to kingdom come over it. I believe he can be quoted as saying in his written report that you were 'unruly', 'uncooperative', 'insolent' and 'disrespectful' among other choice words."

"Did he not suggest locking me up?" Jamie asked.

"No but then he probably hoped his negative report regarding your alleged behaviour in itself would be enough to rescind the agreement with you and cause you to be imprisoned. I'm not going to put words in his mouth when it might not even be the case though but regardless, he seemed rather ticked off with you for some reason."

"That might be down to me all but calling him inferior in getting the job done with me about," Jamie honestly stated.

"Ah, that would explain things."

"So what's going to happen to me then?" Jamie asked, though not feeling too worried given Brody's jovial tone of voice.

"Well as far as the higher-ups are concerned, you're proving yourself a valuable commodity to the operation and want to continue seeing the partnership flourish in the meantime."

"So no blowback whatsoever then?"

"Well you may very well have earned the everlasting enmity of Detective Layne over your words to him but other than that, I would say no. I wouldn't mind having a catch-up with you to go over what

went down with those two teenage thieves you managed to up-end though when you have a moment spare?"

Jamie sat up in her bed feeling chuffed with herself, though with fresh memories of her last pat on the back being rewarded with intervening in a school shooting, she decided not to get too complacent, particularly with Layne looking to cause trouble for her more than ever.

"I'm not available today but I can come in tomorrow during the day if you'd like?" she responded.

"That's no problem. I'll see you at midday if that's okay?"

"Yeah, that's okay with me."

"Good. See you tomorrow then."

Jamie hung up the line and decided to lie back down while snuggling into her duvet. It amused her that Layne had failed to get what he wanted, even though it probably meant he was going to try even harder to make her life a living hell. Standing up to him and throwing his abusive attitude right back in his face, however, had been empowering and her reputation among the police force was growing which, if Rachel was correct, would give her more leeway on what she was able to put up with from the loathsome detective in the future.

The latest addition of enhanced speed had probably left her with the largest pool of abilities she had ever contained within her body, which thankfully was having no negative effect or overwhelming her system to house them all. It could just be likely that her natural powers were becoming stronger with every use of them and her overall handling of those she controlled had improved along with them.

But that was the least of her concerns for the moment as she made her way downstairs to prepare breakfast in anticipation of the day's events to come.

"Not all of us are naturally good at playing instruments, y'know!"

"Just as well you only have to play the one string at a time on yours then!"

"Well I've only been playing bass for a fortnight and already I've heard the 'bassists are just failed guitarists' joke a dozen times," Sissy laughed.

"Yeah but you're also managing to fail at bass too," Jamie joked. "Kidding!"

"It's a work in progress, love."

"Better get good eventually if we want to give Ryan a run for his money. Is he ready for tonight then?"

"He should be; he's been practicing for it nearly every day this week," Sissy replied while trying to get her finger position correct on the fretboard of her bass guitar. "I was in the rehearsal room with them for one of their jams, I think they're tight enough."

"How will the crowd perceive them?"

"I would say pretty well. They'll always have us as a cheering section of course and anyone who comes down as usual will add to the crowd. Is your friend aware of what she's getting into?"

"Probably not fully but she's tough. She'll be able to handle herself."

"What's her name anyway?"

"Gabrielle," Jamie replied. "Or Gabby as she likes."

"Wow, even her name sounds gorgeous," Sissy remarked.

"You should see her face," Jamie marvelled.

"Just make sure she doesn't wear heels, would hate to see her leaving with a broken ankle."

"Nobody's going to do something like that on purpose, are they?"

"No chance but accidents happen as they say, especially in our kind of crowds. There's always further back to avoid that craziness anyway so she'll be safe."

"I think she'll make the most of it, it's been a rough couple of days for her and she'll be looking to just have fun regardless of whether its her thing or not."

"Anything major at all?" Sissy asked out of curiosity, to Jamie's hesitation.

"It's a bit personal to be honest. Promise not to tell anyone else or bring it up in front of her?"

"Hey, my word is my bond," Sissy replied.

"She found out the other day that her biological father died a year into her life and she felt torn up about it and the fact her adoptive dad of 17 years wasn't her birth father as she was led to believe."

"Pretty mad," Sissy sympathetically responded. "Maybe a little eff'd up too I might add. Still, at least she actually had a dad growing up. All *I've* ever known is my mam but she's been all I ever needed."

"Just the two of you the whole time then, no stepdad figure?"

"Some came and went with none of them ever really lasting too long. I never connected with any of them much for that reason as they would often be gone before I knew it. I wouldn't say a lot of them were worth it in my opinion."

"You ever think about your real dad at all?" Jamie asked.

"Only ever wondering why he never bothered to stick around after I was born," Sissy bitterly said. "It's like, why have me in the first place if you had no interest in being a dad to me from the start? It was never easy for my mum trying to rear me with barely any money but I give respect to her for trying the best she could with what she had."

"I suppose I was one of the lucky ones in that aspect," Jamie remarked. "But I've since learned that family can be whoever you want it to be so you're never missing out on too much if you have that much on your side."

"Your folk not around anymore then?" Sissy asked.

More than you know.

"They're absent nowadays but I have a close knit but small circle of close friends," Jamie expertly skirted through the enquiry. "They are family to me, I don't feel alone as much as I used to."

"I hear ya – the guys and I have a good connection with one another," Sissy replied, referring to her punk friends. "My mum's great of course, despite our occasional rows but it's nice to have company with the same interests as you too and they generally fill in for the lack of solid male presence I've dealt with all my life."

"That's cool," Jamie replied warmly as Sissy attempted to play a sequence of notes on her bass guitar.

"Argh, how the hell do you move across strings so easily?" Sissy bemoaned as she fumbled the riff.

"Practicing it over and over. All it takes is getting used to it really, then it feels natural."

"Well you were right about picking and fretting the same note and string over and over while watching TV; got rid of the fret buzz in the end as you may have noticed," Sissy smugly pointed out.

"There you go," Jamie smiled back. "I'm sure we'll be playing songs together soon enough."

"I'm actually looking forward to that prospect, should be loads of fun doing what Ryan does on stage."

"We'll get there eventually," Jamie replied, though also feeling weary at the idea of being stared at by a crowd of people.

"By the way, we're going to get there for around 7 tonight," Sissy mentioned. "You and Gabrielle planning on meeting us there?"

"Can you meet us outside when we arrive?" Jamie asked.

"Sure, just text us when you plan on getting there and I'll make sure I come grab ya."

"Nice one. Knowing Gabby, we'll prob be a bit later while she messes around with what she's going to be wearing."

"Can't blame the gal for wanting to look her best!" Sissy joked.

"And ironically she accuses me of being late for everything," Jamie laughed back. "Think she's looking to have fun though despite it not really being her thing."

"Maybe we'll turn her over to it, you never know!"

"True, it worked on me only last year after all."

"I can't really picture you looking like anything else," Sissy said.

"I can't much either now myself really," Jamie replied while picking her guitar back up. "Wanna crack on with the jam though while we have time?"

"If we can call it a 'jam' with my bass-playing," Sissy jested while positioning her fretting hand once more.

"Gabbs, if you are not ready by the time I order the cab, I am dragging you out the way you are!"

"What if I'm naked when the cab arrives?" Gabrielle cheekily yelled down the staircase.

"The threat still stands, girl!" Jamie called back up with a laugh.

"Didn't everyone get naked anyway at rock shows back in the sixties?"

"Don't think they do at punk shows," Jamie said while levitating up onto the balcony to avoid further shouting. "And besides, there'll probably be enough guys thirsting over you as it is with your clothes on!"

"As long as they remember to just look and not touch," Gabrielle replied from inside her bedroom.

"Best to avoid the mosh pit in that case," Jamie said.

"Where do people get fun in fighting and bashing into one another anyway?"

"It's not fighting as such; just everyone unleashing their energy would be a better way of describing it. Only complete pricks go in there intending to deliberately hurt someone."

"And *you* would have no issue jumping into it?" Gabrielle asked.

"As long as it isn't too aggressive or anyone being a knob, I don't see the harm. I've probably dealt with worse in my field of 'work' recently anyway."

"How's that been going anyway? Nothing too crazy I'd hope."

"Nah, I've been well protected for the most part," Jamie lied, not wanting to put a damper on the atmosphere. "Even got a good review over my most recent task from one of the leading detectives just this morning."

"Well that's something positive at least out of the whole thing," Gabrielle responded. "Hopefully they'll let you go sooner than later."

Not with Layne around, they won't.

"Maybe, you never know," Jamie spoke back. "Anyway, how's things going on in there?"

"You mean the getting changed part or me in general?"

"Both I guess."

"Yeah, things have been alright. Not much different than when we spoke yesterday really, just getting on with life."

"But you're alright as a whole?"

"It's always going to be in my mind but at least now it's in there for the right reasons as opposed to any traumatic ones," Gabrielle answered. "Couldn't have said that a few days ago but I think I'll learn to live with it without ending up in the same dire state of mind again."

"You always have me if you do."

"Love you, babes!"

"Love you too!" Jamie replied. "And as for the progress in choosing your wardrobe for tonight?"

"You tell me," Gabrielle responded by opening the door, revealing herself to be only wearing her lower underwear.

"I'd be appalled if I wasn't looking at total perfection," Jamie half-joked while in admiration.

"You'd be looking at total perfection if you were standing in front of a full-length mirror," Gabrielle quipped as she went to her dresser drawer to select a bra. "But I'll have you know that I already chose what I plan to wear for tonight yesterday before I went to bed so all I have to do is put it on."

"And what about your two hours of make-up?"

"The cheek," Gabrielle replied in jest. "And it's only *one* hour, thank you very much! I can do half while we're waiting for the cab and the rest on the ride over."

"Nah, do it all here. We're in no rush, the band doesn't start until half seven apparently. Sissy and her friends are planning on getting there for bang on seven."

"Well it's just gone six now so what time did you plan on getting there for?"

"Around quarter past seven?" Jamie asked. "Be in time for the band and a bit of hanging around after?"

"Might as well make a full night of it," Gabrielle replied, pulling up her leggings. "When do we ever go out raving anyway?"

"Don't know if I call it 'raving' at a rock club."

"Well having fun anyway. Think we've earned it after everything that's happened of late."

"Shall I book the cab to arrive here for quarter to seven then?"

"Yeah, makes sense," Gabrielle said while pulling her t-shirt over her torso before stepping back out into Jamie's view. "Whaddya think?"

Jamie stared at her friend who was dressed in a black skirt with matching tights complete with the same cropped t-shirt she had bought at the shopping centre with Jamie and the Webster siblings present.

"I think I need an inhaler 'cause you just took all my breath away," Jamie replied as humorously as she could think though no less impressed. "I didn't know you owned a black belly bar with spiked ends?"

"Ordered it the other day when I bought the top so it'd match. Looks cute, doesn't it?"

"Looks 'hot', more like. I'll leave you to do your make-up for a bit then while I call the cab place up."

"No problem, won't be long!"

"And I'm the queen of England(!)" Jamie joked on her way back downstairs.

True to form, Gabrielle was still scrambling to finish her make-up as the cab arrived two minutes before quarter to seven, opting to indeed complete the job in the back seat of the car ride over though garnering compliments from Jamie nonetheless for the rock-inspired design.

A part of her was nervous for her friend actually enjoying herself in what was no doubt going to be a very unsuited environment but she could imagine Sissy being understanding if they chose to leave

256

immediately after Ryan's band's set. She still didn't know what to expect herself from the set considering she had never heard the band play but based on Sissy's description, one would either like it or not with no in-between.

"Well it looks better than I expected," Gabrielle spoke aloud as she and Jamie got out of the cab outside the venue. "Bit isolated, isn't it though?"

"Probably for the best in regards to the noise," Jamie replied while simultaneously texting Sissy.

"Where's your friend?"

"Just messaged her now, she should be out in a minute."

"It's actually nearly half past now, the band we're supposed to be watching should be coming on soon."

"Yeah, must admit it's a lot quicker getting here via flying," Jamie replied. "Didn't think it would take as long to drive."

"Just means we don't have to wait about for the band to start," Gabrielle said, Jamie almost interpreting the response as a hint.

"Jamie!" Sissy called out from the entrance.

"Hey, Sissy!" Jamie called back as Sissy came over to greet her.

"Thought you were going to miss it," Sissy said before turning to the wavy, blonde-haired person next to Jamie. "And are you Gabrielle?"

"'Gabby' if you'd prefer," Gabrielle replied with a smile.

"You weren't wrong, girl; she *is* stunning," Sissy said to Jamie within blatant earshot of Gabrielle.

"Oh, Jamie!" Gabrielle said out of embarrassment.

"Well that's two of us who think it so must be true!" Jamie laughed as the muffled sound of a drum kit being played could be heard.

"Right, they sound like they're about to start so let's get you sorted out," Sissy said as she led the duo to the front door to pay the entry fee.

Once inside, Gabrielle looked around to find a large hall that contained at least fifty teenagers and young adults in their early twenties all dressed like Sissy and Jamie respectively (and herself at that moment in time). On the stage at the far end of the room was a band preparing to begin playing.

"Guess you feel right at home here!" Gabrielle partially yelled to Jamie over the background music.

"Kinda!" Jamie replied. "I don't really know a lot of people though so it's a bit anxiety inducing at the same time but I would say I feel safe!"

"I'm going to get some drinks, what do you and Sissy want?"

"She'll have a cider and I'll just have a beer I suppose!"

"Coming up!" Gabrielle said as she walked to the bar. Jamie admitted to herself that she really wasn't feeling as comfortable as she would have liked despite being in her element, hoping that she would be able to drink herself into enough of a tipsy state to be a bit sociable and enjoy herself more.

Suddenly, a loud noise erupted as Ryan and his band began playing their instruments without warning, calming down only briefly for Ryan to welcome the audience and introduce the first song. As soon as they launched into the opening number, Sissy and her fellow punks immediately took to the centre of the floor in front of the stage and began crashing into one another. Jamie felt the overwhelming urge to join in but was still too nervy to want to step forward, opting for the time being to simply watch the mayhem from her standing position.

At the bar area, Gabrielle yelled to the bartender her drinks order over the noise before turning her head towards the stage area, thinking that it was the loudest thing she had ever heard with very little melody to it. She then eyed Jamie standing by herself while watching what she guessed was the 'mosh pit' right in front of her, assuming that her friend wasn't as nuts as she thought she might be to want to take part in it.

Then again, I did watch you beat up that rapist quite soundly…

After the first song, Ryan thanked the crowd who responded positively. Jamie found herself surprised at just how abrasive the music was, far heavier than she was used to listening to but could nonetheless feel the raw energy of the performance getting her pumped up with adrenaline, albeit without the added urge to join Sissy and the others in slamming each another across the floor.

"This next one, I wanna see you all moving down there!" Ryan screamed into the microphone as the band kicked off again with another song that Jamie couldn't help but feel sounded just like the first one though nonetheless began banging her head to it anyway in support.

"Here you go!" Gabrielle surprised her from behind, barely being heard as she passed on the beer she had just bought to Jamie, who relented her head-bopping in favour of sipping at the drink. By the end of the modestly short but aggressive song, Sissy came back over to claim her cider.

"Cheers, sister!" she said to Gabrielle.

"No worries!" Gabrielle replied while looking at the stage to see the singer having a problem with his guitar. "What's going on up there?"

"Think he's pulled out the guitar cable by accident," Jamie responded.

"Yeah, he does that a lot on stage, the muppet," said Sissy. "He always gets carried away up there, should probably save up for a wireless kit or something."

"How have you managed to survive that pit?!" Jamie exclaimed with a mix of intrigue and admiration.

"It's all about using everyone else's momentum against them!" Sissy replied. "You should give it a try when Ryan sorts himself out."

"Don't think I've had enough for that yet," Jamie said while holding her beer bottle up.

"Go on, down it!" Sissy encouraged.

"Yeah, I dare ya," Gabrielle egged her friend on as well. Jamie then reluctantly put the bottle to her mouth and began trying to drink it all in one go, almost retching from the taste but ultimately succeeding with minor spillage.

"Alright, we're back!" Ryan yelled into the microphone, having dealt with his technical issues. "Get this one down you!"

"Come on!" Sissy said while grabbing Jamie's hand and leading her straight into the mosh pit that immediately proceeded once more following the resumption of the band's set. With the beer barely settled in her stomach, Jamie nonetheless attempted to do as Sissy suggested and use everyone else in the pit's momentum against them, taking a few knocks in the process but managing to hold her own by the end of the song. She noted how exhausting it was but also extremely enjoyable.

"Have fun in there?" Gabrielle asked Jamie who was smiling from ear to ear.

"Well I didn't get knocked over so I think I did well!" Jamie replied as the next song kicked off behind her with Sissy remaining amongst the action, deciding to stay with Gabrielle watching away from the melee for the rest of the set in order to give her some company.

"We want to thank you for watching us tonight!" Ryan bellowed once more to the crowd through the microphone. "This is our last song so make sure you all make it count!"

Without warning, Jamie threw herself straight back into the pit with Sissy one last time, acting on pure adrenaline and tipsiness. Although done on impulse, she admitted to herself that she preferred moshing to actually listening to Ryan's band's music which she just couldn't find herself getting on with despite her best efforts.

As she attempted to move her hair out of her face, Jamie found herself being knocked off balance and straight into the stray elbow of another reveller and subsequently crashing to the floor with the band continuing to play.

Disorientated, Jamie struggled to get to her feet as Sissy and her punk friends opened up a protective perimeter around her with Gabrielle rushing in to try and aid her. As the song came to an end, Ryan immediately realised something was up in the small crowd.

"Everything all right over there?" he spoke into the microphone. He eventually witnessed Jamie being hauled up by his friends.

"She's cool, just got clattered in the pit!" Sissy yelled back as she helped the dazed Jamie to walk towards the front entrance.

"A round of applause for Jamie, everyone!" Ryan spoke aloud to the entire room who responded by clapping in appreciation to the injured teenager. Jamie threw up a fist in response in acknowledgement as she was escorted to the outside.

"Rob, go grab a glass of water, can you?" Sissy said to her friend upon sitting Jamie down with Gabrielle against the wall outside the venue.

"You okay, Jame?" Gabrielle asked worriedly.

"Did I get the other guy as good as he got me?" Jamie joked through the headache.

"Only an accident, babe," Sissy smiled. "Otherwise he'd have been flattened by everyone around him by now."

"Guess I'll call a cab to get us back," Gabrielle said, getting her phone out of her handbag.

"Oh it's not that bad, Gabbs," Jamie protested weakly, though still very obviously out of it.

"Might be best to call it a night, babes," Sissy concurred. "You took quite a heavy blow, you'll probably need to rest it off."

"Sorry, kinda ruined the night," Jamie replied.

"Please, you kicked arse in there!" Sissy responded. "And don't worry about it anyway, there'll be other nights and at least you gave Ryan some support."

"Well he definitely knows how to work a crowd," Jamie feebly spoke.

"Here you go," Rob said, appearing with a glass of water.

"Thanks," Jamie replied as Gabrielle ended her phone call in the background.

"Lucky us – they're going to be here in two minutes as they had someone nearby coming off another fare," Gabrielle stated.

"Hey, Jamie!" Ryan said as he entered the outside area. "Did you take a whack in the pit then?"

"Meh, was a lucky shot," Jamie jokingly responded.

"Well who did it? We'll give 'em what for."

"She's kidding, Ry," Sissy jumped in. "She got slammed into some dude's elbow. All good. Her and Gabby here are heading back now to sleep it off."

"What did you think of us up there then?" Ryan asked.

"I thought it was good!" Jamie answered, referring to the performance itself rather than the music. "Really got the crowd going."

"Glad you liked it," Ryan said, pleased with himself.

"Wow, they're here already," Gabrielle said as the cab arrived. "Must literally have dropped off the last lot down the next street or something. Alright Jame, up you come."

"Text me when you arrive home, girl," Sissy said as she and the punks helped Jamie up and wished her goodbye.

"You know it," Jamie replied as she and Gabrielle made their way to the cab.

"Whoa, is she drunk?" the driver asked from the window, seeing the purple-haired teenager staggering towards his vehicle.

"She had one drink before getting clumped in the head by some klutz on the dance floor; we're going home to put her to bed," Gabrielle responded, trying to mask her annoyance.

"Okay, no worry," the driver said as the girls entered the back of the cab.

"Sure know how to show a girl a good time," Gabrielle said to Jamie.

"Sorry, hun," Jamie responded. "Guessing it wasn't really your thing though, was it?"

"I won't lie and say I had any interest in the music whatsoever, especially your mate's band which was virtually unlistenable to but it was great just going out somewhere with you," Gabrielle replied. "Even if it was only for half an hour(!)"

"I'll try and make it twice as long next time," Jamie jested.

"You'll forgive me for picking the place next time though, or at least pick a night there that has endurable rock music on."

"It's fine, that kind of hardcore music isn't for everyone I admit. Even I don't listen to anything that abrasive. And they played regular stuff last time I was there so I say we give it another go in the future."

"At least I didn't stick out like a sore thumb blending in with my new gear on," Gabrielle remarked.

"Wouldn't say that looking as gorgeous as you do," Jamie replied.

"Oh dear, the blow to the head's turned you insane!" Gabrielle sarcastically said.

"If only!"

"Love you, my Jamie baby," Gabrielle said lovingly while gripping her friend's hand.

"Love you too, bubs," Jamie responded, squeezing back. As short as the night had been, she was happy for it having happened regardless especially after all that had gone on as of late in her 'professional' life.

It did recur to her that she would be seeing Brody again at noon the following day and whether it was for an actual friendly talk or a secret ambush by Layne, she couldn't really care less. As long as she still had her friends and her steadily growing social life, Layne's personal vendetta could only affect her so much.

Chapter 15

"Uh oh, too many drinks last night?" Rachel asked as a slightly dishevelled-looking Jamie approached her desk in the precinct office.

"I wish," Jamie grumbled. "My face headbutted someone's elbow at a gig last night, or so I'm told. Should've grabbed some painkillers on the way out of my house."

"Ouch. I'd offer you some of mine but I've only got one remaining to last me the whole day and I just came on so I need all the pain relief I can get."

"Nah, it's alright. I'm gonna see my mate afterwards, they'll sort me out with something."

"Did you have fun though?"

"For the half an hour I was there, yeah. It was nice to be out."

"That's the spirit, lovely," Rachel responded. "What brings you in on this Saturday morning then?"

"Business with Brody and hopefully *not* a certain other arsehole detective in the process," Jamie answered.

"Well according to his rota, he's scheduled to be off today so I wouldn't worry about it," Rachel replied, easily sussing the source of Jamie's irritation.

"Hopefully having surgery to remove that king-sized rod from his backside. Between putting me down and trying to get me killed in a school shooting, the guy is such a douchebag."

"Wait, he did *what*?" Rachel asked out of shock.

"Oh he had his bosses send me in to deal with that shooting situation once he found out it involved some idiots with powers. I took care of them in the end."

"He sent *you*, an untrained member of staff, into *that* kind of high-risk and deadly scenario?!"

"I wouldn't worry about it too much, Rachel," Jamie shrugged. "I made him look like a complete tosser in front of his colleagues the other day anyway while proving my worth; if he's got anything planned on the horizon, I'll outsmart him as always."

"I guess I'm going to have to go a bit further than signing his mobile up for annoying spam messages then," Rachel schemed. "Is getting him placed on the sex offender's register too much?"

"Probably too far," Jamie replied, unsure if Rachel was joking or not. "Although wouldn't surprise me if he already was with his opinion on women's choice of clothing when going out."

"Y'know the sad part about that is he probably chats to either his mates or similar-minded colleagues about stuff like that and they probably just dismiss it as 'banter' or 'locker room talk'," Rachel said. "What I hear is a load of macho, tone-deaf and offensive trash but what do I know? After all, I'm just a 'femi-nazi' running her mouth off and being all 'woke'."

"Yeah – 'scuse me for not wanting to be treated like a second-class citizen," Jamie jested. "Ah well, better go see what surprise Brody has lined up for me, if any."

"Go get 'em, tiger," Rachel said as Jamie made her way to the staircase and up to Brody's office on the next floor up. Knowing Layne was absent had made the visit so much more bearable, as long as Brody really wasn't about to dump something undesirable on her as she half-expected.

Walking up to the door of the office, Jamie could see the blinds covering all the windows in the room.

Now why so private all of a sudden?

Jamie knocked on the door to hear Brody's voice calling her in.

"Afternoon, Jamie," Brody said from behind his desk. "I hope you're doing well."

"Better than other days this week anyway. So what's on your mind?"

"Well just a check-up on you really," Brody answered. "I want to know what's going on up there in your head after that nightmare situation earlier in the week and all the crap Layne's been giving you. Plus I do feel I've let you down a bit in that regard, not protecting you as I said I would try to."

"I'll admit the whole politics-at-work thing is new to me, Brody" Jamie replied. "But I get that you're limited in your position to be able to do everything you would prefer to do including reining

Layne in when he's being a jerk. At least I got the last laugh on him the other day though."

"It's not exactly been the easiest start to your employment with us, I will state that," Brody said. "You've adapted well though and four suspects apprehended in one week is a huge achievement, especially for someone new to the place."

"Well I *have* had practice in the past, y'know. I'm surprised you didn't get that impression from any of the footage of me in Ryan Sharp's videotape library.

"Well that's another thing I wanted to bring up with you today, actually," Brody said.

"What about?" Jamie asked, feeling confused.

"Nothing serious depending on how you take it but I was reviewing camera footage from one of the outdoor cameras on the grounds of the school that was recently the victim of David Oliver and his unidentified assailants' shooting rampage."

Jamie suddenly felt extremely worried.

"Why were you looking at that?" she asked nervously.

"Trying to see if his two super-powered cohorts were careless enough to expose themselves at any point seeing as they're still at large but no such luck owing to the very limited camera footage available and Dawn not being able to catch them using their powers since the incident. I did happen upon another individual though who was caught literally flying onto the scene at one point as well as leaving in the same manner."

Jamie's heart then skipped a beat; Jesse had been revealed to the police. If this was Brody's way of having a friendly chat, he had a warped sense of humour that even Layne would envy.

"Based on the backlog of footage we have from Ryan Sharp's secret building where he conducted his research and experiments into empowered human beings, the young man caught on the school grounds is the same one whom Sharp captured outside his building a couple of weeks ago. His name is Jesse Webster, and the person he is seen accompanying in Sharp's building footage just happens to be a Miss Jamie Avonoit."

"So what is this?" Jamie replied, accepting that there was no point denying the facts of the matter with the readily available evidence. "A confrontation? Or are you telling me this because you want to throw him in prison?"

"On the contrary, I want to offer him a job."

Jamie looked back at Brody with surprise. "A job?"

"Yes," Brody replied. "But level with me first though; this Jesse person aided you in bringing down the school shooters, am I correct?"

"What gave you that impression?" Jamie asked, playing coy for clarification's sake.

"Well other than the fact that he appears to be on friendly terms with you, I was speaking to Bennett of the tactical team that accompanied you during the raid on the school. Among his version of events that went down inside, there was witnessing you being thrown into a set of metal lockers from the force of an exploding attack from one of the super-powered suspects just before he himself was incapacitated. And seeing as Jesse entered the building roughly around the same time as you guys did, it just seems to add up that he helped you out in some manner with the team taken out."

"I suppose that's why you're the detective, Brody," Jamie remarked. "I *am* friends with him and he was indeed there giving me a hand when we apprehended David Oliver. In fact, he probably saved all our lives at one point when he took out the culprit behind the explosive attacks on all of us. But I'm not really comfortable with the idea of him joining this operation though."

"Why do you feel that way?" Brody asked.

"Because I do not like the fact *I* am currently bound to this thing whether I like it not and I certainly don't want the same to happen to him. And he's got other responsibilities in his life that require his attention more than being tied to this project."

"That's a fair enough explanation," Brody replied.

"That it?" Jamie asked.

"Yes, actually. I asked if he'd be interested and you gave a valid enough reason why he wouldn't. Which is a shame because he seems like quite the useful person to have around, much like yourself."

"Aren't you just going to blackmail him into it like me?"

"Well firstly, I'm not blackmailing anyone," Brody responded in a tone suggesting that he had taken offence to Jamie's comment. "If it were down to me, you would be here of your own free will but Layne has his own ideas as you very well know by now. And secondly, your friend's involvement in the school incident is known only to me at the moment."

"Layne doesn't know?" Jamie asked with a sense of relief.

"No and I don't plan to let him know either. Whether he finds out on his own is a different matter but he won't be doing so with help from me. And if you two are as good friends as you seem, it'll just be another thing that Layne will try to use against you."

"Thank you," Jamie meekly replied, feeling bad for her accusing tone prior to the explanation.

"What I instead would like to do is extend an emergency contact detail swap with him where he can act in a 'consultant' role whenever we need his help."

"You mean when the job is too big for me alone or if I'm not available," Jamie caught Brody's drift. "But you don't even know what he's capable of."

"Well I know he can fly at the very least," Brody responded. "And as you mentioned, if he can take out someone who you yourself had some trouble confronting, he must be powerful to some extent."

"He took the guy out from behind, Brody," Jamie said. "It was pure luck. But if you want to know what powers he has, you'd need to ask him yourself."

"Well if he wants to talk to me personally, you can give him this next time you see him," Brody replied while holding out a business card for Jamie to take, which she subsequently put in her cargo trouser pocket.

"Honestly, Brody. Why aren't you running this show instead of that walking egomaniac, Layne?" Jamie spoke. "Your attitude towards recruiting people like us is far more approachable."

"Layne mainly got the nod over me owing to his extra years of experience but he was also aware of the nature of these abilities before I was," Brody replied. "But remember that you're in the minority of good ones we've brought in – the rest are normally beyond any approach at all and Layne's sterner attitude, for better or worse, is ideally suited for that. The fact that we do actually arrest some decent empowered beings who choose to co-operate with us is where I take centre stage because I am recognised as being more down-to-Earth, as you've come to know by now. As you've also come to know unfortunately, Layne oversteps his boundaries and makes unwitting enemies out of people who he'd be better off keeping on his side."

"Do you have any idea at all why he hates me and my kind? Or at least it seems like it."

"He's never said anything to me but maybe he doesn't want to, or can't afford to. It's possible that he does indeed have it in for people with abilities but to be openly prejudiced against a certain type of person, even those with powers, is risking one's career."

"Didn't seem to have a problem commenting on women dressing more conservatively to avoid being raped the other day," Jamie retorted. "One could argue he has it in for women with remarks like that."

"He would simply argue that that was an opinion and not a sexist remark," Brody replied. "These things do have a tendency to be hard to prove at tribunals which is why it doesn't often get pursued."

"Sounds accurate," Jamie quipped.

"Anyway," Brody swiftly moved on. "I also wanted to have a chat regarding your collar the other night. How did you manage to track them down?"

"Luck if I'm honest. I used analysis to target a specific ability being used to phase through walls," Jamie said while concealing the empathy ability use for Kayleigh's sake.

"And it came up with the super-speed teenager and her mate with, what ability again?"

"Analysis referred to it as 'problem solving' and it appears to give a subjective solution to an issue or dilemma that someone presents it with."

"And what do you mean by '*subjective* solution'?"

"That it seems to pick the most viable or effective solution to a problem but not a universally correct one. I must admit, I was quite impressed to see the other girl using her enhanced speed to create a phasing effect, presumably by speeding up or vibrating her molecules to pass through solid matter."

"I'm no science boffin but that sounds more like science-fiction," a sceptic Brody replied.

"Well more like quantum mechanics to a degree, yet I'm glad she just stuck to her speed abilities while fighting me. She was lucky not to blow up the walls she passed through during those heists unless her ability just happens to help aid her in properly executing that 'tunnelling' process. It's surprising she was even able to use her ability in such a manner in the first place."

"Nothing really surprises me with these powers now, after everything I've seen" Brody remarked.

"Guess so," Jamie replied. "Though it's still highly advanced stuff that even I barely understand despite my interest in it. Off-topic, what's happening with that pair anyway?"

"Well they're both in the special cells right now with the enhanced speed individual under sedation owing to the nature of her powers allowing her to walk through walls. Her mate is simply under surveillance in the room she occupies to make sure her specific powers don't enable an escape."

"Has she come up with anything yet?"

"Not so far but we'll be keeping an eye on her at all times. It's taking in youth like them that's problematic for our operation as we often end up having to reveal to their parents why they're under arrest in such max security conditions and the whole notion of human abilities in the process."

"Does that ever go down well?" Jamie asked.

"Hardly. Even when we show them security footage of the crimes being committed, they seldom believe it and accuse us of showing them doctored videos featuring some sort of special effects. But seeing as we have to keep all knowledge of powers on a need-to-know basis, they're normally threatened with arrest themselves if they even as much whisper what they learn to anyone and most accept a pay-off for keeping quiet. It's not ideal but it's all we really have at this moment in time."

"It's such a surreal thing to believe even when dealing with it first hand," Jamie commented.

"I know it was for me the first time I witnessed such activity," Brody replied.

"Oh well, they're still bank thieves in the end and they deserve what they've got."

"Exactly. And congratulations on successfully bringing them in to face justice of course," Brody said with Jamie giving an awkward smile in response, not entirely content with the pair being put in the same position as she was under Ryan Sharp but nonetheless accepting it was necessary in their cases.

"Is there anything else you wanna discuss?" Jamie asked.

"No, that's all," Brody answered. "I've got nothing floating around at the moment so make the most of your weekend I'd suggest."

"Okay, I'll see you soon then," Jamie replied as she made her way towards the door.

"Can you let me know in advance if your friend, Jesse, is interested in speaking to me by the way?" Brody called out quickly.

"Will do," Jamie replied before turning back around to head out the door.

From her position in the air, Jamie descended onto the nearest rooftop to Jesse's workplace and used flight to aid clambering down a drainpipe attached to the wall of the alley beside the building. It was strange reminiscing the fact that their very first encounter had occurred in an alley and had been a catalyst in getting to know each other better on the second occasion. Other than that, her contempt for everything else that had ever happened within a narrow passage still remained.

It was also interesting to catch Jesse at work, and having a conversation about what Brody had spoken of would be far easier with just the two of them as opposed to Kayleigh being present also.

As she walked in, Jamie failed to see Jesse on the shop floor.

"Sorry, is Jesse in today?" she asked one of the staff members on the till.

"Yeah, he's just having his lunch break," the man replied. "Should be around still if you want me to get him quick."

"It's alright, I'll just give him a quick bell," Jamie said as she whipped out her phone and dialled his number.

"Hi Jamie, what's up?"

"I'm at your workplace," Jamie replied. "By the till."

"Oh really? Okay, I'll meet you by the front of the store, we can go hang round the local park."

"Okay, see you in a minute," Jamie responded and made her way back outside. Jesse re-entered the shop floor and headed towards the entrance with Jamie catching sight of him approaching.

"Good to see you," he said while opening the door. "Never thought you'd want to see me at work."

"Technically I still haven't seeing as you're on lunch break," Jamie quipped. "Doesn't seem like a bad place though."

"At least not during the sales and Christmas season," Jesse remarked. "Shall we head off then?"

"Yeah, how far is the park?"

"Literally five minutes."

"And you have how long exactly?"

"Twenty five minutes until I'm back on duty."

"Thank goodness Brody's chat was relatively short then," Jamie said. "Do have something to talk to you about saying that."

"About what?" Jesse asked, curious.

"Nothing bad but let's go sit down to discuss it."

"Guess I should've kept those shades on after all," Jesse said upon Jamie finishing relaying to him about Brody discovering his identity.

"Well I'd have to shoulder the blame on that front," Jamie responded, having indeed made the suggestion to forgo any attempt at a disguise. "At least he offered you a choice of what you can do."

"Yeah, that's something. Although I'm flattered, I would have to respectfully turn him down though, Jame; I've got too much going on with home and work to take something like that on and I don't have a desire to throw myself into situations that involve super-powered maniacs and criminals if I can help it."

"I would say that's a smart call," Jamie replied, feeling good about the declination.

"Though I wouldn't mind holding onto Brody's details in case you ever needed my help and were unable to contact me."

"You sure about that, Jess?" Jamie asked worriedly.

"Hey, I only found you due to sheer luck with Kayleigh's ability when that Satanist nut took over your mind. Could be easier to find you with Brody's help next time."

"I suppose. How is the Kayster anyway?"

"She's doing fine. Aunt Trish is home today looking after her seeing as I'm working but she'll just amuse herself in her own ways."

"Seeing as it's just us right now, you mind if I ask you something about her?" said Jamie.

"Sure."

"Does it bother her that she's separated from her mother who she's known since she was born? I worry that she hasn't really dealt with it properly."

"Well…" Jesse attempted to reply, clearly caught out by the question. "I really don't know to be honest, Jamie. She had a few bad nights when we first moved into our aunt's house which involved crying her eyes out and sleeping next to me until she got used to the new situation we found ourselves in. I think it was less of a blow that I was still with her because we tried to be there as much as possible for one another during those darker years of living under our mum's scumbag of a partner who really just didn't like us."

"I can't really act like I know what it's like to grow up separated from my parents, at least before I was sixteen when I lost my dad," Jamie replied. "Kay just seems so much stronger than I'd imagine for someone as young as she is who had gone through that much turbulence."

"I guess the shock of having to leave our mother behind when we moved out changed how she viewed everything around her. She and mum were quite close, not as much as she is with me but enough to miss her being around. Between that and our mother's partner's disinterest in us as well as his abusive nature, I think in her pre-adolescent mind somewhere she subtlely engaged a survivalist-type mode where she blocked out how the trauma affected her to prevent it from destroying her emotionally. I may just be making up some psycho-babble there in trying to analyse her but she's had to be strong since she was very young to tolerate the often-hostile environment we had at our last place."

"Is that how you approached it when you were effectively abducted away from your dad?" Jamie asked.

"I'd be lying if I said I wasn't extremely upset over that," Jesse replied. "I was still just a kid at the time and I grew to resent my mum for a while after that when it became obvious we were not going to be having my dad in our lives anymore. She tried to compensate in her own ways but I also really hated her partner from the start as I blamed him for my life being upended and he never liked having me around either so that only contributed to the dysfunctional and neglectful hellhole that we lived in.

"With Kayleigh around, I had something to be happy about. She was such a happy and beautiful child that she made waking up each day worthwhile, especially when I entered secondary school and was bullied there too so I had barely any respite from all the aggravation. As she grew older, we became closer as siblings despite the age gap because we were united in being each other's safe space. But as I mentioned before, I numbed myself to my own negative feelings in order to be strong for her. A psychologist would probably have a field day with me one day but it's how I've been half my life now and I'm kind of set in those ways."

"You're in a safer place now though, Jess," Jamie replied while taking her friend's hand. "You'll never be separated from Kayleigh either while I still have a house to offer you both to stay in, if you worry about that ever happening."

"That probably is my biggest fear," Jesse replied. "I hide my vulnerable side to protect her but she *is* my weakness – I would struggle to feel alive without her in my life."

"It won't happen," Jamie said. "There's very little reason for it to occur."

"Well there's always the chance that mum could claim her back or my dad resurfacing and doing the same I suppose which would only complicate things more."

"Are you insinuating that you don't want them back in your life to prevent any likelihood of Kayleigh from being taken away from you?" Jamie asked.

"I guess it sounds awful, and I have missed the pair of them a lot but I really can't not have my baby sister in my life. I have often thought about going back to my mother and pummelling her partner using my powers and also trying to track down my father but what from there? I know we could never live as a family again after everything that has happened between the pair of them and being a minor, Kayleigh could end up being fought over quite viciously. That wouldn't be fair to her after all she's gone through as it is. I don't want anything like that to happen. I don't like the situation but it seems the safest option to keep us together at the moment. Besides, nobody said life was supposed to be easy, it's the small things we can get out of it that make it worthwhile in my opinion and Kay's definitely worth everything."

"You know she cares deeply about how you feel too though?" Jamie added, recalling her personal conversation with Kayleigh at the funfair about having potential feelings for Jesse. "She knows you've suffered a lot too and you can allow yourself to drop the older brother act and show your vulnerable side if you want."

"I don't know, Jame," Jesse sighed. "As I said, it's what I've come to be over the last decade and it's allowed me to get through my teenage years while allowing Kayleigh to indulge more in her own youth, of which I myself didn't really have. And as is obvious, she acts way older than she should for her age."

"She also probably wants you to act yours too," Jamie cut in. "What say you, me and Gabby all go out sometime, just the three of us? I'm sure she'll be fine on her own for one night."

"I'll consider it," Jesse replied. "I've never actually tried bowling before saying that if you wanted to give that a go?"

"Never? Really?" Jamie exclaimed in surprise, though immediately calming down upon realising it was quite logical owing to his lack of a close group of friends and his devotion to his sister. "Well we'll sort something out sometime soon."

"Sounds good," Jesse smiled. Jamie realised she had yet to relinquish Jesse's hand throughout their talk, having enjoyed the feeling too much to let go in addition to providing a supportive gesture. According to her (sneaky) use of her empathy powers though, the feeling was completely one-sided as Jesse's emotive state had only indicated a warmth from the camaraderie he felt towards her rather than any yearning beyond friendship. She bemoaned to herself the ongoing unrequited feelings she continued to endure, particularly given the fact even she didn't really know whether she wanted anything beyond being friends anyway.

"Sorry, didn't mean to take the conversation in a depressive direction," Jamie said, interrupting her thoughts.

"Nah, you know what? I actually don't mind being this deep," Jesse replied, finally taking his own hand back. "I prefer having more meaningful conversations that just talking crap so it's been quite nice despite the sombre nature of the subject matter."

"Do you feel any better for getting some of that off your chest?" Jamie asked.

"A little bit. Doesn't change things of course but sometimes you need that release. Thanks for listening anyhow."

"Pfft, don't mention it," Jamie replied. "You going back to work now then?"

"Probably should head off before the afternoon shift starts," Jesse said while standing up. "Even if it does involve working the tills."

"You'll survive," Jamie joked, almost regretting her choice of words following the previous conversation. "Give my love to Kay as always."

"Always do," Jesse said as he allowed Jamie to kiss him on the cheek before walking off towards the park entrance in the direction of his shop. Whether he actually intended to give Brody a call was anyone's guess, though probably not if it involved interfering with his time spent with Kayleigh. Jamie didn't feel too bothered either way considering he had a habit of joining in her escapades at a moment's notice as it was and staying out of the operation officially kept him away from being used by Layne at any point.

It was a wonder Layne hadn't already checked Ryan Sharp's extensive video collection himself and found out about her connection to Jesse. On the other hand, he probably left such trivial things to any underling to take care of, knowing what he was like by now.

Using a forested area of the park for cover, Jamie ascended into the air using flight and hazing to make her way home. Had Gabrielle not been working an evening shift later on, she would have suggested visiting the bowling alley later on that day. But then even her own free time as of late was no longer set in stone thanks to the empowered human being operation effectively being a twenty-four hour job compared to her two close friends' respective work rotas. How ironic that she had lacked a social life at all while she was free of any commitment compared to the present moment in both aspects.

Guess this is what being in my twenties is going to feel like.

Jamie suddenly stopped in mid-air as her analysis ability went off in her head, having picked up on the use of a familiar ability.

Teleportation!

Jamie assumed it to be Nate again. With a chance that it was merely a different version of the same ability being used by an entirely different person, Jamie promptly locked onto the sensation with empathy to try and determine who exactly it was.

Within seconds, she then got her answer.

Nate, my boy. Prepare yourself.

284

Jamie altered her course of direction and headed towards the power usage's location being indicated to her in her head. Though she had been given leave of the operation for the day and Nate wasn't even on the list of people to hunt down, she relished the opportunity to have someone who tried to cause her serious injury thrown into the cells, not to mention a member of Bill and his inept gang too.

Within two minutes, Jamie landed on a nearby rooftop very close to where Nate's current location was based on the empathy ability honing in on him. Remembering that she still possessed x-ray vision courtesy of Marcella, Jamie activated it and used it on the buildings surrounding her, not wanting to risk missing Nate teleporting away before she had a chance to confront him.

Where are you…?

Among the several different people within each of the buildings, Jamie eventually spotted a gang of individuals running amok on the second floor of what looked like a sportswear shop. She then saw several light beams emerging from one of the miscreants which immediately was identified as the same laser power that a certain ringleader was known to use by the analysis ability.

Jamie decided to fly over to the store, landing on the rooftop and sailing down the back of it. Her x-ray vision confirmed that right behind the wall was the floor that the gang were currently occupying.

With no window to enter, Jamie considered utilising the enhanced speed within her to try and phase through the wall. The Issy girl had demonstrated that it was possible, though had probably practiced well in advance of the robberies she had committed. Failure to get it correct could hypothetically excite the atoms in the wall into exploding as she feared but utilising the super speed aspect of the ability would put her clear of the blast regardless of it occurring.

Throwing caution to the wind, Jamie began concentrating on internally focusing on enhanced speed to vibrate her molecules, pressing against the wall in the midst of the attempt. She could feel her heart beating furiously, terrified of any negative effects of doing so but also taking confidence in the fact that Issy had been successful with her execution.

To her surprise, Jamie felt her hand push through the solid matter with her whole body, then following with an unexpected assist from the actual speed function of the ability combining with the phasing attempt to shunt her past the wall and into the room.

Stabilising herself with flight, she quickly swooped across the store floor towards where the gang members were amassed.

"Right, enough fun. Grab your gear and let's blow this place," Bill announced. "Nate, get ready to teleport us."

As the gang all came towards Nate, the teleporter was then hit by an invisible force from out of nowhere and knocked several feet away.

"What happened?" Johnny exclaimed.

"Oh, not her again!" Bill groaned loudly upon seeing the black-hooded girl beside them.

"As much as I've enjoyed our times together, I think I'm going to have to bring them to an end," Jamie taunted, knowing apprehending any empowered member of the gang would suffice for Brody though she would prefer to bring in Bill, Johnny or Nate as a matter of principle owing to her enmity towards them specifically.

"Good luck with that, love!" Johnny sneered. "Bill, waste her!"

Bill stepped forward and aimed a flurry of quick laser blasts straight at the girl, only to watch them all blocked by an invisible shield. Jamie then hurled a kinetic energy wave in response which slammed him straight into the floor.

"Is it possible for you to just leave us in peace, lass?!" Johnny yelled in frustration while attempting to flee with the other two gang members in pursuit towards the escalator. Jamie prepared to take to the air once more to head them off, only to feel a set of arms wrapping around her body from behind before she could do so.

"Not this time!" Nate growled as he then teleported with Jamie in tow, leaving the rest of the gang to continue fleeing as Bill picked himself up in the background.

Nice one mate, he thought before departing too with some stolen merchandise in hand.

Jamie found herself re-materialising in a random car park with Nate still holding onto her, noticing the store across the road. She then caught sight of Johnny and the others exiting through the main entrance seconds later as she tried to wrench herself free, finally managing to do so by smashing her head backwards into Nate's face who let go from the pain of the physical blow.

"Looks like I'll just be bringing *you* in by yourself then," Jamie said aloud as she turned the tables by grabbing a disorientated Nate, who was now suffering from a bleeding nose.

"Get off me, you psycho!" Nate roared as he fought back in spite of the intense pain emanating from his face, regretting having not used his future sight aspect of his powers to see the girl's interference in advance. "Let go!"

Beginning to panic, he tried to escape by unwittingly concentrating a large amount of energy into the latest teleportation effort. Only this time though, he felt an unusual sensation as he activated his ability.

Wha...?

Knowing something was wrong, Nate could only watch helplessly as everything before his eyes immediately disappeared with the almost-involuntary teleportation attempt.

Less than a second later, he instead found himself staring at an empty London street with tall buildings either side of him featuring varying broken windows.

"I remember this..." he burbled aloud with Jamie, still clinging on, looking past Nate's head partially obscuring her view to see what the hapless teleporter was murmuring about.

How did we...?

Jamie released her hold as she too stared in bewilderment at her surroundings, realising where she had witnessed the same scene from previously.

"What is this place? How did you send us here?" Jamie yelled at Nate.

"I don't know what this is about!" Nate protested. "I thought I was teleporting, I don't have any idea where this is."

Jamie looked around again at the eerie sight upon her empathy ability conforming the truthfulness of Nate's answer. Annoyingly she had been so busy focused on trying to take Nate down prior to the teleportation that she had completely failed to analyse the latest aspect of his ability on top of teleporting and seeing the future.

"Ay-"

Jamie looked back again to the see that Nate had completely disappeared.

No!

The sound of thunder burst out of nowhere from the darkened sky. In the midst of panicking over Nate leaving her stranded in such a confusing and unworldly place, Jamie could see a figure hovering over from the distance.

Her analysis ability subsequently kicked in, detecting flight being used as well as 'weather manipulation'.

It's really you, she thought with a mix of horror and fear at the person now standing only a short distance away.

"Hello Jamie," Jesse stated.

Chapter 16

Jamie looked straight into Jesse's eyes – or at least who it appeared to be – and seeing heavy dark marks around them. The exact same marks she witnessed in Nate's vision. Activating her remaining empathy powers, she attempted to feel any sensation she could from the person before her to confirm if it was really her friend or someone masquerading as him.

"Heh, that's one lame ability I don't regret not absorbing," the person resembling Jesse spoke. Jamie's analysis ability then picked up on the exact same power being used, realising the person before her was aware of her attempt to feel their emotions. From what she could feel though, whoever they truly were just happened to be giving off a particularly ominous vibe.

"Jesse?" she asked, almost at a loss at what else to do.

"I suppose if nothing else," the person vaguely replied.

"*Are* you Jesse?" Jamie reiterated, trying to make sense of the situation.

"And I thought *you* were the smart one," the person replied sarcastically. "Yeah; I'm Jesse and that's all you're going to know before I wipe you off this planet!"

Jamie felt the empathy ability confirm the claim as true, or at least whoever the person was believed themself to be Jesse anyway, as she quickly dodged a flight-assisted lunging punch that came her way using her enhanced speed.

"Now that's an interesting ability," 'Jesse' stated as he turned around to face Jamie upon his physical attack being evaded, having detected the brief use of the enhanced speed power being activated.

Jamie then felt the ground underneath her shaking before she was forced to take to the air as the tarmac surface she was standing on completely collapsed into itself, leaving a deep, endless-looking crater where she had been standing. The analysis ability informed her that it was being caused by the use of a 'terrakinetic' power, or the ability to affect the earth.

"Duh, of course; you get that power from me," Jesse remarked as he witnessed Jamie hovering above the now-destroyed ground. "Okay then – try this one!"

Jamie felt the analysis power going off in her head again as it indicated that the previously detected 'weather manipulation' ability was being reactivated. She then instinctively looked up to hear thunder rumbling above as the sky turned even darker than before.

Using empathy, Jamie could feel a malicious intent coming from Jesse as she sought to quickly fly away from her current position to avoid whatever he was planning on doing.

A lightning strike suddenly filled the sky as Jamie froze in mid-air. Deducing that Jesse was planning on trying to electrocute her, she instead flew directly towards him in a bid to dissuade him from attempting to do so at the risk of putting himself in the line of fire.

As she approached, Jesse then disappeared into thin air.

What the...?

Jamie then gathered her senses, realising that analysis had just detected teleportation being used.

"Nice try, Jamie!"

Jamie turned around to see Jesse looking as though he was concentrating heavily on something from the short distance he had teleported away from her to. Once again, the analysis ability was picking up on activity from him.

Weather manipulation, water manipulation...

A spiralling funnel of water then emerged from the thunderclouds above. Jamie looked on in horror at the overwhelmingly terrifying sight as she realised it was heading straight for her at a significant speed, too fast and too large to simply out-fly.

As the funnel mouth came down to engulf her, Jamie combined her flight with enhanced speed to rapidly move several hundred feet away out of the path of the huge elemental attack that instead crashed straight into the street, causing an instantaneous flood.

Looks like you've got a lot of tricks up your sleeve, Jesse thought to himself upon witnessing the miraculous dodge which his own version of the analysis ability confirmed as enhanced speed and flight. He remained unconcerned, however; he felt as though he had finally found a good way to test out all his acquired power on a combative subject as he then began to conjure up gale force winds.

Jamie held her face in agony as she felt a damaged layer of skin across her cheek, a severe friction burn as a result of moving at such an intense speed through the air. Luckily she noted that the burst of energy used in the evasive movement had not drained her overall reserves of the ability too much as she was going to need as much of it as possible to keep up with the ongoing empowered affront from the polar opposition version of her close friend.

She was then hit by the strong gales, causing her additional searing pain as she felt the wind against her facial wound. Jamie used her flight to try and avoid being blown away but the strength of the wind was too much for her ability to handle on its own, opting to enhance it with super speed which in itself struggled to help her maintain her position. The gales were so powerful that they were akin to what being caught in a tropical cyclone would feel like.

Out of desperation, Jamie turned direction and used the momentum of the wind to fly into an alley between two buildings to shelter from the onslaught.

"Nice try," Jesse muttered to himself as he activated terrakinesis again while losing partial focus on manipulating the high winds, exerting seismic control over the ground directly around the buildings where Jamie was situated.

Within her makeshift shelter, Jamie began to feel the earth shake again as the gales died down slightly. She heard a loud creaking as the buildings either side of her began to slump into one another with debris falling from them down towards her.

Forced to evacuate, Jamie flew straight into the winds again and propelled herself as far down the street as she could in the complete opposite direction of Jesse in order to regroup. However, as she felt the gales behind her cease with immediate effect, she realised a figure had materialised from out of nowhere in the near distance towards where she was flying.

Jesse then flew straight at Jamie, hoping to collide straight into her head on. In response, Jamie activated her absorbed shielding that she had managed to hold on to, allowing her rampaging foe to smash straight into the barrier shoulder-first with such force that the invisible shield was severely damaged upon impact and dealing recoil to Jamie as well. Jesse yelled in pain as he gripped his shoulder immediately after as Jamie recovered quickly to inspect the aftermath of the kamikaze attack.

Have you gone insane with whatever transformation you've undergone? Jamie thought to herself over Jesse's reckless surge against her; even if she hadn't activated the shield, the collision would have still caused physical damage to his body in either scenario. She looked at her injured foe as he nursed what appeared to be a nasty-looking dislocated shoulder with his connecting arm motionless by his side. She noted that for all his offensive capabilities, now she would be able to have a better chance at overcoming him until she could figure out what to do next.

Her analysis ability kicked back in, already detecting flight being used of course but now was coming up with an additional power being activated.

Regeneration?

Jamie watched in disbelief as Jesse's arm began to contort back into its regular position from its dislocated state. Within a few seconds, it appeared as though he had made a full recovery with no lasting aftereffects.

"Didn't think I could do that, eh?" Jesse taunted as Jamie looked back at him with a worried expression on her face, realising that no matter what she could do it would ultimately prove futile against a body that could repair itself in no time whatsoever.

Or, a body at least with an *active ability* that could repair itself, she then thought. And based on the extremely reckless charge he had just unsuccessfully tried, believing himself to be invincible while possessing a regenerative power appeared to have made 'Jesse' overconfident in viewing it as an insurance policy allowing him to go over the top with whatever he chose to do regardless of the risk.

To Jamie, it was a way in to getting the upper hand.

"Where were we then?" Jesse smirked as he attempted to fly straight into Jamie again but teleported just before coming into contact in anticipation of another shield effort. However, Jamie correctly guessed that he expected the same counter and instead swooped downwards as Jesse reappeared behind her, subsequently missing a timed punch as a result.

While descending towards the ground, Jamie found herself cut off again by Jesse teleporting in front of her, dodging to the side in response which was met with the same response each time she tried to evade his approaches.

"You can't escape me, Jamie," Jesse mocked. "How about actually trying to fight back instead?"

Who says I'm trying to escape?

Jamie lunged forward with a straight punch that Jesse easily dodged but failed on his own following-up swinging blow as Jamie activated enhanced speed to quickly move out of his reach, then delivering a flying kick straight into his upper back.

Angered, Jesse teleported a short distance away and reactivated his weather manipulation ability to launch another howling gale in Jamie's direction, who put up a shield to deflect the debilitating effects of the hindering winds away from her body though still found herself being pushed backwards by the sheer force of them regardless.

Undeterred, Jesse commanded a rain of hail to continue the onslaught, gleefully watching the destructive precipitation heading in Jamie's direction.

Just about seeing the oncoming hail thanks to her shielding ability preventing the strong gusts from affecting her eyesight, Jamie abandoned her defensive stance and again flew towards the nearest shelter she could find that could protect her from the array of frozen pellets swarming towards her. This time she settled for a nearby petrol station, hiding under the forecourt roof which took the brunt of the attack.

Annoyed, Jesse thought about launching a lightning strike against the metal framework of the petrol station forecourt in order to electrocute Jamie, though quickly convinced himself to instead draw out killing her as a means of prolonging his fun.

Instead, the empowered maniac chose to use terrakinesis to crumble the ground beneath it, causing the roof to quickly collapse and forcing Jamie to take to the sky once more as she narrowly escaped the destruction.

You can't run from me all day long, my dear, Jesse thought to himself. Caught between attacking Jamie physically and continuing an ability-based affront, he opted to engage in the former and decided to teleport within close proximity to her, appearing right next to her current position and launching a double-footed kick at her head.

Jamie, however, quickly countered with enhanced speed enabling her to move out the way fast enough but then flew backwards instead of counter-attacking.

Jesse steadied himself, feeling slightly baffled at the lack of follow-up from his opponent but nonetheless continued the pursuit and tried to hit another punch square in Jamie's face, only for it to once again be avoided with enhanced speed.

With another few attempts all thwarted, Jesse began to feel his frustration beginning to get the better of him before taking a moment to calm himself. He did not consider himself a patient person but he knew he was only playing his part in some strategic defence scheme that Jamie was conducting and knew better than to get sucked into it.

Jamie watched as Jesse then paused his onslaught, remaining motionless in mid-air facing her. She attempted to feel what he was planning next using her empathy powers but felt nothing but a coldness coming from him, creeping her out somewhat.

However, her analysis then sprung into life and detected the use of weather manipulation about to be used once more with Jesse looking up into the heavens, assumedly to see the next attack he was about to summon from above.

You won't even get a chance to nail it.

Jamie took her opening and lunged forward with enhanced speed and flight, hoping to cut off the attack and absorb Jesse's powers to neutralise the threat he posed.

As she rapidly approached, Jamie unexpectedly found herself colliding straight into an invisible barrier, rebounding in tremendous agony having smashed straight into it at vehicular-like speed with her left shoulder taking the brunt of the impact as well as some of the side of her head.

Next thing she knew, both her arms were pinned to her sides by a pair of legs wrapping around her torso from behind with a chokehold applied firmly around her neck and injured head.

"Thought you were being smart trying to lure me in to try and absorb my powers, huh?" Jesse sneered as he clung on tightly. "I didn't believe you'd fall for the same trick you pulled on me though. Let's see you fight your way out of this one!"

Jamie was in too much pain to properly register what was being spoken to her, though fully aware that she was in deep trouble unless she could escape the hold around her neck slowly cutting off her oxygen supply. Unfortunately her left arm was all but useless in aiding her following the collision with the barrier and her right arm alone was not enough to wrench free of the leg scissors currently pinning it down which would enable an absorption attempt. Whatever she was still able to do, it had to be fast.

With great reluctance but seeing no other option as she began fading into unconsciousness, Jamie aimed her right hand towards Jesse's body and activated her electrical manipulation ability.

As the analysis power activated to notify him of it, Jesse felt a surge of electricity instantly paralysing his muscles and causing immense pain throughout his nervous system as Jamie then ended the attack after only a few seconds.

Both enhanced humans fell to the floor, Jesse barely able to summon the will to control his flight ability with his body in a state of shock and agony to prevent an extremely hard landing from fifty feet in the air. His wobbly descent ended with a minor slam into the ground, relatively smoother than what would have been without the flight ability. Jamie then slowly floated down, still heavily injured herself as she made way over to the helpless Jesse.

Looking down at her fallen foe, Jamie saw Jesse's extensive electrical burns beginning to heal as the discoloured, charred flesh steadily restored itself to normal.

Perfect.

Jamie weakly placed her hands on areas of Jesse's skin that had already reverted to a healthy state and began absorbing the regeneration power as efficiently as she could, leaving him semi-immobile from the remaining damaged parts of his body causing too much agony to even try moving.

Then, the analysis ability activated once more, alerting Jamie to an additional power being used at that moment.

Problem solving?

Aware of the power's capabilities and already in the process of gaining one ability, Jamie started draining the problem solving power too at the same time while it was in active use while simultaneously preventing Jesse from turning it off with her ability manipulation skills. Soon, she had both problem solving and regeneration at her full disposal, feeling relief as her injuries immediately healed with the absorption of the latter.

"Painful?" Jamie taunted Jesse who scowled in response. "It'll be a while before you can heal properly now that I have your regenerative powers."

"Make good use of them," Jesse fired back as he teleported from sight. Less than a second later, Jamie heard a tortured scream behind her as she saw an upright Jesse slowly float down to the ground onto his back once again.

"I guess that teleportation ability isn't as powerful with your body heavily damaged right now," Jamie said upon flying over to Jesse's position, remembering the pain Nate felt when he attempted to teleport with insufficient energy. "Now, I want to know exactly what happened to me and how I ended up here."

"Leave it out, alright?" Jesse defiantly responded.

"Care for another round?" Jamie threatened while emitting a few electrical arcs from within her open hand.

"And risk killing me now that I'm unable to heal myself if you try it? Your move."

Jamie stared back at Jesse with reluctance, not needing her empathy ability to know that he was right. The actual worry was whether the *real* Jesse was dormant within the deranged and murderous person that was currently lying before her or not for whatever reason, making inflicting further punishment too much of a risk.

"Are you Jesse or are you someone else, for the last time?" she said with a stern tone.

"Jog on, love," Jesse rebuked her, leading to a swift kick straight into a cluster of burns on the right side of his torso and eliciting another horrific yell of agony.

"Try that again," Jamie growled. "And remember, I can tell when you're lying."

"I don't have a name," 'Jesse' replied. "I just go by what everyone has ever called the other personality within this body."

"'Other personality'?" Jamie repeated back out of confusion. "What does that mean?"

"There's two sides to every coin, isn't there?" he replied cryptically. "I'm just one side."

"I'm not interested in riddles, mate. Tell me what I want to know."

Without saying a word, Jesse instantly teleported away from the scene again. Jamie listened out for another scream or even a detection of an ability being used, only to be disappointed by nothing forthcoming on either front. Ironically, the passive regeneration ability that she had just absorbed would have made tracking her heavily wounded opponent with analysis a lot easier.

Jamie still lacked the answers to her questions regarding where she was exactly – a parallel universe? The future? It seemed finding that out took priority over hunting down some evil version of Jesse who wasn't interested in telling her what she wanted to know and whom she had already defeated anyway.

While confounded by the situation, Jamie then realised she could utilise the problem solving ability she had just absorbed to try and get the answers she sought. She then activated it and waited for the most accurate or likely solution to generate in her head.

Locate Gabrielle.

Although the answer seemed generic at best, Jamie decided to try and contact Gabrielle anyway. She took her phone, surprisingly undamaged, from her cargo trousers pocket and attempted to dial her friend's number, noticing that at least the reception was working. To her delight, a ringtone was established. She hoped Gabrielle would answer it.

"Jamie?!" Gabrielle spoke through the receiver, almost hysterical.

"Yeah, babes. It's me," Jamie replied, taken back by the emotion in Gabrielle's voice.

"Jamie, where are you? Where have you been this whole time?" Gabrielle responded, audibly in tears.

"Calm down, Gabbs, I'm okay. I was teleported to what appears to be some London street but the idiot who teleported me here disappeared soon after."

"Teleported?" Gabrielle's voice tone changed to incredulity. *"Jamie, you've been gone for two weeks!"*

"I've *what?*" Jamie replied in astonishment. "What do you mean I've been gone for two weeks?"

"Brody showed me security footage of you and some teleporting thief having a tussle in a car park and you both disappeared shortly after with only him making the jump back. This is the first anyone's heard from you in a fortnight!"

Jamie stood momentarily stunned by the revelation, to the point she could hear Gabrielle mistaking the silence for the phone call going dead through the receiver.

"Gabby, I'm fine! Are you at home?"

"Yes! Please come back now!"

"I will, I'll see you shortly."

"Okay, please be quick."

Jamie hung up the call, still reflecting on what she had just been told. It especially confused her as to how Nate had managed to apparently travel through time without her analysis ability picking up on it when it occurred, the only reasoning that it was an unintentional blending of his teleporting and future sight powers, the latter of which he hadn't appeared to have full control over as it was.

But knowing that did not solve the issue of locating him in order to return to the moment when she was thrown two weeks into the future timeline. Without his ability, she was stranded in a version of her world that really didn't seem appealing to live in based on the very limited experience she had already endured within it.

Using analysis and empathy combined, Jamie tried to root out Nate's power in the hope of locating him. After a minute of trying, Jamie realised the current futility of chancing Nate using his ability randomly, noting that it wasn't even picking up 'Jesse's' version of it. Unfortunately, her combined powers were failing to detect any of his other powers either, leaving her out of luck.

Then she remembered that she had the power to attempt exactly what Kayleigh had done, which was using her empathy to act as a form of clairvoyance. Jamie knew it would be a faint hope as she had never tried it herself or had a proper chance to ask Kayleigh how precisely she had achieved it but imaginably it was through the strong bond and emotional attachment that they shared with each other that had allowed it to occur.

Jamie then tried to feel out Jesse based on their own relationship, which she assumed would be boosted by the fact she held strong feelings for him as it was, possibly even bordering on love. However, she found that the empathy ability was not allowing her to pick up on him.

Maybe because this isn't the version of Jesse I'm acquainted with?

Jamie tried again, only this time attempting to harness how she felt towards Jesse in his current persona, which conversely was nothing but contempt but still came up with nothing. It could have been down to a myriad of reasons, be it a lack of proper strong connection or her own inability to utilise clairvoyance properly as Kayleigh had but regardless, Jesse was gone for the time being.

With no other recourse, Jamie decided to travel to her house to meet Gabrielle and at least find out everything that had gone down in the fortnight since she had vanished in her regular time.

In the near distance, Jesse stared angrily at the figure ascending into the air and immediately setting off in the opposite direction from where he lied a street over from where the battle had taken place. He didn't know what felt worse – the physical agony that he was currently in or the humiliation of his defeat.

Yet, he considered himself lucky that he had managed to hold back from yelling at the top of his lungs upon teleporting again as well as connecting his burnt torso with the surface of the ground.

Vengeance would be swift, he vowed as soon as the regeneration ability restored itself enough to enable the continuation of his burnt flesh to heal itself. It was to his regret that he had also lost access to the problem solving ability, especially given the fact that it had merely suggested teleporting away when he didn't need an ability to inform him of, which would have prevented exposing it's usage to Jamie's power absorption in the first place.

Nonetheless it had succeeded in allowing him to escape from an impossible predicament, something that only regeneration was going to fix once it returned. Until then, he remained rueing the loss in the pain of his charred skin while plotting his retribution.

Flying over the city landscape, Jamie realised she was actually close to Jesse and Kayleigh's home from her current position. Not thinking that Gabrielle would notice her being a few minutes later than expected, she decided to make a detour towards the siblings' abode in the hope of finding Kayleigh safe at the very least considering what had happened to her brother.

Upon touching down outside the house, Jamie felt a wave of horror flooding her system; the front garden area was completely sectioned off by police tape. Not wanting to consider the possibilities behind the reasoning for it, Jamie immediately took off once more into the sky to continue her journey.

A further ten minutes later, Jamie landed in the front lawn of her house, still not mindful of being seen using her powers in public seeing as the entire neighbourhood was deserted. The emptiness of the city and suburbs felt surreal, like something out of a disaster film she thought to herself, though still unable to shake off what she had witnessed at the Webster house as much as she would rather forget. Potentially, it was merely in response to Jesse going bad and becoming a homicidal maniac rather than any crime being committed on the property. It was a farfetched notion but still better than picturing Kayleigh and her aunt being slain.

"Jamie!" Gabrielle exclaimed upon answering the door, following up by hugging Jamie tightly.

"Gabby, what on earth has been happening?" Jamie said, close to tears herself.

"Oh Jamie, it's all messed up!" Gabrielle replied solemnly. "We're common knowledge now and Jesse has turned into an evil lunatic and turned the country upside down…"

"Slow down, Gabby. Let's go inside and talk," Jamie attempted to calm her friend as she led them both into the living room and sitting down on the couch. "Okay, I need you to tell me everything."

"I wouldn't even know where to start, hun."

"Then let's start at the beginning."

Chapter 17

"It all started when you disappeared," Gabrielle began. "Well tell a lie – it kicked off several hours *after* you disappeared, not that we knew what happened to you of course. I got in touch with Jesse to see where you were, only for him to tell me you had left his place ages ago. Naturally we were worried shitless and discussed filing a missing persons' report with the police.

"Then Jesse told me he had the business card of someone belonging to the secret police operation that dealt with people like us and we opted to call them up instead of doing the report. It was a guy named Brody and he was well aware of who you were. He actually had a lot of good things to say about you but we relayed to him that you were missing and no-one knew where. It was then that he said he would look into any reports of empowered human being activity that had been phoned into his department in the last day."

"I'm guessing my excursion with the teleporter and his mates in the shop came up," Jamie cut in.

"Yeah, it did. I even saw the footage and it showed you taking all of them on at once. Is that really what they have you do as part of that operation?"

"Focus, Gabby(!)" Jamie remarked.

"The footage itself didn't show what happened to you but Brody managed to acquire footage of a neighbouring car park that caught your struggle with the teleporter after you appeared within it. After a few seconds, you both disappeared and only the teleporter returned. That was the last time anyone saw you alive."

"Almost feel like a murder victim," Jamie said, failing to read the seriousness etched on Gabrielle's face. "So what happened from there?"

"We did the only thing we could do really – try and figure out where you had ended up with help from contacts within the department. Rachel was really lovely, using her powers to scour the internet for any mention of your name popping up on social media or phone texts. A young woman named Dawn even allowed Jesse to replicate her power tracking ability using his powers."

"Almost wish I had seen that for myself, Jesse's own absorption process," Jamie said, noting the irony of Dawn helping Jesse out after previously having helped imprison him. "Have wondered what it actually looks like in use."

"He used his new powers to try and locate you using your abilities for hours on end, only for him to find nothing of course owing to you not even being in this time it turns out. At the same time, Brody identified the gang members including the teleporter from the security footage and began targeting them for arrest with

Jesse helping out. Apparently Brody had wanted to recruit him anyway so Jess didn't exactly turn down the opportunity to join in."

"So they planned a raid on the gang?"

"Jesse and that Dawn bird had little progress in tracking their known abilities based on the security footage, which they were probably suppressing the use of to avoid being noticed while lying low. Fortunately though, Rachel was able to detect the use of one of the gang member's phones being used which led to Brody and his boys tracking the entire gang down to a house in the suburbs which belonged to a relative of one of them who was helping them hide from law enforcement."

"Probably posted something on social media out of boredom, I imagine," Jamie attempted to joke. "Did the raid go ahead?"

"Well, that's where things get a bit turbulent," Gabrielle responded.

"How so?"

"The last I heard from Jesse personally was just before they headed off to do the raid, calling me up to let me know what was happening. I had no idea what went down in that house at the time and I heard nothing from anyone until Brody showed up at our door in person a day later."

"I'm guessing it was something pretty bad," Jamie remarked, hiding the fact she had already met Jesse in his 'deranged' persona for the moment.

"'Pretty bad' would be putting it mildly," Gabrielle replied. "Brody told me there had been an incident during the raid and that Jesse had accidentally absorbed an unstable ability."

"What ability could it have been for it to be 'unstable'?"

"Apparently Jesse's analysis powers had identified the power bizarrely as 'shadow manifestation' – one of the five gang members possessed it and tried to attack him while in this state which caused Jesse to instinctively replicate it while trying to defend himself. Evidently it causes the user to involuntarily switch personalities; the side of them that is otherwise dormant and based on the complete opposite of their regular personality."

Jamie raised an eyebrow, realising that the version of Jesse she had fought earlier must have been the result of the 'shadow manifestation' ability that he had absorbed, which made perfect sense given his destructive and merciless nature in comparison to the otherwise docile dominant personality he held.

"Obviously Jesse was distraught over now possessing such an unpredictable ability so he asked Brody if he could have access to any other ability that might help counteract the effects of the shadow manifestation. Brody told me that he recommended for Jesse to accompany him to the holding cells for the empowered humans they had imprisoned in order to determine that for himself."

"And which one did he acquire?" Jamie asked though having a good idea.

"Brody told me that he led Jesse to the captives and he found an individual called 'Olivia' who had an ability called 'problem solving'," Gabrielle answered, leaving Jamie unsurprised but curious nonetheless to the subsequence of events. "I assume the reason was obvious why he chose that one."

"I'm guessing it didn't work if you haven't heard from Jesse since then though?"

"No; it worked perfectly according to Brody," Gabrielle replied. "Apparently as Jesse attempted to copy the ability into himself, the shadow manifestation ability kicked in out of nowhere and Jesse took on his 'shadow' personality as a result."

"I'm guessing nothing good?"

"Well the first thing he did in this state was to replicate the problem solving ability and then kill the Olivia girl he copied it from," Gabrielle said with a remorseful tone.

"Cold," Jamie put simply.

"It got worse from there – Brody claimed to have fled the basement immediately upon witnessing this and locked Jesse inside to prevent him getting loose."

"Although not a particularly great idea in the sense that he had a whole shopping aisle of abilities to choose from to absorb," Jamie cut in.

"Brody acknowledged that but justified it to me on the grounds that Jesse did not know what abilities every prisoner had without him there pointing them out. Unfortunately, aside from a few of the captives that he decided to kill outright anyway, Jesse apparently gained a few abilities from the unconscious ones that remained before murdering them too."

"Wasn't even aware that he could absorb powers from unconscious people," Jamie said. "He once told me that he could acquire a power that he had witnessed the use of and wanted for himself and Ryan Sharp confirmed it as a form of coveting other people's powers. Then again, Jesse himself was never fully aware of how it worked properly."

"However he did so, one of the abilities that he gained was the power to control the earth around him," Gabrielle continued. "He then proceeded to level the entire building before escaping. Brody said it was a miracle that he and several other survivors managed to get out in time, only doing so because they were watching a live feed of the security cameras broadcasting the whole thing."

"What happened from there?"

"That was all Brody saw before coming to the house to relay everything to me. I honestly couldn't believe what he was telling me; first you disappeared into thin air and then Jesse turned into a murderous rampaging lunatic."

"I suppose it was a rough time," Jamie quipped, almost trying to make light of the situation.

"Not as rough as it got in the days to come," Gabrielle grimaced. "Everything changed forever after that."

"I'm guessing it's the reason why every street I've stood in so far has been completely devoid of life?" Jamie asked.

"They're all afraid to come out no doubt. In the first day alone, parts of London were struck by devastating floods and extreme weather like tornados and hail the size of toasters. Then a series of earthquakes struck the capital. The death toll was in the thousands."

"Man…."

"As if that wasn't enough, the disasters then spread to neighbouring counties and even in Wales which was all but submerged by the sea and Scotland which suffered a heavy blizzard out of nowhere after enjoying a spell of pre-summer warmth. People were frozen in their homes"

"That's just crazy," Jamie replied, astounded at what she was hearing despite having witnessed such destructive power herself first hand earlier. "The Jesse we know must truly have a heart of gold if his 'other side' is capable of all this death and destruction."

"The news didn't report on the reasoning behind the several phenomena happening initially, possibly because they themselves didn't know what the cause was. We had everyone making their own assumptions like the religious crowd with claims of 'Judgment Day being upon us' and talk of global warming despite the lack of scientific explanation behind it all happening out of nowhere. It was just nuts."

"So when *did* the true cause get explained?" Jamie asked. "Or was it at all?"

"Oh, it did," Gabrielle answered. "It was announced by the Prime Minister himself in a rare live broadcast to the whole nation in which he explained that super-human abilities were actually real and that an individual with access to many of them was responsible for the chaos and also everyone should stay off the streets as much as possible."

"Anyone believe that?"

"Hard to tell. A couple of newspapers were sceptical and even denied it was the case outright. A lot of people on social media mocked the official explanation and those who did believe it were generally ridiculed too. The widespread mass-murder spree didn't end there though; in fact Jesse took it intercontinental."

"What, meaning he began killing people abroad too?"

"He wasn't directly blamed for what happened but it seemed more than obvious when you look at the circumstances of how things unravelled," Gabrielle began. "A few days after the devastation in Britain kicked off, a report came in that a landslide had occurred on a Spanish island in the Atlantic as a result of a powerful earthquake which had caused a large mass of rock to collapse into the ocean. The result was a huge wave that battered the east coast of America several hours later."

"A tsunami," Jamie cut in with the technical term. "With an impact in the water like that, the wave must have been dozens of feet high approaching the shores."

"The entire side of the country was engulfed by water," Gabrielle continued. "It was absolutely incredible to watch on live TV but no less terrifying what power he was capable of."

"I don't suppose the narrative began to focus on the possibility of a super-human teenager being behind it?"

"Nope; it was treated as a natural disaster. But if they thought they had endured enough already, the worst was yet to come."

"How can it get worse than a coastline-long tsunami?"

"Well next up was one of the strongest tropical hurricanes ever recorded forming in the same ocean which went on to further annihilate the already-totalled east coast."

"Now I know *that* shouldn't otherwise be possible during this time of year," Jamie remarked.

"See for yourself," Gabrielle responded, getting her mobile phone out and bringing up a news story on her internet browser app before handing it to Jamie to read.

"A 200 mile per hour storm?" Jamie read aloud in disbelief. "868 millibars of pressure? This intensity should not be possible during the spring season."

"Somehow it was. Other new stories I've read have all said the same as what you just came out with; that it is all but impossible for such a storm to achieve the wind speeds and pressure that this one did at this time of year."

"Well the water temperature would be too cold and wind shear too high to allow an overly-powerful tropical cyclone to develop, among other things. How bad was the devastation?"

"A hundred thousand people were estimated to have lost their lives between this and the preceding tsunami," Gabrielle replied. "I read this morning that bodies are still being discovered so the death toll will no doubt be increasing with time to come."

"It probably wouldn't be amiss to suggest that nega-Jesse was indeed capable of all that," said Jamie. "Still unreal how he could generate that much power and control to cause that though."

"You'd think that would be enough for him, wouldn't you?" Gabrielle interjected. "Seemed it wasn't enough just doing those things, he needed to be recognised as having done them too. And seeing as nobody was taking the government and the news claiming it to be him behind it all seriously, he decided to make a statement."

"Which was…?"

"Quite literally interrupting a live news broadcast and informing the whole nation exactly who was responsible while providing a demonstration of his powers there and then so that everyone believed it."

"Dare I ask what he did to prove himself?"

"He simply caused a series of tremors on command. Then he mockingly gave a weather report claiming Manchester was about to be subject to the worst hail storm in history, at which point he teleported from the studio before reappearing less than a minute later to sarcastically thank everyone watching for tuning in. Later news reports confirmed that Manchester had been hit by a catastrophic barrage of hail from out of nowhere."

"Shouldn't come as a huge surprise that this version of Jesse would have a gigantic ego considering the real deal is as humble as they come," Jamie stated. "Just a shame he can no longer live a normal life if he were to revert back to his regular self considering the infamy this evil personality has attained using his body."

"I'm surprised the army hasn't been drafted in to try and stop him," Gabrielle said.

"Probably because they know they would stand very little chance against his multitude of powers," Jamie answered. "The government and the police force have known about our kind for some time now and have of course collaborated to hide our existence from the general public as best they could knowing what kind of distrust and panic that could arise as a result. The fact that they've ended up revealing everything to the nation goes to show how helpless they feel in being unable to contain it now. They got lucky with Ryan Sharp – he would have probably gone on to do similar things had me and Jesse not stopped him before he could really let loose. But this, this is far worse than what I imagined Sharp would've been capable of."

"Hard to believe it was technically their special operation that they recruited you for that inadvertently led to it all happening with Jesse turning into a psychopath and gaining all those powers."

"Were the police or Brody trying to do anything about it at all though?" Jamie enquired.

"I haven't heard anything from Brody at all since he visited the house," Gabrielle responded. "I've tried ringing the number off the business card he gave me but it just goes straight to voicemail every time so either the phone has broke, the phone operator out of service or Brody himself has been killed and his mobile has run out of battery as a result."

"I doubt Brody would have sat back and done nothing at all about it, I just hope though he didn't do anything stupid like trying to take on Jesse by himself."

"If he did, it would certainly explain why he's been unreachable the last few days. It's not exactly been easy to tell what's going on out there at the moment; all televised news has come to a halt since Jesse invaded that broadcast, most likely due to the news staff being too afraid to return to their workplaces as a result. Thankfully the internet is still up and running and the electricity hasn't been affected, yet anyway so being able to keep my phone on to check for updates online has not been too much of an issue."

"Some brave people out there still going to work if that's the case," Jamie said.

"Or people who still don't believe what's happening is actually real maybe," Gabrielle suggested. "The bosses at my supermarket sure don't think it's a hoax; I've been off work since Jesse caused that hailstorm up north with the shop being closed down indefinitely. A lot of other places on the high streets have shut up too out of fear."

"It'll no doubt cause a food shortage among other things with all those outlets closed but honestly, who could blame them?" Jamie said. "People will have to then choose between starving to death or risking going about their usual lives and possibly being killed by an unpredictable maniac and his arsenal of super-human abilities. Does make you wonder why every other empowered being like us haven't all banded together to bring him down seeing as we're now common knowledge?"

"Not everyone has your confidence, Jamie," Gabrielle replied. "But even then it would be a hard task; he's far too powerful."

"I know, I already faced him before I came here," Jamie revealed at last, feeling her own ego needing to establish itself once again.

"You've already encountered him?" Gabrielle reacted with shock. "Why didn't you say so earlier?"

"I thought it would be easier to hear the full story rather than just hearing about the parts of this negative personality of Jesse that I hadn't already dealt with," Jamie responded, to Gabrielle's bewilderment.

"How did you escape him?" she followed up.

319

"I didn't; *he* escaped me."

"What are you talking about?" Gabrielle replied, utterly confused.

"Well he tried to attack me, did some damage but I ultimately managed to strike him with an electrical attack which heavily burned his body and I left him in that state, well after draining his regeneration ability so he couldn't immediately heal himself."

"You managed to defeat him?!" Gabrielle exclaimed. "Jamie, we need to finish him off while we have the chance."

"That's our friend you're talking about killing, Gabby," Jamie replied in a hardened tone. "Or at least he's *my* friend."

"Jamie, I understand where you're coming from but the Jesse we once knew is gone; all that's left is this abhorrent killing machine who's only concern is destroying anything and anyone in his path. We will be signing our death warrants if we do not take care of him now."

"I know I haven't experienced exactly what you and everyone else have had to deal with the last fortnight but I am not a murderer, Gabby," Jamie sternly responded. "And my friend is still in there somewhere – I will bring him back to the forefront somehow and banish that demonic personality from whence it came."

"And what then, Jamie?" Gabrielle fired back. "He'll spend the rest of his days rotting in prison for what he's done and even if he doesn't, he'll face being hunted by vigilantes and baying mobs until the day he dies. I don't like the idea of putting an end to him either but–"

"Then why are you bringing it up?" Jamie scornfully interrupted. "Regardless of what he's done in this wretched, malicious form, the

Jesse we know is completely innocent and would never have done any of these things. I'm actually amazed that you would even suggest killing him in cold blood."

"You might not feel the same way about him if you knew what he did to Kayleigh," Gabrielle mournfully replied, bringing out a wounded expression on Jamie's face.

"No…" she said while feeling overwhelmed by dread.

"I'm sorry, Jamie," Gabrielle said with a heavy look in her eyes as she saw her friend well up. Jamie then fell to her knees in despair as Gabrielle knelt down to offer comfort.

"How?" Jamie said in an almost monotone voice. "How did it happen?"

"I'm not sure when but it's likely it occurred not long after he trashed the building that contained the holding cells," Gabrielle replied. "I ended up reading about it in the online news; apparently the police entered the house in search of Jesse in case he had returned to the property, only to find him long gone and the bodies of a middle-aged woman and a pre-adolescent girl."

"His aunt too," Jamie lamented in her state of grief. "How did they die?"

"I've no idea, it hasn't been revealed. I don't even want to speculate how it went down, it's bad enough that they're both dead."

"You're probably right," Jamie agreed, still struggling to compose herself. "Goodness knows how Jesse would feel knowing that he killed the person he loved the most in this world."

"He'd never need to find out, Jame," Gabrielle said. "He could be reunited with her whether she is now."

"And what then?" a clearly irritated Jamie responded. "Should I kill *my*self so I can perhaps meet my parents again based on that logic? Man, I know you've been through a lot, Gabby, but I'm really finding it hard to believe you're acting like this right now."

"Jamie, I hate to sound like it myself but without being melodramatic, we're facing the end of civilisation here as long as that monster remains within it. And I have all the sympathy in the world for Jesse and everything that's happened to him as well as everything he'll go on to suffer if he's returned to his normal state. I'm just trying to think of the bigger picture here. Not a jury in the world would convict anyone for bringing down that mass murderer, it just makes the most sense."

"Well I'd hate to disappoint you but I won't be killing anybody," Jamie replied resolutely.

"Then we are destined to die ourselves, Jamie," Gabrielle responded.

"On the contrary, I plan to return the world to the way it was without another person dying at all, including Jesse."

Jesse remained on the ground, still finding it too painful to fully move properly but could nonetheless feel the regeneration ability ever so gradually healing the burnt parts of his body as it itself slowly underwent the process of restoration. Half an hour had passed since Jamie had deactivated it as well as his analysis and problem solving abilities and none of the three powers were anywhere close to being fully functional yet.

He had noted though that the lack of passive regeneration within him at the time had probably helped to prevent Jamie tracking him down before she had decided to leave, much to his fortune. But the little regeneration he currently had would still be enough to gradually return his body to a useable and agony-free state.

Enough for him to enact his revenge at the very least.

Jesse then activated the very low amount of analysis power that he had within his body, detecting nothing nearby. Teleportation was still readily available to escape the area with in case Jamie returned to the scene prematurely.

He would have very much preferred to use his trump card ability to deal with the situation but risking exposing that to someone who could just as easily absorb it for themselves if they were to discover it would have been more trouble than it was worth, particularly if said person just happened to be immune to it for whatever reason.

Then, the analysis ability weakly picked up on an another power being used, which would have to be being used very close by in order to sense it via analysis' current low reserves. Jesse subsequently heard some voices in the distance, remaining as quiet as possible to avoid being noticed.

"Dudes, you do realise this is absolutely crazy, don't you?"

"C'mon man, you have a duty to do this!"

"The hell do I want to face that psycho down by myself? He could kill me before I even got the chance to zap him."

"Think about what will happen when you kill that bastard, Lee – we'll be world famous. We'll never have to work again for the rest of our lives."

"Funny, I thought *I* was the one doing the job!"

Jesse listened to the squabbling in the background, realising that not only were the presumably three people talking about taking him out but they were approaching his position in his incapacitated state. But the ability that one of them had in their possession – *electrical manipulation* according to the faint analysis power within him – was an extremely tempting opportunity to replicate for himself. It had been the cause of his downfall against Jamie; possessing it himself would give him a greater means of protecting himself against her use of it as well as having the chance to completely fry her just like she had done to him.

"Gavin, if you think you're getting an equal share of cash, think again," Lee said out loud as he suddenly stopped in his path. "Shit guys, it's him!"

The trio looked down in stunned silence at the sight of what appeared to be the Jesse individual that was responsible for running amok around the country. His eyes were closed and seemed to be dead.

"Guys, I think he's a goner!" Gavin yelled as they slowly approached the seemingly deceased body of the maniac responsible for devastating Britain.

"Well that was easy," Lee said, feeling another charge of electricity surging through his body. "Looks like someone already beat us to him."

"Maybe we should make sure he's definitely history," the third individual among the trio suggested.

"Well seeing as his body's already burnt anyway, won't hurt to cook it a bit extra," Lee said as he moved towards the charred body lying near him.

Continuing to play dead, Jesse realised it was now or never. Teleporting away would be easy enough despite his injuries but missing out on owning electrical powers was too good a chance to miss out on.

As Lee moved forward, Jesse unexpectedly opened his eyes, causing the trio to react in a panic.

"He's awake! Lee, kill 'im!"

"Time to die!" Lee roared as he prepared to discharge a lethal amount of electricity from his body. Jesse quickly teleported a few metres away in the distance, much to the small group's confusion.

"Where he's gone?" Lee yelled out loud in frustration.

From his new position, Jesse's eyes began turning a shade black. Suddenly, he could hear a scream of anguish from where he had been lying previously.

"Lee, what's wrong?" Gavin asked with the third person standing alongside him. Lee then looked up and turned to face them, only now his pupils were completely black and showing little to no emotion whatsoever.

"Are you there, bruv?"

Without warning, the enslaved Lee unleashed a powerful electrical attack against his two friends who were instantly electrocuted where they stood. As they dropped dead to the floor, Lee then turned to face the still-immobile Jesse.

Just as well the user of that power is granted immunity from being attacked themselves, Jesse thought as he began the process of copying Lee's electrical manipulation ability. As soon as he felt the replication process complete, he then used terrakinesis to open up the ground beneath Lee and watched him being swallowed into the resulting chasm towards his own demise.

"Oh Jamie, you're in a world of trouble now!"

Chapter 18

"Jamie babe, how do you plan on doing all that exactly?" Gabrielle questioned her friend. "As far as I know, your powers aren't magic-based."

"No, but I do currently have that lunatic's problem solving ability at full power within me," Jamie answered.

"What, you managed to get that off him as well?" Gabrielle reacted with surprise.

"Yeah, and his analysis power so he can't currently track me down while using my powers."

"So you're going to use the problem solving ability to figure out how to change everything back to the way it was then? Still a long shot if you ask me."

"I already know what I'm going to do to change everything back – I'm going to go hunt down that psychopath by any means necessary and absorb his teleportation ability. The problem solving power is going to inform me how to use it to travel back to the moment that idiot Nate brought me here in the first place and prevent all this from happening."

"Will that really work?" Gabrielle asked, though took comfort in how confident and determined Jamie sounded.

"It's the best and only real option I have," Jamie replied.

"Shouldn't Jesse have been able to do that too seeing as he possessed both abilities? Wouldn't he have tried that already if it was possible?"

"What reason would he have to attempt travelling through time?" Jamie responded. "He's been having too much fun in his own time as it is, I doubt the thought has even crossed his mind."

"I sure hope you're right, sweetness."

"Well to bolster those hopes, let's see what it has to say about achieving time travel to the past first off," Jamie said as she activated the problem solving ability, terrified herself at what the answer was going to be.

After a few seconds, she got a response as Gabrielle looked on with mixed emotions.

"Well?' she asked, feeling as though the weight of the world was on her shoulders.

"It told me to absorb Jesse's teleportation ability," Jamie smiled to an emphatic looking Gabrielle.

"It's doable then?"

"Well let's not get too carried away, hun. The power comes up with the most logical and probable solution to a problem it is presented with. Its answer does vary and is dependent on several factors at play. For instance, it may just be telling me this because it knows that I've seen it being done before by someone with the same ability and therefore assumes it can be achieved again based on that."

"So it's not set in stone after all?" a deflated Gabrielle asked.

"No idea but I can honestly say it's something very much worth pursuing and first thing's first – I need to track down Jesse, or at least that piece of trash that's taken over his body."

"What if he's not using his abilities to be able to locate him?"

"His regeneration is probably kicking back in to a degree so that's at least one to pick up on. However, it's probably still too diminished to locate from this distance but I have another way of finding him."

"How's that?"

"I still have Kayleigh's empathy power within me, quite a sizeable amount remaining too and I can use it as a form of clairvoyance to mentally locate Jesse based on how strongly I feel towards him."

"Well I imagine that won't be hard considering how close you and Jess are," Gabrielle said.

"You'd think but it failed earlier when I tried that," Jamie replied. "It could only be down to the fact that the Jesse I know is currently not among us which prevents me from making it work. And unfortunately it wouldn't work on this other version of him when I tried it again because I didn't feel strongly enough towards him as I do the real deal."

"Okay then, so how *is* this going to work?" a confused Gabrielle inquired.

"By applying how much I now *hate* this miserable scumbag and how much I want to beat him within an inch of his life before I take his teleportation power for murdering Kayleigh for no reason at all," Jamie answered with venom in her voice as she began concentrating. Even she didn't know if the process was going to work in such a manner but it was all she had at her disposal as she focused her anger and loathing inward to try and find out exactly where Jesse was currently hiding.

"Is it working?" Gabrielle asked after a few seconds of watching Jamie sitting completely still with an angry look on her face.

"Babe, this works better when I'm fully concentrating," Jamie snapped, leading an annoyed Gabrielle to sullenly remain quiet for the remainder of the attempt. Channelling all her negative emotions, Jamie hoped to find Jesse before she became angry enough in doing so to want to punch a hole in the wall.

Nearly a minute later, Gabrielle watched Jamie open her eyes though held back from saying anything.

"I've got him," Jamie said as she stood up. "And sorry for snapping; focusing on so much anger and hate can really make a girl irritable."

"I'm sure I'm used to that already being around you when you're on a tough level while playing your video games," Gabrielle joked. "You going after him then?"

"Yeah, and I think it's best you stay here. I don't think it's going to be a hospitable environment," Jamie replied.

"It's going to be weird if you do succeed – I have no idea what will happen if and when you travel back and undo this nightmare reality. Heck, I probably won't even know when it happens."

"Like I'd travel back without saying goodbye to you first, you silly," Jamie affectionately said to an increasingly emotional-looking Gabrielle. "Not that for all my science-based knowledge I have a clue how to describe altering timelines beyond the standard hypothesises on them but I would hope that you're just going to go about your life as if none of this ever happened and Kay and Jess are back, alive and sane."

"Imma hold you to all that," Gabrielle replied warmly as she moved forward to hug Jamie.

Suddenly, she recoiled in what appeared to be a fit of pain stemming from her head.

"Gabby, what's wrong?!" Jamie yelled in panicky confusion as her friend thrashed about while clutching her cranium before eventually collapsing onto her knees, remaining perfectly still.

"Gabbs?"

Gabrielle raised her head to face Jamie, who looked straight back to examine her friend's face; her chocolate brown eyes had turned completely pitch black and were sporting a vacant but creepily malicious look. Jamie took a step backwards, unsure of how to react to the unexpected development.

Before she could do anything else, Gabrielle launched herself straight at Jamie who utilised enhanced speed to quickly dodge the lunge.

"Gabby, what's happening?" Jamie asked in desperation as Gabrielle turned around to attempt another diving tackle. Dodging it once more, Jamie tried to use analysis to see if a telepathic power was at play, though found absolutely nothing within the vicinity in active use.

Gabrielle charged again with Jamie opting to float to the ceiling to stay out of reach of her rampaging friend who clearly was functioning on pure instinct as well as evidently induced malice.

But how?

Undeterred, Gabrielle began flinging multiple kinetic energy waves up towards the airborne Jamie who lamented the destruction of her family living room while avoiding the attacks.

Be cruel to be kind.

Jamie used her flight to propel a double-footed stomp straight into her possessed friend's torso, sending her crashing into the armchair which then flipped backwards and taking Gabrielle with it. Mortified, Jamie descended to the floor.

"You alright, babes?" she meekly called out, only for Gabrielle to rise back up and quickly fire off another kinetic energy wave in her direction. Upon ducking out of the way, Jamie heard a smash as the wave continued its path and took out the window behind her.

Realising the futility of standing her ground, Jamie decided to exit the property through the now-shattered window.

Taking refuge up on the roof, Jamie watched Gabrielle jump through the broken window and slash her arm on the glass shards still embedded in the frame. Clearly still entranced by unknown means, Gabrielle maintained her mindless pursuit of anyone who happened to be within proximity of her, targeting other rampaging individuals across the road with kinetic energy waves.

Jamie looked on with a heavy heart, unable to help her best friend to overcome whatever was afflicting her but having a good idea of how it was occurring.

Jesse.

With anger and hatred coursing through her veins once more, Jamie reactivated her empathy ability and began flying in the direction of the source of her complete and total contempt.

Jesse spied on the chaos going on below amidst the local neighbourhood he was currently overlooking from his position atop a block of flats – the surface was overrun by people mass-infected with the rage-inducing sickness his latest ability use afforded him. Though his burn wounds were still in the process of healing fully, he could at least now tolerate the pain enough to be able to move about. Even at quarter-efficiency, the regeneration power was still relatively effective.

Of course, plunging an entire area of society into unbridled anarchy was easily achieved but now it came with the added incentive of re-establishing his dominance after the bruising defeat he had been handed to him by one mere teenage girl. Jesse knew that the most likely place to find her at that moment was her house along with Gabrielle with or without the problem solving ability telling him that but he considered it far more punishing to have the two girls fight each other to the death in a pure, animalistic state of fury beyond their control.

Jesse kept an eye on the large digital clock mounted on the building directly opposite the block of flats, noting it had been ten minutes since he had activated his rage-inducing ability which would surely have been enough time already to allow a zombie-fied Jamie to unwittingly cause some deadly havoc around her. He was in no rush to reactivate the ability in order to relinquish its effects; the more time he left everyone in said state, the more time he bought for his body to continue its slow rehabilitation.

Even if Jamie *were* able to maintain some cognitive function to enable hunting him down, her ability manipulation powers would be useless in trying to turn off the rage-inducing power as it was only active when initialising or diminishing the effects, such was the handiness of its nature.

Jesse then felt an unexpected, albeit subdued sensation go off in his head courtesy of the analysis ability.

Flight, empathy.

Jesse stood up on the rooftop in shock; it could only be Jamie heading towards him and owing to the analysis power currently working at only a percentage of its full capability, she had to be very close to his location. He fretted slightly at the fact his wounds were still in the process of healing but teleportation was still available to him to enable a quick escape.

Running from you *though…*

No, he thought. As far as he was concerned, a score was yet to be settled. Jamie had overpowered and bested him once before, he was not going to allow it to happen again. His pride towards being the undisputed scourge of the country and eventually the world could not be hampered by some pathetic and depressed brat who was unworthy of the power she held. He would allow it no further.

Utilising the decreased problem solving power within, Jesse attempted to formulate a strategy to overcome his current physical limitations. Despite operating at reduced strength, the ability managed to come up with a somewhat unorthodox solution to the problem.

Absorb electricity to accelerate regeneration.

As he saw a figure rapidly approaching through the air from the distance, Jesse struggled to comprehend exactly how to use the information just given to him, specifically on how to utilise taking in electricity to cause his wounds to heal faster. *Is it supposed to work in conjunction with regeneration?*

He nonetheless kept teleportation at the ready in case a mindless, instinctive Jamie was about to relentlessly assault him, not entirely content with the idea of having to take another electrical attack after having suffered greatly as a result of the previous one.

He then watched what was now clearly Jamie come to a halt a short distance in front of him before lowering herself down to the rooftop. Jesse couldn't help but feel puzzled at the fact she seemed to be functioning as normal.

"I see you've managed to heal yourself to an extent," Jamie spoke, confusing Jesse even further. "Don't worry; I won't be making the mistake of leaving you able to do that again."

"Why are you not under the effects of the ability?" he demanded to know, though feeling foolish for having to ask.

"Ah, so it *was* you behind that," Jamie responded. "I have come to find that mind control powers don't always succeed in affecting those with similar abilities. I guess in my case, my empathy powers have granted me some immunity to you. Funny how you mocked Kayleigh's ability earlier, huh?"

Jesse glared back at her.

"Also funny though how I'm not picking up anything being used by you to induce all this madness going on down there. Care to reveal how you're doing it?"

"If you must know," Jesse replied, sensing an opportunity to brag and restore some personal pride. "It's a lovely power I picked up in the police station's basement from one of their sedated prisoners. Of course I didn't know what I had absorbed but when asking myself how I could lay waste to an entire neighbourhood with minimal effort, my problem solving ability informed me that I needed only to activate what it referred to as 'darkness envelopment'."

A truly nefarious ability, Jamie thought to herself.

"Learning the effects of what that could do was indeed a delightful discovery, as I imagine you just found out," Jesse sneered.

"Well I just had to ditch Gabrielle who started acting like a possessed lunatic which dismayed me a lot," Jamie replied flatly. "But what really pissed me off more than that was finding out exactly what you've been up to in the two weeks since I went missing; namely the senseless murder of your own sister."

"Oh yeah, that wasn't too hard despite her realising that something was off about me the second I walked in the door," Jesse responded with an evil smile. "That wretched empathy ability did ruin the surprise a bit but seeing the fear in her eyes and hearing her scream as I ended her life there and then more than made up for it, not to mention throwing Trish down the stairs when she came up to see what the commotion was about. It's amazing how easily a person can die from landing on their head(!)"

"Have you enjoyed yourself the last half an hour then?" Jamie seethed, brimming with anger amidst a tear running down her cheek from hearing the details of Kayleigh's demise.

"What do you reckon?" Jesse sarcastically rebuked, taking immense pleasure in seeing the emotional pain in Jamie's face.

"I hope it was worth the agony I'm now going to put you through," Jamie said, aiming a surge of electricity straight at Jesse in the hope of paralysing him before being able to teleport away.

To her complete bewilderment, Jesse instead absorbed the electrical attack through unknown means as her analysis ability sprung into life.

Electrical manipulation.

"How did you…?" Jamie muttered to herself in disbelief as she saw the burns that had previously covered Jesse's body all but disappear.

"And to think I doubted that would work myself but thanks for the help, love," Jesse grinned, feeling almost completely rejuvenated.

Jamie thought about asking where he got his own version of the ability from but then decided to let it go, not wanting to give the egomaniacal fiend any more gratification than she already had. It

337

surprised her greatly that he had been able to convert her electrical blast into a form of accelerated healing but it didn't matter overall – with his body back to near-full health, she hoped the return of Jesse's overblown self-confidence would enable her to exploit it as weakness rather than the strength he considered it to be.

"Think fast!" Jesse smirked as he instantly disappeared via teleportation. Not to be caught off-guard, Jamie swooped forward with combined flight and enhanced speed as the psychopath rematerialized behind her. Aiming a flight-assisted punch at Jamie in response, Jesse immediately teleported again before his fist collided with the shield Jamie activated instantly in anticipation of a follow up ambush.

Sensing Jesse now on the other side of the rooftop, Jamie fired off a kinetic energy wave in his direction hoping to use it as a distraction as she prepared to launch herself at him with an enhanced speed-infused flying lunge. However, Jesse simultaneously activated his weather manipulation power and unleashed near-hurricane force winds right back at her, causing the energy wave to dissipate before reaching him.

Jamie activated her shielding once more while pushing back against it with all the strength her flight power could afford her. As she realised it was becoming a futile effort, she instead allowed herself to fall backwards and take refuge from the gale by the side of the building.

Failing to catch her breath, Jamie narrowly avoided a hard punch from Jesse as he instantly appeared next to her, watching as he drove his closed-hand straight into a window.

Taken aback momentarily by the pain of the resulting bloodied scrapes in his arm, Jesse quickly surrounded his body by an electrical aura as he felt Jamie grabbing the back of his neck. She immediately recoiled from the shock as he turned to face her while clutching his injured arm.

"You really think I'm going to let you anywhere near me to absorb my powers after the last time, girlie?" Jesse taunted.

"I don't need your powers to put an end to you," Jamie replied defiantly.

"Then why so eager to get close up?" Jesse replied before teleporting below Jamie in an attempt to blindside her. However, she responded instantly by moving out of the way of the subsequent charge with enhanced speed and retaliated with a swift elbow into Jesse's spine, causing him considerable discomfort as he teleported once more to a safer distance.

"Because it's a lot more satisfying hurting you with my own physical attacks," Jamie answered the previous taunt, much to Jesse's indignation.

Opting to utilise his powers more, Jesse teleported high into the sky and launched a hailstorm directly downwards to prevent the block of flats acting as a shelter. Jamie considered briefly using electricity to heat up the air around her to melt the hail before it could hit her but realised the resulting water could risk 'short-circuiting' her if it were to make contact, instead choosing to fly away from the oncoming barrage of precipitation.

Though struggling to see Jamie from his lofty position, Jesse expanded the hail to affect a greater area in the hope it would strike

Jamie regardless of where she was. The effort was taxing on his energy reserves but his permanent powers would replenish while her temporary absorbed ones would not as she continued to expend them to avoid the deadly onslaught.

Jamie found shelter under a large bus station canopy, though realised that even the fortified roofing was eventually going to sway under the battering it was receiving from the relentless and powerful hail raining down.

She watched as several mentally-enslaved individuals from the ongoing 'darkness envelopment' power were bludgeoned by the falling, rock-sized ice balls striking them from above, turning away to avoid witnessing the horrific sight. She knew she needed to find a way to get close to Jesse to absorb his teleportation; coaxing him into letting his ego run wild was one step but actually taking advantage of that fact in order to make physical contact with him was something else entirely. And so far, it wasn't going well at all.

Growing fatigued by the continued ability use, Jesse finally ended the hailstorm and teleported down to the surface to inspect his handiwork. There was no sign of Jamie and his weakened analysis powers were unable to detect her nearby, though he was satisfied with the carnage surrounding him as a result of the weather affront. Anything that brought him further fear and acknowledgement of his immense power was worth continuing the hunt for his elusive quarry.

But she could only avoid him for so long, both in physical terms and in still being alive – her death would be the only thing that would satisfy him now and he aimed to make it as torturous as possible to avenge his previous loss.

Jesse then began channelling all the analysis power he could muster into trying to locate Jamie in order to begin his final assault on her.

Analysis sensing.

He laughed to himself upon realising that she was currently doing the same thing to him, except that she was most likely trying to avoid his presence rather than his attempts to hound her out.

Jesse immediately teleported in the direction of the sensation in his head, ending up at a completely disfigured bus station that had bore the brunt of the hail in addition to several bloodied corpses littering the street.

"You can only hide so long!" Jesse called out, hoping to draw out his target upon her realising that she could not continue evading him forever. When she failed to emerge, though notably still utilising her analysis ability, Jesse engaged his electrical manipulation power.

Good luck stopping this, he thought to himself as he launched an overwhelming surge of electrical energy at the entire metallic bus canopy in a bid to overwhelm Jamie's own personal supply of the ability to prevent from absorbing the electricity. The remaining working lights instantly exploded, raining glass down to the underneath of the shelter which no doubt would have landed on the hiding Jamie if she had dared to stay where she was to ride out the attack.

Jesse was suddenly alerted to the use of flight and enhanced speed being used at close range, turning to his right to see Jamie rapidly charging at him with an outstretched hand.

With milliseconds to respond, Jesse put up his right arm to generate a barrier using his shielding ability, just barely managing to block the sneak attack as Jamie's arm bounced off the invisible blockade with an audible bone snapping, causing a scream to ring out.

Jesse then redirected his electricity surge straight towards Jamie as she instinctively flew far enough out of range to prevent it making contact.

Knowing Jamie's absorbed regeneration would heal her arm in less than a minute based on his own experience, Jesse gave chase but was met with an unexpected reverse stomp straight to the gut as Jamie clutched her slowly healing limb, the counter-strike buying her valuable seconds to recover from her grievous injury. Fighting through his own pain, however, Jesse teleported above Jamie and attempted to drop his elbow directly into her head but was instantly shocked by an electrical discharge of her own in turn, having been too focused on landing the physical blow in retaliation to anticipate the defensive offence.

As she watched Jesse descend to the ground to regroup, Jamie felt her arm completely straighten up as the bone set itself back into place, fully healed as a result of her regeneration power.

Suddenly though, she began to involuntarily fall through the air herself.

No, not now!

Stabilising her own descent, Jamie touched down to the surface having been too distracted by her own accord dodging Jesse's deadly onslaught to realise just how low her flight reserves were.

Only a few dozen metres away, Jesse gave a malicious smile upon realising what had just happened.

"No more flying for you then, eh girl?" he mockingly called out as Jamie responded angrily with an electrical attack in his direction, only for her to see it absorbed and integrated by the insidious enhanced human into advancing his healing capabilities once more.

"Getting careless as well too! All the better for me!" Jesse exclaimed joyfully as he rose into the air as a gesture of disrespect owing to his opponent's forced grounding.

Jamie looked on with a vexed stare, knowing she had gotten carried away with trying to attain revenge first and foremost than trying to achieve the actual main objective. Now with her bloodlust mostly gone, she activated the problem solving ability once more to try and determine how to deactivate the shadow manifestation ability within Jesse to revert him to his normal self, something she knew she should have pursued from the beginning.

To her dismay, it could not come up with a direct answer, only suggesting to weaken Jesse's resolve enough to allow the ability to reactivate on its own as it had in the first place and banish the negative persona in favour of her friend.

"That's not going to help you now!" Jesse yelled, detecting the problem solving ability via analysis. "But if you really want to try and get at me, here's your chance!"

With that, a chunk of the road began to rise up from the ground and settled into a makeshift ramp which Jesse aimed directly towards his position in the sky.

"Here it is; if you can use your speed to reach me, you can absorb some of my flight to continue the bout up here!" he called out.

Jamie surveyed the situation – it was possible to achieve such an elevated jump with a fast enough run-up, as long as she could endure the pain of the resulting friction burns which would easily be corrected with regeneration. The obvious flaw was that Jesse was plainly planning to either teleport out of the way and let her fall to her death from a height of fifty feet or block her with shielding at the last second.

Then she realised she had a trick up her sleeve that he wasn't aware of and wouldn't be until only after she had achieved it.

"You're just gonna teleport out the way, you lying bastard!" Jamie called back.

"Scout's honour I won't!" Jesse replied

"Say it and mean it!" Jamie fired back, activating empathy to tell if he was lying or not which Jesse would notably be picking up on.

"You have my word; no teleporting!" he responded truthfully which empathy confirmed.

"Or flying out the way!"

"You got it!" he again confirmed, as did empathy of the veracity of the answer. With that, Jamie began making her way as far back as she could to begin her attempt.

Jesse looked gleefully on, just waiting for the moment to activate the barrier to prevent Jamie reaching him. Knowing he had managed to use Kayleigh's wretched empathy ability against Jamie in her own use of it was the icing on the cake in finally getting his hard-earned revenge. He then watched as she began activating her enhanced speed ability.

Fully prepared but with a rapidly beating heart no less, Jamie sped forward towards the ramp at breakneck speed; with her skin peeling rapidly as she ran, she executed the perfect jump off the edge of the angled tarmac and leapt straight towards Jesse with enough propulsion to make a grab for him.

Jesse snickered as Jamie hurtled right at him in the air.

Enjoy your landing!

He then activated the barrier with seconds to spare, knowing there was nothing Jamie could do to alter her trajectory in any instance.

However, Jamie then proceeded to pass straight through the invisible shield and quickly clamped her hand round Jesse's face while wrapping her legs around his body to prevent his arms from flailing about. In a blind panic, he instinctively attempted to teleport away instead of activating electrical manipulation.

Thank you! Jamie thought to herself as she instantly began absorbing every bit of the teleportation ability that she could with both hands. Her analysis power then detected electrical manipulation emerging, activating her own in response to absorb the electricity being used to try and electrocute her. Once she felt the teleportation ability fully absorbed, she then quickly took some of Jesse's flight before relinquishing the hold on him and quickly descending back to the ground.

345

"How?!" Jesse raged as he slowly made his own way down to the floor before taking a place opposite Jamie on the road.

"Your own idiotic ego, that's how," Jamie smirked. "I admit I was careless myself in getting caught up in wanting to hurt you for killing Kayleigh but you left yourself wide open at the same time by trying to make sport out of making me suffer too. You didn't know that I could convert my enhanced speed into a form of phasing, did you?"

Jesse's eyes widened upon the revelation before squinting in anger at the fact he had been completely outsmarted.

"All I had to do was get confirmation you weren't going to move when you offered me a way up to you. Like I thought for any instant that you were going to allow me near you without some sort of double-cross, you idiot! You yourself said earlier that I had little chance of getting up close following what happened the last time we met, so how does it feel to be taken down by your own baby sister's ability?"

You son of a–

"Oh and in case you didn't know," Jamie continued her gloat. "The teleportation ability has a second function of being able to see the future, which combined with the main aspect of it enables time travel. So now I'll be going back to my own time to undo everything you've done and preventing this version of you from ever existing. Maybe had you used it yourself, you could've seen this happening in advance(!)"

As she turned to leave, Jamie heard glass breaking in the background as she and Jesse both looked towards the commotion.

Gabrielle!

Still under the darkness envelopment power's influence, a mindlessly-enraged Gabrielle was seen by both enhanced humans taking out two similarly inflicting individuals with her kinetic energy wave power.

She then instinctively turned her attention to her two friends, immediately firing off another wave in Jamie's direction which was swiftly blocked by her shielding ability.

Seizing his opportunity, Jesse reactivated his electrical manipulation ability and charged a powerful ball of electrical energy before throwing it straight in Gabrielle's direction.

"NO!" Jamie screamed upon realising what Jesse was doing, quickly teleporting to try and intercept the attack.

As she reappeared just before Gabrielle to absorb the ball of electricity, she turned around to realise she had missed it by mere milliseconds. An electrocuted Gabrielle then fell to the floor, lying motionlessly.

Chapter 19

Jamie couched down by Gabrielle's side in total shock and anguish. She didn't need empathy to realise her friend was dead, having had no chance to survive upon the electrical attack making contact with her body.

In the background, Jesse felt enjoyment at having managed to deliver such a heavy blow to his nemesis, even it was just an emotional one.

Jamie then turned around with angry tears in her eyes, the merriment being enjoyed by Jesse having not gone unfelt by her empathy ability. She then got back to a standing position as all logic and common sense dissipated in favour of immense rage at the killing of her beloved Gabrielle.

Overwhelmed by her vitriol, Jamie launched herself into the air and made a beeline towards Jesse with reckless abandon.

Jesse braced himself, happy to have finally dealt Jamie a crushing blow but nonetheless prepared to face the resulting vengeful onslaught head on. Without his ability to teleport, this would truly be a fight for survival but proving himself once and for all against such a versatile opponent would be the pinnacle of achievements; moreso than devastating the nation of Britain singlehandedly or laying waste to the east coast of America. Although he would never admit it out loud, defeating Jamie Avonoit was without a doubt the most prestigious conquest he could find himself succeeding in.

As he tried to form a barrier, Jesse found himself being outpaced by an enraged Jamie who proceeded to use enhanced speed to bypass the shield attempt to deliver a hammering fist straight to Jesse's face, followed up by an array of punches and kicks that the embattled psychopath struggled to defend against.

Though trying to fight back by summoning another windstorm via his weather manipulation, Jesse was again intercepted by the relentless physical assault by Jamie who seemed as though she was intent on bringing his life to a violent end.

Jesse then tried to flee the scene but found himself being outpaced by Jamie and her enhanced speed who embarked on yet another round of vicious blows that were starting to take its toll on the pair of them – Jesse with his swollen face and generally bruised body and Jamie quickly wearing herself out with the endless and brutal offensive.

Catching Jamie being forced to take a moment to recuperate, Jesse soared high into the sky and determined to end the battle once and for all, prepared to launch a lightning strike using his weather manipulation ability. Though the odds of actually connecting a bolt of lightning with Jamie were slim, it was virtually the best chance he had of gaining the upper hand taking everything into consideration.

Jamie looked up towards the heavens and despite her exhaustion, vowed to continue exalting her wrath upon the murderer of her closest friend as she began ascending towards Jesse at immense speed.

"Hope you like suffering ten times what your friend just did," Jesse spoke aloud as he readied himself to meet Jamie head on with a flurry of lightning to put an end to the affair once and for all.

Out of nowhere though, he began to feel an incapacitating migraine-like pain in his head that completely scuppered his counter-attack. Overwhelmed, Jesse helplessly began to plummet through the air towards the ground as Jamie watched on, stopping her own approach in confusion at the development.

Shadow manifestation.

Jamie's analysis ability appeared to indicate that Jesse's shadow persona had lost control of the very power that allowed him to exist beyond the confines of his mind.

As his polar opposite form returned to dormancy, a dazed Jesse opened his eyes amidst his rapid descent.

"Jamie?" he said upon seeing his friend looking at him from her position in the sky.

And then, the world was gone.

Jamie teleported down to where Jesse lay motionless, having landed sickeningly on the ground with no chance to break his fall. She looked down at his face, no longer sporting the black smears under his eyes having returned to his former self unexpectedly in the midst of his attempted attack.

Sadly, it had come at such an inopportune moment that had resulted in an outcome she had hoped to avoid as much as humanly possible.

"Jesse?" Jamie whimpered as she looked into her friend's lifeless eyes. Her volatile mood had completely gone, replaced with the familiar feeling of loneliness and sadness that she had been forced to endure for months on end as the reality sank in; her one remaining close friend was dead. Beyond all consolation, Jamie collapsed in grief beside Jesse's body and broke down, beside herself with sorrow at the loss of her entire circle of loved ones.

With tears still streaming down her face, Jamie slowly rose back to her feet as she surveyed the rest of the scene – upended roads, broken windows, an entire bus station destroyed and bodies scattered all over, including those of Gabrielle and Jesse. Although her plan had been successful, she hardly felt as though she had come out the victor in such a woeful conclusion to the fight.

In spite of her despair, Jamie quickly came to terms with the fact she now had exactly what she needed to fix the timeline.

Activating the problem solving ability, it quickly gave her the likeliest method to achieve the desired time travelling effect from the absorbed teleportation powers she had just gained, which was to simply use both teleportation and future sight simultaneously, though in her case, view the past as opposed to the future.

Engaging both aspects of the ability and envisioning the moment in which she had departed her own timeline, Jamie then vanished into thin air, leaving the carnage of her future world behind forever.

*   *   *

351

"What is this place? How did you send us here?"

"I don't know what this is about!" Nate protested to the purple-haired girl. "I thought I was teleporting, I don't have any idea where this is."

A moment later, Nate felt his teleportation ability involuntarily activating again as the girl looked around the deserted London street in total confusion.

"Ay–" he yelled as he was forcibly thrown back to the current timeline.

Upon returning to the present, Nate took a moment to comprehend what had just happened; somehow he had travelled to a different realm or version of the city that had been devastated by unknown means, of which the meddlesome girl had just been left behind in.

Far from feeling guilty over the act, Nate felt mostly relieved and victorious at having permanently removed the interfering empowered human responsible for consistently thwarting his friends' gang's schemes from society. With her gone, committing their crimes would be far easier from that point on.

As he saw the others fleeing the sports shop, he decided to call out to them.

"Hey guys! There's no need to worry – I got rid of the bitch!" Nate yelled across the road.

Out of nowhere, Nate heard the sound of someone landing on the car park floor near to him. He turned to face the source of the noise, feeling faint as he stared directly at what appeared to be the girl, albeit in a bedraggled state compared to how she was a minute prior.

"I think I owe you some payback," she spoke as Nate attempted to teleport away from the area, only for her to use enhanced speed to quickly grab a hold of him as he did so. Simultaneously disappearing, the two quickly rematerialized owing to Jamie's own use of the ability before delivering an electrical shock to Nate, flooring the enhanced miscreant instantly as she then eyed his cohorts across the road.

"Flee!" Bill yelled as he and his fellow gang members attempted to run away with their stolen goods.

In the mood for delivering punishment, Jamie then teleported and reappeared in front of the escaping gang, cutting them off from their route. Desperately, Bill fired off numerous laser beams only to see the girl teleporting again to avoid the blasts.

"Behind ya!"

Bill turned around to see his nemesis deliver a straight kick to his crotch, followed up by a knee square into his forehead as he bent over in agony which was enough to completely knock him out cold.

"Gareth, take her out!" Johnny yelled to one of the newest recruits, with the person in question forcing their ability to manifest.

Within seconds, familiar dark marks appeared around his eyes as he launched himself at the troublesome girl. Instead of taking her down, however, Jamie instead took Gareth out with a quick-fire kinetic wave before electrocuting Johnny and the other remaining gang member with bursts of non-lethal electricity.

Triumphant, Jamie approached the still-conscious Gareth who was attempting to get back to his feet, having reverted to his regular form. Before he could make a move, Jamie turned him around and looked straight into his eyes.

"You'll never get a chance to infect anyone with that again," she said while discharging another round of electricity to shock the terrified youth into unconsciousness like his fellow thieves.

Having neutralised everyone involved in the robbery, Jamie pulled out her phone to dial Brody's number.

"Hi, Brody. I believe you may have some wanted empowered criminals to come arrest…."

Epilogue

Jamie sat against the door on the rooftop where she and Jesse became acquainted, looking blissfully into the skyline as her analysis ability indicated the approach of an individual using flight and hazing.

A familiar and welcome face soon touched down beside her.

"Hi," Jesse spoke.

"Aren't you a sight for sore eyes?" Jamie remarked.

"So what did you want to meet about?" Jesse asked as Jamie got to her feet.

"Nothing in particular really."

"You feeling alright?" Jesse questioned his friend who then wrapped her arms around him in a warm embrace which lasted for several seconds. Upon relinquishing the hug, Jamie stared back into Jesse's eyes.

"Seriously, Jamie. What's up?"

"Nothing," Jamie replied. "Just thought I'd get a hug in."

"Something happen to you recently?"

"I guess so," she answered. "I mean I suppose I already knew but I don't want to go a single day without letting you know how much you mean to me from this point on."

"Okay," Jesse responded, unsure of what else to say. "Where's this coming from anyway?"

"Don't need a reason to express how much I appreciate your friendship, do I?"

"Well, no, of course not. And I appreciate you a lot too."

"I know," Jamie smiled. "But if there's one thing I've learned from my parents' deaths, it's that nothing is guaranteed in this world; anyone we love can be taken away from us at any given moment so it's best to enjoy their company as much as possible while we have them around."

"Jamie, with my ability to heal and your ability to absorb *my* ability to heal, we'll be in each other's lives for many years to come. Count on that."

"I hope so," Jamie replied. "Because you and your sister are my family now and I'll be doing everything humanly possible to make sure that lasts a lifetime."

"I'm glad," Jesse said, still ever confused. "Are you sure nothing else has happened recently to bring this on though?"

"Nothing worth going into," Jamie replied. "By the way, do you still have Brody's business card on you?"

"Actually I do, yeah."

"Can I see it?

Still baffled, Jesse handed over Brody's card with his contact details on. Jamie then proceeded to tear the card in half before discarding the two torn pieces, much to Jesse's surprise.

"Trust me, it's for the best," she said.

Acknowledgements

And here we are again! I must say that round two was a bit more of a frenetic writing process but it was nonetheless a fun journey in seeing how the characters all progressed in their adventures. I don't know what feels more surreal - the fact that I have two books out to my name or that I somehow managed to write the second one in only 5 months compared to the 10 years it took the first novel to be released!

What also surprises me that I somehow found the time to write the sequel throughout 2021 to begin with. Having recovered from a mental breakdown and with the global pandemic still very much ongoing, I definitely felt determined to get out and make up for lost time and try and enjoy life as much as I could. Thankfully I can safely say that not only did I achieve that but also had one of the best years of my life. And as always, I owe a lot of that to the people closest to me for helping me do so. You know who you are and I'm forever grateful to you all for the opportunities I get to have fun in your company.

When it came down to writing *Insurgence*, I did already have a lot of plot elements in mind to form the basis of the story but as far as acknowledgements go, I couldn't really not mention the societal ills that inspired some of the book's content on this occasion.

One thing I've always found myself being fascinated with is the occurrence of high school shootings and why they happen so much, particularly across the pond. Having suffered during my time in school myself, I could've felt myself sympathising with those who went on to commit vengeful shooting rampages in their schools upon a time (though thankfully I don't and never will). But recent incidents did bring another notable theme besides bullied students to my attention – the thought process of several of these young, predominantly male shooters doing so on the grounds of taking revenge against girls for rejecting them and refusing to grant them sexual access to their bodies. And it just seems to continue the underlying misogyny in society as far as I was concerned, particularly at a relatively young age.

As Jamie probably put bluntly in several chapters of this novel, we'll be doing the world a favour in eradicating that toxic masculinity mindset from everyone's heads at every opportunity we get. Or better yet, teaching it in the very schools that tend to be on the end of these violent acts of revenge. Who knows if we don't at least try?